JOHN CREASEY'S
CRIME COLLECTION 1982

JOHN CREASEY'S CRIME COLLECTION 1982

*An Anthology by members of the
Crime Writers' Association*

edited by

HERBERT HARRIS

St. Martin's Press
New York

JOHN CREASEY'S CRIME COLLECTION 1982. Copyright © 1982 by
[...] Printed in the United
[...] may be used or
[...] ithout written
[...] ɔtations embodied in
[...] ɔn address St. Martin's
[...]. 10010.

[...] ᴊer: 81-52640

First published in Great Britain by Victor Gollancz Ltd.

First U.S. Edition

10 9 8 7 6 5 4 3 2 1

CONTENTS

ACKNOWLEDGMENTS

Six original stories appear in this edition, those by Ernest Dudley, Peter Godfrey, Herbert Harris, H. R. F. Keating, Jean McConnell and Jeffry Scott.

We are grateful to *Ellery Queen's Mystery Magazine* for "The Nuggy Bar" (published by *EQMM* as "Metaphor for Murder") by Simon Brett; "A Case of Maximum Need" by Celia Fremlin; " 'To the Editor, Dear Sir—' " by Michael Gilbert; "Captain Leopold Incognito" by Edward D. Hoch; and "The Sensitive Ears of Mr Small" by Julian Symons.

"Death of an Old Dog" by Antonia Fraser and "The Victim" by P.D. James first appeared in *Winter's Crimes*, a series of anthologies published by Macmillan; "Deerglen Queen" by Bill Knox first appeared in *Crime Without Murder* (Scribners, New York).

Acknowledgments to *Alfred Hitchcock's Mystery Magazine* for "The World According to Uncle Albert" by Penelope Wallace; to *Mike Shayne's Mystery Magazine* for "Dead Giveaway" by Dan J. Marlowe; and to *Woman* for "The Reckoning" by Margaret Yorke.

INTRODUCTION

This volume is the twenty-first collection of short stories by members of the Crime Writers' Association, a club founded by the late John Creasey in 1953 and still flourishing as lustily as ever.

Because the Association comprises, as it were, a coven of crime-writers, it is natural enough to call an anthology of its members' stories a "Crime Collection". Yet that generic term suggests a rather limited range, and, quite to the contrary, the reader will find in these pages a variety of themes which embrace different nuances of mystery and suspense designed to thrill or puzzle; indeed, we are occasionally led down paths which excite our curiosity or whet our appetites for the unexpected without the aid of mayhem or skulduggery.

Surprisingly few of the leading exponents of crime-writing attempt the difficult short-story form, and it is our aim to cull some of the best examples from those who stubbornly do, and to introduce them to a wider public. We believe we have catered for most tastes with these versatile and ingenious stories, and feel sure you will find this year's Collection every bit as entertaining as the Collections of previous years.

HERBERT HARRIS

THE NUGGY BAR

Simon Brett

Murder, like all great enterprises, repays careful planning; and, if there was one thing on which Hector Griffiths prided himself, it was his planning ability.

It was his planning ability which had raised him through the jungle of the domestic cleaning fluids industry to be Product Manager of the Gliss range of indispensable housewives' aids. His marriage to Melissa Wintle, an attractive and rich widow with a teenage daughter, was also a triumph of planning. Even his wife's unfortunate death two years later, caused by asphyxiation from the fumes of a faulty gas heater while he was abroad on business, could be seen as the product of, if not necessarily planning, then at least serendipity.

But no amount of planning could have foreseen that Melissa's will would have left the bulk of her not inconsiderable wealth to Janet, daughter of her first marriage, rather than to Hector, her second husband.

So when, at the age of fifty-two, Hector Griffiths found himself reduced to his Gliss salary (generous, but by no means sufficient to maintain those little extras—the flat in Sloane Street, the cottage in Cornwall, the Mercedes, the motor-boat—which had become habitual while his wife was alive) and saddled with the responsibility of an unforthcoming, but definitely rich, step-daughter, he decided it was time to start planning again.

Hector Griffiths shared with Moses, Matthew, Mark, Luke, John and other lesser prophets and evangelists the advantage of having written his own Bible. It was a series of notes which he had assembled during the planning build-up to the launch of New Green Gliss—With Ammonia, and he was not alone in appreciating its worth. No less a person than the company's European Marketing Director (Cleaning Fluids) had congratulated him on the notes' cogency and good sense after hearing Hector use them as the basis of a Staff Training Course lecture.

Hector kept the notes, which he had had neatly typed up by his secretary, in a blue plastic display folder, of which favoured Management Trainees were occasionally vouchsafed a glimpse. On its title page were two precepts, two precepts which provided a dramatic opening to Hector's lectures and which, he had to admit, were rather well put.

A. *Even at the cost of delaying the launch of your product, always allow sufficient time for planning. Impatience breeds error, and error is expensive.*

B. *Once you have made your major decisions about the product and the timing of its launch, do not indulge second thoughts. A delayed schedule is also expensive.*

A third precept, equally important but unwritten, dictated that, before any action was taken on a new product, there should be a period of Desk Work, of sitting and thinking, looking at the project from every angle, checking as many details as could be checked, generally familiarizing oneself with every aspect of the job in hand. Thinking at this earlier, relaxed stage made it easier to deal with problems that arose later, when time for thought was a luxury and one had to act on impulse.

It was nearly three months after Melissa's death before Hector had time to settle down to the Desk Work for his new project. He had been busy with the European launch of Gliss Scouring Pads and had also found that clearing a deceased's belongings and sorting out a will, even such a simple and unsatisfactory one as Melissa's, took a surprising amount of time. Janet had also needed attention. Her mother's death had taken place at Easter, which meant that the girl had been home from her Yorkshire boarding school. Janet, now a withdrawn fifteen-year-old, had unfortunately been asleep at the time of Melissa's accident, had heard nothing and so been unable to save her. Equally unfortunately, from her step-father's point of view, she had not been in the bathroom with her mother when the gas fumes started to escape, which would have solved his current difficulties before they arose.

But, as Hector always told the eager young men in beige suits and patterned ties on the Staff Training Courses, success rarely comes easily, and the wise manager will distrust the solution that arrives too readily.

No, Janet was still with him, and he did not regret the time he had devoted to her. His plans for her future had not yet crystallized, but, whatever it was to be, prudence dictated that he should take on the role of the solicitous step-father. Now she was such a wealthy young woman, it made sense that he should earn at least her goodwill.

He smiled wryly at the thought. Something told him he would require more of her than goodwill for the occasional handout. The flat in London, the cottage in Cornwall, the motor-boat and the Mercedes demanded a less erratic income. He needed permanent control of Janet's money.

But he was jumping to conclusions. He always warned Management Trainees against prejudging issues before they had done their Desk Work.

Hector Griffiths opened the blue folder on his desk. He turned over the page of precepts and looked at the next section.

1. Need For Product (Filling market void, increasing brand share)
It took no elaborate research to tell him that the product was needed. Now Melissa was dead, there was a market void, and the product required to fill it was money.

Unwilling to reject too soon any possibility, he gave thought to various methods of money-making. His prospects at Gliss were healthy, but not healthy enough. Even if, when the Marketing Director (U.K.) retired and was replaced by the European Marketing Director (Cleaning Fluids), Hector got the latter's job (which was thought likely), his salary would only rise by some twenty-five per cent, far off parity with the wealth he had commanded as Melissa's husband. Even a massive coincidence of coronaries amongst the senior management of Gliss which catapulted Hector to the Managing Director's office would still leave him worse off.

Career prospects outside Gliss, for a man of fifty-two, however good a planner, offered even less. Anyway, Hector didn't want to struggle and graft. What he had had in mind had been a few more years of patronizing his underlings in his present job and then an early, dignified and leisured retirement, surrounded by all the comforts of Melissa (except for Melissa herself).

So how else did people get money? There was crime, of course—theft, embezzlement and so on—but Hector thought such practices undignified, risky and positively immoral.

No, it was obvious that the money to ease his burdens should be Melissa's. Already he felt it was his by right.

But Janet had it.

On the other hand, if Janet died, the trust that administered the money for her would have to be broken, inevitably to the benefit of her only surviving relation, her poor step-father, desolated by yet another bereavement.

The real product for which there was a market void, and which would undeniably increase Hector Griffiths' brand share, was Janet's death.

2. Specific description of product
Fifteen-year-old girls rarely die spontaneously, however convenient and public-spirited such an action might be, so it was inevitable that Janet would have to be helped on her way.

It didn't take a lot of Desk Work to reach the conclusion that she would have to be murdered. And, following unhappy experiences with the delegation of responsibility over the European launch of Green Gliss Scouring Pads, Hector realized he would have to do the job himself.

3. Timing of Launch

This was the crucial factor. How many products, Hector would rhetorically demand of the ardent young men who dreamt of company Cortinas and patio doors, how many products have been condemned to obscurity by too hasty a schedule? Before deciding on the date of your launch, assess the following three points:

A. *How soon can the production, publicity and sales departments make the product a viable commercial proposition?*
B. *How long will it be before the market forces which revealed a need for the product alter? (N.B. Or before a rival concern also notes the need and supplies it with their own product?)*
C. *What special factors does your product have which create special needs in timing? (E.g. You do not launch a tennis shoe cleaner in the winter.)*

Hector gave quite a lot of Desk Work to this section. The first question he could not answer until he had done some serious Research and Development into a murder method. That might take time.

But, even if the perfect solution came within days, there were many arguments for delaying the launch. The most potent was Melissa's recent death. Though at no point during the police investigations or inquest had the slightest suspicion attached to him, the coincidence of two accidents too close together might prompt unnecessarily scrupulous inquiry. It also made sense that Hector should continue to foster his image of solicitude for his step-daughter, thus killing the seeds of any subsequent suspicion.

The answer to Question A, therefore, was that a launch should be delayed as long as possible.

But the length of this delay was limited by the answer to Question B. Though with a sedately private matter like the murder of Janet, Hector did not fear, as he would have done in the cut-throat world of cleaning fluids, a rival getting in before him, there was still the strong pressure of market forces. The pittance Melissa had accorded him in her will would maintain his current lifestyle (with a conservative allowance for inflation) for about eighteen months. That set the furthest limit on the launch (though prudence suggested it would look less suspicious if he didn't run right up against bankruptcy).

In answer to Question C (what he humorously referred to, to his

Management Trainees, as the "tennis shoe question"), there was a significant special factor. Since Janet was at boarding school in Yorkshire, where his presence would be bound to cause comment, the launch had to be during the school holidays.

Detailed consideration of these and other factors led him to a date of launch during the summer of the following year, some fifteen months away. It seemed a long time to wait, but, as Hector knew, *Impatience Breeds Error.*

4. Research and Development of Product (A. Theoretical)

He was able, at his desk, to eliminate a number of possible murder methods. Most of them were disqualified because they failed to meet one important specification: that he should not be implicated in any way.

Simplified, this meant either a) that Janet's death should look like an accident, b) that her step-father should have a cast-iron alibi for the time of her death, or, preferably, c) both.

He liked the idea of an accident. Even though he would arrange things so that he had nothing to fear from a murder inquiry, it was better to avoid the whole process. Ideally, he needed an accident which occurred while he was out of the country.

A wry instinct dissuaded him from any plan involving faulty gas heaters. A new product should always be genuinely original.

Hector went through a variety of remotely-controlled accidents that could happen to teenage girls, but all seemed to involve faulty machinery and invited uncomfortably close comparisons with gas heaters. He decided he might have to take a more personal role in the project.

But if he had to be there, he was at an immediate disadvantage. Anyone present at a suspicious death becomes a suspicious person. What he needed was to be both present and absent at the same time.

But that was impossible. Either he was there or he wasn't. His own physical presence was immovable. The time of the murder was immovable. And the two had to coincide.

Or did they?

It was at this moment that Hector Griffiths had a brainwave. They did sometimes come to him, with varying force, but this one was huge, bigger even, he believed, that his idea for the green tear-off tag on the Gliss Table-Top Cleaner sachets.

He would murder Janet and then change the time of her murder.

It would need a lot of research, a lot of reading of books of forensic medicine, but, just as Hector had known with the green tag, he knew again that he had the right solution.

4. Research and Development of Product (B. Practical)

One of Hector's favourite sentences from his Staff Training lecture was: "The true Genesis of a product is forged by the R and D boys in the white heat of the laboratory." Previously, he had always spoken it with a degree of wistfulness, aware of the planner's distance from true creativity, but with his new product he experienced the thrill of being the real creator.

He gave himself a month, the month that remained before Janet would return for her summer holidays, and at the end of that time he wanted to know his murder method. There would be time for refinement of details, but it was important to get the main outline firm.

He made many experiments which gave him the pleasure of research, but not the satisfaction of a solution, before he found the right method.

He found it in Cornwall. Janet had agreed to continue her normal summer practice of spending the month of August at the cottage, and early in July Hector went down for a weekend to see that the place was habitable and to take the motor-boat for its first outing of the season. While Melissa had been alive, the cottage had been used most weekends from Easter onwards and, as he cast off his boat from the mooring in front of his cottage and breathed the tangy air, Hector decided to continue the regular visits.

He liked it down there. He liked having the boat to play with, he liked the respect that ownership of the cottage brought him. Commander Donleavy, with whom he drank in the Yacht Club, would often look out across the bay to where it perched, a rectangle of white on the cliff, secluded but cunningly modernised, and say, "Damned fine property, that."

The boat was a damned fine property, too, and Hector wasn't going to relinquish either of them. Inevitably, as he powered through the waves, he thought of Melissa. But without emotion, almost without emotion now. Typical of her to make a mistake over the will.

She came to his mind more forcibly as he passed a place where they had made love. During the days of their courtship, when he had realised that her whimsical nature would require a few romantic gestures before she consented to marry him, he had started taking her to unlikely settings for love-making.

The one the boat now chugged past was the unlikeliest of all. It was a hidden cave, only accessible at very low tide. He had found it by accident the first time he had gone out with Melissa in the boat. His inexperience of navigation had brought their vessel dangerously close to some rocks and, as he leant out to fend off, he had fallen into the sea. To his surprise, he had found sand beneath his feet and caught a glimpse of a dark space under an arch of rock.

Melissa had taken over the wheel and he had scrambled back on board, aware that the romantic lover image he had been fostering was now seriously dented by his incompetence. But the cave he had seen offered a chance for him to redeem himself.

Brusquely ordering Melissa to anchor the boat, he had stripped off and jumped back into the icy water. (It was May.) He then swam to the opening he had seen and disappeared under the low arch. He soon found himself on a sandy beach in a small cave, eerily lit by reflections of the sun on the water outside.

He had reappeared in the daylight and summoned Melissa imperiously to join him. Enjoying taking orders, she had stripped off and swum to the haven, where, on the sand, he had taken her with apparent, but feigned, brutality. When doing the Desk Work on his project for getting married to Melissa, he had analysed in her taste for Gothic romances an ideal of a dominant, savage lover, and built up the Heathcliff in himself accordingly.

It had worked, too. It was in the cave that she had agreed to marry him. Once the ceremony was achieved, he was able to put aside his Gothic image with relief. Apart from anything else, gestures like the cave episode were very cold.

When, by then safely married, they next went past the cave opening, Melissa had looked at him wistfully, but Hector had pretended not to see. Anyway, there had been no sign of the opening; it was only revealed at the lowest spring tide. Also by then it was high summer and the place stank. The council spoke stoutly of rotting seaweed, while local opinion muttered darkly about a sewage outlet, but, whatever the cause, a pervasively offensive stench earned the place the nickname of "Stinky Cove" and kept trippers away when the weather got hot.

As he steered his boat past the hidden opening and wrinkled his nose involuntarily, all the elements combined in Hector's head, and his murder plan began to form.

4. Research and Development of Product (C. Experimental)

Commander Donleavy was an inexhaustible source of information about things nautical, and he loved being asked, particularly by someone as ignorantly appreciative as Hector Griffiths. He had no problem explaining to the greenhorn all about the twenty-eight-day cycle of the tides, and referring him to the tide tables, and telling him that yes, of course it would be possible to predict the date of a spring tide a year in advance. Not for the first time he marvelled that the government didn't insist on two years in the regular Navy as the minimum qualification for anyone wishing to own a boat.

Still, Griffiths wasn't a bad sort. Generous with the pink gins, anyway.

And got that nice cottage over the bay. "Damned fine property, that," said Commander Donleavy, as he was handed another double.

The cycle of the tides did not allow Hector Griffiths to become an "R and D boy" and get back into "the white heat of the laboratory" again until his step-daughter was established in the cottage for her summer holiday. Janet was, he thought, quieter than ever; she seemed to take her mother's death hard. Though not fractious or uncooperative, she seemed listless. Except for a little sketching, she appeared to have no interests, and showed no desire to go anywhere. Better still, she did not seem to have any friends. She wrote duty postcards to two elderly aunts of Melissa in Stockport, but received no mail and made no attempt to make new contacts. All of which was highly satisfactory.

So, on the day of the spring tide, she made no comment on her step-father's decision to take the boat out, and Hector felt confident that, when he returned, he would still find her stretched lethargically in her mother's armchair.

He anchored the motor-boat in shallow water outside the cave entrance, took off his trousers (beneath which he wore swimming trunks), put on rubber shoes, and slipped over the side. The water came just above his knee, and more of the entrance arch was revealed. On his previous visit the tide could not have been at its very lowest. But the entrance remained well hidden; no one who didn't know exactly where it was would be likely to find it by chance.

He had a flashlight with him, but switched it off once he was inside the cave. The shifting ripples of reflection gave enough light.

It was better than he remembered. The cave was about the size, and somehow had the atmosphere, of a small church. There was a high pile of fallen rock and stones up the altar end, which, together with the stained glass window feel of the filtered light, reinforced the image.

But it was an empty church. There was no detritus of beer-cans, biscuit packets or condoms to suggest that anyone else shared Hector's discovery.

Down the middle of the cave a seeping stream of water traversed the sand. Hector trod up this with heavy footsteps, and watched with pleasure as the marks filled in and became invisible.

The pile of rubble was higher than it had at first appeared. Climbing it was hard, as large stones rocked and smaller ones scuttered out under the weight of his feet. When he stood precariously on the top and looked down fifteen feet to the unmarked sand below, he experienced the sort of triumph that the "R and D boys" must have felt when they arrived at the formula for the original Gliss Cleaning Fluid.

In his pocket he found a paper bag and blew it up. Inflated, it was about the size of a human head. He let it bounce gently down to the foot of the rubble pile, and picked up a large stone.

It took three throws before he got his range, but the third stone hit the paper bag right in the middle. The target exploded with a moist thud. Shreds of it lay plastered flat against the damp sand.

Hector Griffiths left the cave and went back to get his step-daughter's lunch.

5. *Packaging (What Do You Want the Product to Look Like? What Does the Public Want the Product to Look Like?)*

"The appearance of your product is everything," the diligent young men who worried about their first mortgages and second babies would hear. "Packaging can kill a good product and sell a bad one. It can make an original product look dated, and an old one look brand new."

It could also, Hector Griffiths believed, make the police believe a murder to be an accident and an old corpse to be a slightly newer one.

As with everything, he planned well ahead. The first component in his murder machine was generously donated by its proposed victim. Listless and unwilling to go out, Janet asked if he would mind posting her cards to Melissa's aunts in Stockport. She didn't really know why she was writing to them, she added mournfully; they were unlikely ever to meet again now Mummy was dead.

Hector took the cards, but didn't post them. He did not even put stamps on them. You never knew how much postal rates might go up in a year. He put them away in a blue folder.

There wasn't a lot more that could be done at that stage, so he spent the rest of his time in Cornwall being nice to Janet and drinking with Commander Donleavy at the Yacht Club.

He listened to a lot of naval reminiscences and sympathised with the pervading gloom about the way the world was going. He talked about the younger generation. He said he had nothing to complain of with his step-daughter, except that she was so quiet. He said how he tried to jolly her along, but all she seemed to want to do was mope around the cottage or go off on long walks on her own. Oh yes, she did sketch a bit. Wasn't that her in a blue smock out by the back door of the cottage? Commander Donleavy looked through his binoculars and said he reckoned it must be—too far to see her clearly, though.

If he was in the Yacht Club in the evening, Hector might draw the Commander's attention to the cottage lights going off as Janet went to bed. Always turned in by ten-thirty—at least he couldn't complain about late hours. She was a strange child.

Commander Donleavy laughed and said there was no accounting for the ways of women. Good Lord, within a year that little mouse could have turned into a regular flapper, with boyfriends arriving every hour of the day and night.

Hector said he hoped not (without as much vigour as he felt) and laughed (without as much humour as he manifested). So the holidays passed.

When he got back behind his desk at Gliss, he found a letter telling him that an international domestic cleaning exhibition, Intersan, would be held in Hamburg from the 9th to the 17th September the following year.

This was better than he had dared hope. He called in his assistant, a former Management Trainee, who was in charge of the undemanding and unexciting Gliss Spot-Remover range and who constantly complained about his lack of responsibility, and asked him to represent the company at the exhibition. Hector knew it was a long way off, but he thought it would give the young man something to look forward to. He was beginning to feel his age, he added tantalizingly, and thought there might be other responsibilities he would soon wish to delegate.

On the 14th September, Hector Griffiths set aside that day's copy of the '*Daily Telegraph*'. He put it with the postcards in the blue folder.

There was little more he could do for the time being, except to go over his planning in detail and check for flaws. He found none, but he still thought there was something missing. He needed one more element, one clinching piece of evidence. Still, no need to panic; it'd come. Just a matter of patient Desk Work. So, while he devoted most of his energies to the forthcoming launch of Gliss Handy Moppits (Ideal for the Kitchen, Nursery or Handbag), he kept a compartment of his mind open to receive another inspiration.

So the months passed. He and Janet spent Christmas quietly in London. To his relief, she did not appear to be fulfilling Commander Donleavy's prognostications; if anything, she was quieter still. The only change was that she said she hated school, was getting nowhere there, and wanted to leave. Her indulgent step-father suppressed his glee, thought about the matter seriously, and finally agreed that she should leave at the end of the summer term, then join him for August at the cottage, so that they could decide on her future.

6. Publicity (Make Sure Everyone Knows About Your Product Exactly When You Want Them To.)

This was the only one of Hector Griffiths' headings which might, while vital for any Gliss product, seem to be less applicable in the case of a murder.

But publicity is not only making things public; it is also keeping things secret until the time is right, and Hector's experience at Gliss had taught him a great deal about this art. Though lacking the glamour of military secrets, cleaning fluid secrets were still valuable and had been the subjects of espionage. So Hector was trained to keep his plans to himself.

And, anyway, there was going to come a time when publicity of the conventional sort was necessary, indeed essential. If the police never found Janet's body, then the plan was incomplete. Not only might there be difficulties in releasing her money to her step-father, he might also have to suffer the stigma of suspicion. As with the launch of a product, what was important was the moment of public revelation. And the timing of that, with this product as with any other, Hector would dictate personally.

It was, incidentally, while he was thinking of publicity that he came upon the missing element in his campaign. Some months before the launch of Gliss Handy Moppits (Ideal for the Kitchen, Nursery or Handbag) Hector had to go to his advertising agency to agree the publicity campaign for the new product. He enjoyed these occasions, because he knew that he, as Product Manager, was completely in command, and loved to see his account executive fawn while he deliberated.

One particular ploy, which gave him a great deal of satisfaction, was simply delaying his verdict. He would look at the artwork, view the television commercial or listen to the campaign outline, then, after remaining silent for a few minutes, start talking about something completely different. The executive presenting to him, fearful above all else of losing the very lucrative Gliss account, would sweat his way up any conversational alley the Product Manager wished to lead him, until finally Hector relented and said what he thought.

After seeing the television commercial for Gliss Handy Moppits (Ideal for the Kitchen, Nursery or Handbag), Hector started playing his game and asked what else the executive was working on.

The young man, a fine sweat lending his brow a satisfying sheen, answered sycophantically. His next big job was for one of the country's biggest confectionery firms, the launch of a brand new nut and nougat sweet—the Nuggy Bar. It was going to be a huge nationwide campaign, newspapers, cinema, television, radio, the lot. The product was already being tested in the Tyne-Tees area. Look, would Mr Griffiths like to try one? Nice blue and gold wrapper, wasn't it? Yes, go on, try—we've got plenty—the office is full of them.

Well, what did Mr Griffiths think of it? Pretty revolting? Hmm. Well, never mind. Yes, take one by all means. Well, anyway, whatever Mr Griffiths thought of them, he was going to be hard put to avoid them. After the launch on 10th September, he would see them in every shop in the country.

Hector Griffiths glowed inwardly. Yes, of course there was skill and there was planning, but there was also luck. Luck, like the fact that the old Gliss Floor Polish tin had adapted so easily to metric standards. Luck, like suddenly coming across the Nuggy Bar. It was a magnetism for luck that distinguished a great Product Manager from a good Product Manager.

The Nuggy Bar was secure in his pocket. His mind raced on, as he calmly told the account executive that he found the Gliss Handy Moppits (Ideal for the Kitchen, Nursery or Handbag) commercial too flippant, and that it would have to be remade, showing more respect for the product.

7. Run-Up to Launch (Attend to Details. Check, Check and Recheck.)
Hector Griffiths checked, checked and rechecked.

In June he went to an unfamiliar boat dealer in North London and bought, for cash, an inflatable dinghy and outboard motor.

The next weekend he went down to Cornwall and, after much consultation with Commander Donleavy, bought an identical dinghy and outboard from the boatyard that serviced his motor-boat.

Three days later he bought some electrical time-switches in an anonymous Woolworths.

Then, furtively, in a Soho sex shop, he bought an inflatable woman.

In another anonymous Woolworths, he bought a pair of rubber gloves.

At work, the Gliss Handy Moppits (Ideal for the Kitchen, Nursery or Handbag) were successfully launched. Hector's assistant, in anticipation of his exciting trip to Hamburg for Intersan, took his holiday in July. One of his last actions before going away was to prepare the authorization for the continued production of Gliss Spot-Remover. This was the formal notice to the production department which would ensure sufficient supplies of the product for November orders. It was one of those boring bits of paperwork that had to be prepared by the individual Product Manager and sent to the overall Gliss Product Manager for signature.

Hector's assistant did it last thing on the day he left, deposited it in his out-tray, and set off for two weeks in Hunstanton, cheered by the fact that Griffiths had said he was going to take a longer holiday that summer, all of August plus two weeks of September. Another indication, like Intersan, that the old man was going to sit back a bit and give others a chance.

So Hector's assistant didn't see the old man in question remove the Gliss Spot-Remover authorization from his out-tray. Nor did he see it burnt to nothing in an ash-tray in the Sloane Street flat.

Janet left her Yorkshire boarding school as quietly as she had done everything else in her life, and joined her step-father in London. At the beginning of August they went down to Cornwall.

She remained as withdrawn as ever. Her step-father encouraged her to keep up her sketching, and to join him in occasional trips in the motor-boat or his new rubber dinghy. He spoke with some concern to Commander Donleavy in the Yacht Club about her listlessness. He pointed her out sketching outside the cottage, and the Commander almost saw her figure through his binoculars. Once or twice in the evening, Hector commented to the Commander about the early hour at which she switched the lights out.

On the 16th August, Hector Griffiths went out fishing on his own and unfortunately cut both his hands when a nylon line he was reeling in pulled taut.

That evening he tried to talk to his step-daughter about a career, but found it hard going. Hadn't she discussed it with friends? With teachers at the school? Wasn't there someone he could ring and talk to about it?

After a lot of probing, she did give him the name of her French mistress, who was the only person she seemed to have been even slightly close to at the school. Had she got her phone number? asked Hector. Yes. Would she write it down for him? Here, on this scrap of paper.

Reluctantly she did. She didn't notice that the scrap of paper was a piece torn from a copy of the *Daily Telegraph*. Or that the only printing on it was most of the date—"14th September, 19. . ."

Her step-father continued his uphill struggle to cheer her up. Look, here was something he'd been given. A new sort of chocolate bar, nut and nougat, called the Nuggy Bar. Not even on the market yet. Go on, try a bit, have a bite. She demurred, but eventually, just to please him, did take a bite.

She thought it was "pretty revolting".

8. The Launch

The spring tide was to be at its lowest at 19.41 on 17th August, but Hector Griffiths didn't mention this when he persuaded his step-daughter to come out for a trip in the motor-boat at half past six that evening. Janet wasn't keen, but nor was she obstructive, so soon the boat, with its rubber dinghy towed behind, was chugging along towards "Stinky Cove". Her step-father's hands on the wheel wore rubber gloves, to prevent dirt from getting into the wounds made by his fishing line the previous day.

Janet seemed psychologically incapable of enthusiasm for anything, but Hector got very excited when he thought he saw an opening in the rocks. He steered the boat in close and there, sure enough, was an archway. The stench near the rocks was strong enough to deter any but the most ardent speleologist—in fact, there were no other vessels in sight—but Hector still seemed keen to investigate the opening. He anchored the motor-boat and urged Janet into the dinghy. They cast off and puttered towards the rocks.

Instructing his step-daughter to duck, Hector lined the boat up, cut the motor, and waves washed the dinghy through on to the sand of a hidden cave.

With expressions of wonder, Hector stepped out into a shallow stream, gesturing Janet to follow him. She did so with her usual lethargy. Her step-father pulled the dinghy some way up on to the sand. Crowing with childlike excitement about the discovery they'd made, he suggested exploring. Maybe this little cave led to a bigger one. Wasn't that an opening there at the top of the pile of rubble? He set off towards it. Without interest, but cooperative to the last, Janet followed.

It was on the precarious top of the pile that Hector Griffiths appeared to lose his balance and fall heavily against his step-daughter. She fell sideways down the loose surface to the sand of the cave floor. Fortunately she fell face down, so she didn't see the practised aim of the rock that went flying towards her head.

The damp thud of its impact was very similar to that an earlier missile had made against a paper bag, but louder. The commotion was sufficient to dislodge a shower of small stones from the roof of the cave, which gave very satisfactory credibility to the idea that Janet had been killed by a rockfall.

Hector also found it a source of satisfaction that she had landed away from the stream. When her body was finally discovered, he didn't want her clothes to be soaked through; it must be clear that she had entered the cave in the dinghy, in other words, at the lowest ebb of a spring tide.

Hector stepped carefully down the rubble. Keeping his feet in the stream, he inspected Janet. A little blood and brain from her crushed skull marked the sand. She was undoubtedly dead.

With his gloved hands, he slipped the scrap of *Daily Telegraph* with her French mistress's phone number and the opened Nuggy Bar with its blue and gold wrapper into Janet's pocket.

He then walked down the stream to the opening, already slightly smaller with the rising tide, waded into the sea and swam out to the motor-boat.

On board he removed a tarpaulin from his second rubber dinghy, attached its painter to the back of the larger boat and cast it behind. Then he chugged back to his mooring near the cottage, as the tide continued to rise.

9. The Vital First Month (Your Product Is Your Baby—Nurse It Gently.)

Hector Griffiths still had nearly a month of his six-week holiday in Cornwall to go, and he passed it very quietly and peacefully. Much of the time he was in the Yacht Club drinking with Commander Donleavy.

There he would complain to the Commander, and anyone else who happened to be listening, about his step-daughter's reticence and ask advice on what career he should guide her towards. Now and then at lunch-time he would point out the blue smock-clad figure sitting sketching outside the back door of the cottage. At night he might comment on her early hours as he saw the cottage lights go off.

In the mornings, before he went out, he would check the time-switches and decide whether or not to use the inflatable woman. He didn't want the sketching to become too predictable, so he varied the position of the dummy in its smock and frequently just left it indoors. Once or twice, at dusk, he took it out in the dinghy past the harbour and waved to the fishermen on the quay.

At the end of August he posted Janet's cards to Melissa's aunts in Stockport. Their messages had the timeless banality of all postcard communications.

In the first week of September he continued his nautical rounds and awaited the explosion from Gliss.

Because the cottage wasn't on the telephone, the explosion, when it came, on the 5th September, was in the form of a telegram. (Hector had kept the sketching dummy out of the way for a few days in anticipation of its arrival.) It was from his assistant, saying a crisis had arisen, could he ring as soon as possible.

He made the call from the Yacht Club. His assistant was defiantly guilty. Something had gone wrong with the production authorization for Gliss Spot-Remover. The factory hadn't received it and now there would be no stock to meet the November orders.

Hector Griffiths swore—a rare occurrence—and gave his assistant a lavish dressing-down. The young man protested he was sure he had done the paperwork, but received an unsympathetic hearing. Good God, couldn't he be trusted with the simplest responsibility? Well, there was nothing else for it, he'd have to go and see all the main buyers and apologise. No, letters wouldn't do, nor would the telephone. Gliss's image for efficiency was at stake and the cock-up had to be explained personally.

But, the young man whimpered, what about his forthcoming trip to Intersan in Hamburg?

Oh no! Hector had forgotten all about that. Well, it was out of the question that his assistant should go now, far too much mopping-up to be done. Damn, he'd have to go himself. Gliss must be represented. It was bloody inconvenient, but there it was.

After a few more demoralizing expletives, Hector put the phone down and, fuming, joined Commander Donleavy at the bar. Wasn't it bloody typical? he demanded rhetorically, can't trust anyone these days—now he was going to have to cut his holiday short just because of the incompetence of his bloody assistant. Young people had no sense of responsibility.

Commander Donleavy agreed. They should bring back National Service.

Hector made a few more calls to Gliss management people, saying how he was suddenly going to have to rush off to Hamburg. He sounded aggrieved at the change of plan.

On his last day in Cornwall, the 6th September, he deflated the dinghy and the woman. He went a long way out to sea in the motor-boat, weighted them with the outboard motor and a few stones, and cast them overboard. The electrical time-switches and the rubber gloves followed.

That evening he said goodbye to Commander Donleavy in the Yacht Club. He confessed to being a little worried about Janet. Whereas previously she had just seemed listless, she now seemed deeply depressed. He didn't like to leave her in the cottage alone, though she spoke of going up to London, but he wasn't sure that he'd feel happier with her there. Still, he had to go on this bloody trip and he couldn't get her to make up her mind about anything. . .

Commander Donleavy opined that women were strange fish.

As he drove the Mercedes up to London on the 7th September, Hector Griffiths reviewed the necessary actions on his return from Hamburg. Because of the Gliss Spot-Remover crisis, he could legitimately delay going back to Cornwall for a week or two. And, since the cottage wasn't on the phone and she hadn't contacted him, he'd have to write to Janet. Nice, fatherly, solicitous letters.

Only after he had received no reply to two of these would he start to worry and go down to Cornwall. That would get him past the next low tide when the cave was accessible.

On arriving and finding his letters unopened on the mat he would drive straight back to London, assuming that he must somehow have missed his step-daughter there. He would ring her French mistress and Melissa's aunts in Stockport and only after drawing blanks there would he call the police.

When they talked to him, he'd mention Janet's talk of going up to London. He'd also mention her depressed state. He would delay as long as possible mentioning that his rubber dinghy appeared to be missing.

Then, preferably as much as four months after her murder on August 17th, by which time, his reading of forensic medicine told him, it would be difficult to date the death with more than approximate accuracy, he would remember her once mentioning to him a hidden cave she'd found at low tide round "Stinky Cove".

The body would then be discovered.

Because of the lack of accurate timing from its state of decomposition, the police would have to date her death from other clues. The presence of the dinghy and the dryness of her clothes would indicate that she had entered the cave at a low spring tide, which at once limited the dates.

Local people would have seen the dinghy, if not the girl, around until shortly before Hector's departure on the 7th September. But other clues would be found in the girl's pocket. First, a Nuggy Bar, a new nut and nougat confection which was not available in the shops until the 10th September. And, second, a phone number written on a scrap of newspaper dated 14th September. Since that was the date of a spring tide, the police would have no hesitation in fixing the death of Janet Wintle on the 17th September.

On which date her step-father was unexpectedly, through a combination of circumstances he could not have foreseen, in Hamburg at Intersan, an international domestic cleaning exhibition.

So Hector Griffiths would have to come to terms with a second accidental death in his immediate family within two years.

And the fact that he would inherit his step-daughter's not inconsiderable wealth could only be a small compensation to him in his bereavement.

10. Is Your Product a Success? (Are You Sure There's Nothing You've Forgotten?)

On the day before he left for Hamburg, Hector Griffiths had a sudden panic. Suppose one of Melissa's aunts in Stockport had died? They were both pretty elderly and, if it had happened, it was the sort of thing Janet would have known about. She'd hardly have sent a postcard to someone who was dead.

He checked by ringing the aunts with some specious inquiry about full names for a form he had to fill in. Both were safely alive. And both had been so glad to get Janet's postcards. When they hadn't heard from her the previous year, they were afraid she had forgotten them. So it was lovely to get the two postcards.

Two postcards? What, they'd got two each?

No, no, that would have been odd. One each, two in all.

Hector breathed again. He thought it fairly unlikely, knowing Janet's unwillingness to go out, that she'd sent any other postcards, but it was nice to be sure.

So everything was happily settled. He could go abroad with a clear conscience.

He couldn't resist calling Gliss to put another rocket under his assistant and check if there was anything else urgent before he went away.

There was a message asking him to call the advertising agency about the second wave of television commercials for Gliss Handy Moppits (Ideal for the Kitchen, Nursery or Handbag). He rang through and derived his customary pleasure from patronizing the account executive. Just as he was about to ring off, he asked, "All set for the big launch?"

"Big launch?"

"On the 10th. The Nuggy Bar."

"Oh God. Don't talk to me about Nuggy Bars. I'm up to here with Nuggy Bars. The bloody Product Manager's got cold feet."

"Cold feet?"

"Yes. He's new to the job, worried the product's not going to sell."

"What?"

"They've got the report back from the Tyne-Tees area where they tested it. Apparently 47% of the sample thought it was 'pretty revolting'."

"So what's going to happen?"

"Bloody Product Manager wants to delay the launch."

"Delay the launch?"

"Yes, delay it or cancel the whole thing. He doesn't know what he wants to do."

"But he can't pull out at this stage. The television time's been contracted and the newspapers and—"

"He can get out of most of it, if he doesn't mind paying off the contracts. He's stuck with the magazine stuff, because they go to press so far ahead, but he can stop the rest of it. And, insofar as he's capable of making a decision, he seems to have decided to stop it. Call came through just before lunch—Hold everything—the Nuggy Bar will not be launched on the 10th September!"

The Mercedes had never gone faster than it did on the road down to Cornwall. In spite of the air-conditioning, its driver was drenched in sweat.

The motor-boat too was urged on at full throttle until it reached "Stinky Cove". Feverishly Hector Griffiths let out the anchor cable and, stripping off his jacket and shoes, plunged into the sea.

The water was low, but not low enough to reveal the opening. Over a week to go to the spring tide. He had to dive repeatedly to locate the arch, and it was only on the third attempt that he managed to force his way under it. Impelled by the waves, he felt his back scraped raw by the rocks. He scrambled up on to the damp sand.

Inside all seemed dark. He cursed his stupidity in not bringing a flashlight. But, as he lay panting on the sand, he began to distinguish the outlines of the church-like interior. There was just enough glow from the underwater arch to light his mission. Painfully, he picked himself up.

As he did so, he became aware of something else. A new stench challenged the old one that gave the cove its name. Gagging, he moved towards its source.

Not daring to look, he felt around in her clothes. It seemed an age before he found her pocket, but at last he had the Nuggy Bar in his hand.

Relief flooded his body and he tottered with weakness. It'd be all right. Back through the arch, into the boat, back to London, Hamburg tomorrow. Even if he'd been seen by the locals, it wouldn't matter. The scrap of *Daily Telegraph* and the dry state of Janet's clothes would still fix the date of her death a week ahead. It'd all be all right.

He waded back into the cold waves. They were now splashing higher up the sand, the tide was rising. He moved out as far as he could and leant against the rock above the arch. A deep breath, and he plunged down into the water.

First, all he saw was a confusion of spray, then a gleam of diluted daylight ahead, then he felt a searing pain against his back and, as his breath ran out, the glow of daylight dwindled.

The waves had forced him back into the cave.

He tried again and again, but each time was more difficult. Each time the waves were stronger and he was weaker. He wasn't going to make it. He lay exhausted on the sand.

He tried to think dispassionately, to recapture the coolness of his planning mind, to imagine he was sitting down to the Desk Work on a cleaning fluid problem.

But the crash of the waves distracted him. The diminishing light distracted him. And, above all, the vile smell of decomposing flesh distracted him.

He controlled his mind sufficiently to work out when the next low tide would be. His best plan was to conserve his strength till then. If he could get back then, there was still a good chance of making the flight to Hamburg and appearing at Intersan as if nothing had happened.

In fact, that was his only possible course.

Unless. . . He remembered his lie to Janet. Let's climb up the pile of rubble and see if there's an opening at the top. It might lead to another cave. There might be another way out.

It was worth a try.

He put the Nuggy Bar in his trouser pocket and climbed carefully up the loose pile of rocks. There was now very little light. He felt his way.

At the top he experienced a surge of hope. There was not a solid wall of rock ahead, just more loose stones. Perhaps they blocked another entrance. . . A passage? Even an old smugglers' tunnel?

He scrabbled away at the rocks, tearing his hands. The little ones scattered, but the bigger ones were more difficult. He tugged and worried at them.

Suddenly a huge obstruction shifted. Hector jumped back as he heard the ominous roar it started. Stones scurried, pattered and thudded all around him. He scrambled back down the incline.

The rockfall roared on for a long time and he had to back nearer and nearer the sea. But for the darkness he would have seen Janet's body buried under a ton of rubble.

At last there was silence. Gingerly he moved forward.

A single lump of rock was suddenly loosed from above. It landed squarely in the middle of his skull, making a damp thud like an exploded paper bag, but louder.

Hector Griffiths fell down on the sand. He died on the 8th September.

Outside his motor-boat, carelessly moored in his haste, dragged its anchor and started to drift out to sea.

It was four months before the police found Hector Griffiths' body. They were led to it eventually by a reference they found in one of his late wife's diaries, which described a secret cave where they had made love. It was assumed that Griffiths had gone there in his dinghy because of the place's morbidly sentimental associations, been cut off by the rising tide and killed in a rockfall. His clothes were soaked with salt water because he lay so near the high tide mark.

It was difficult to date the death exactly after so long, but a check on the tide tables (in which, according to a Commander Donleavy, Griffiths had shown a great interest) made it seem most likely that he had died on the 14th September. This was confirmed by the presence in his pocket of a Nuggy Bar, a nut and nougat confection which was not available in the shops until 10th September.

Because the Product Manager of Nuggy Bar, after cancelling the product's launch, had suddenly remembered a precept that he'd heard in a lecture when he'd been a Management Trainee at Gliss . . .

Once you have made your major decisions about the product and the timing of its launch, do not indulge second thoughts.

So he'd rescinded his second thoughts and the campaign had gone ahead as planned. (It may be worth recording that the Nuggy Bar was not a success. The majority of the buying public found it "pretty revolting".)

The body of Hector Griffiths' step-daughter, Janet Wintle, was never found. Which was a pity for two old ladies in Stockport who, under the terms of a trust set up in her mother's will, stood to inherit her not inconsiderable wealth.

A CASE OF MAXIMUM NEED

Celia Fremlin

"No, NO TELEPHONE thank you, it's too dangerous," said Miss Emmeline Fosdyke decisively; and the young welfare worker, only recently qualified, and working for the first time in this Sheltered Housing Unit for the elderly, blinked up from the form she was filling in.

"*No telephone?* But, Miss Fosdyke, in your—I mean, with your . . . well, your arthritis, and not being able to get about and everything . . . ? You're on our House-Bound list, you know that, don't you? As a House-Bound Pensioner, you're entitled—well, I mean, it's a *necessity*, isn't it, a telephone? It's your link with the outside world!"

This last sentence, a verbatim quote from her just-completed Geriatric Course, made Valerie Coombe feel a little more confident. She went on:

"You *must* have a telephone, Miss Fosdyke! It's your *right*! And if it's the cost that you're worrying about, then do please set your mind at rest. Our Department . . . anyone over sixty-five and in need . . ."

"I'm not in need," asserted Miss Fosdyke woodenly. "Not of a telephone, anyway."

There'd been nothing in the Geriatric Course to prepare one for this. Valerie glanced round the pin-new Sheltered Housing Flatlet for inspiration, but there was none. Its bland, purpose-built contours were as empty of ideas as was the incompletely-filled-in form in front of her. *Telephone Allowance. In cases of Maximum Need . . .*

It was a case of maximum need, all right. Valerie took another quick look at the papers in her file.

Fosdyke, Emmeline J. Retired dress-maker, unmarried. No relatives. Hundred-percent disability: arthritis, diabetes, cardiovascular degeneration, motor-neurone dysfunction . . .

The case-notes made it all so clear. Valerie glanced up from the precise, stream-lined data, and was once again confronted with a person. An actual, quirky, incomprehensible person: a creature whose eyes were sunk in helpless folds of withered skin, yet glittered with some impenetrable secret defiance.

Why couldn't old, sick people just *be* old and sick, the poor girl wondered despairingly? Why did they have to be so many other things as well—things for which there was no space allotted on the Form, and which just didn't fit in *anywhere*?

"But suppose you were *ill*, Miss Fosdyke?" she hazarded, her eyes fixed, for moral support, on all that list of incapacitating disabilities. "Suppose . . .?"

"Well, *of course* I'm ill!" snapped back Miss Fosdyke. "I've been ill for years, and I'll get iller. Old people do. Why do I have to have a telephone as well?"

Valerie's brain raked desperately through the Course Notes of only a few months ago. Dangers to Watch Out for in Geriatric Practice. Isolation. Mental Confusion. Hypothermia. Lying dead for days until the milkman happens to notice the dozen unclaimed bottles . . .

An *easy* job, they'd told her back in the office. An easy job for Valerie's first solo assignment: simply going from door to door in the Sheltered Housing Block, and fixing up with a free telephone those who qualified for it, either by age or disability or both. She'd pictured to herself the gratitude in the watery old eyes as she broke the good news: imagined the mumbling but effusive expressions of gratitude.

Why couldn't Miss Fosdyke be like that? Eighty-seven and helpless—why the *hell* couldn't she?

"Miss Fosdyke, you *must* have a telephone!" Valerie repeated, a note of desperation creeping into her voice as she launched into these unknown waters beyond the cosy boundaries of the Geriatric Course. "Surely you can see that you must? I mean, in your situation . . . suppose you were taken ill suddenly? Suppose you needed a doctor?"

"Nobody of my age needs a doctor," Miss Fosdyke retorted crisply. "Look at my case-notes there, you can see for yourself the things I've got. Incurable, all of them. There's not a doctor in the world who can cure a single one of them, and so why should I have to be bothered with a doctor who can't?"

Obstinate. Difficult. Blind to their own interests. Naturally, the Course had dealt with these attributes of the aging process, but in such bland, non-judgemental terms that it was only just recognizable as the real thing, when you finally came upon the real thing.

But recognizable, nevertheless. Be friendly, but firm, and don't become involved in argument. Smilingly, Valerie put Miss Fosdyke down for a free telephone, and left the flat, all optimism and bright words.

"Hope you'll soon be feeling better, Miss Fosdyke," she called cheerfully as she made her way out, and then on her long lithe young legs she almost ran down the corridor in order not to hear the old thing's riposte:

"Better? Don't be silly, dear, I'll be feeling worse. I'll go on feeling worse and worse until I'm dead, everyone does at my age. Don't they teach you *anything* but lies at that training-place of yours?"

"*What* a morning!" Valerie confided, half-laughing, and sighing with relief, among her lunch-companions in the staff canteen. "There was this poor old thing, you see, getting on for ninety, who was supposed to be applying for a free telephone, and do you know what she said . . . ?"

And while the others leaned forward, all agog for a funny story to brighten the day's work, Valerie set herself to making the anecdote as amusing as she knew how, recalling Miss Fosdyke's exact words, in all their incongruous absurdity: "No telephone, thank you. It's too dangerous!"

Too dangerous! What *could* the old thing mean? Ribald suggestions about breathy male voices late at night ricocheted round the table; anecdotes of personal experiences on these lines almost took the conversation right away from this Miss Fosdyke and her bizarre attitude, and it was only with difficulty that Valerie brought it back.

At *eighty-seven!*—she should be so lucky!—this was the general reaction. Of course (the girls admitted), one did read occasionally of old women being raped as well as robbed—look at that great-grandmother found stripped and murdered behind her own sweet-shop counter only a few months ago. And then a few years back there'd been that old girl in an Islington basement defending her honour with a carving knife. Still, you couldn't say it was common. The chances of being knocked down by a flying saucer were surely considerably greater.

"At *eighty-seven!*" they kept repeating, wonderingly, giggling a little at the absurdity of it. Consciously and gloriously at risk themselves, triumphantly exposed to all the dangers of being young and beautiful, they could well afford to smile pityingly, to shrug their shoulders, and to forget.

It was nearly five months after the telephone had been installed that Miss Fosdyke heard the heavy masculine breathing. It was late on a Sunday night—around midnight, in fact, as is usual with this type of anonymous caller—and it so happened that Miss Fosdyke was not in bed yet, but dozing, uneasily, in her big chair; too tired, after her hard day, to face the slow and exhausting business of undressing and preparing for bed.

For it *had* been a hard day, as Sundays so often were for the inhabitants of the Sheltered Housing Block. Sunday was the day when relatives of all ages, bearing flowers and pot-plants in proportion to their guilt, came billowing in through the swing-doors to spend an afternoon of stunned boredom with their dear ones; or, alternatively, to escort the said dear ones, on their crutches and in their wheel-chairs, to spend a few hours in the tiny, miserable outside world.

Just *how* tiny and miserable it was Emmeline Fosdyke knew very well, because once every six weeks or so her old friend Gladys would come with her husband (arthritic himself, these days) to take Emmeline to tea in their tall, dark, bickering home; hoisting her over their awkward front-door-step, sitting her down in front of a plate of stale scones and a cup of stewed tea, and expecting her to be envious. Envious not of their happiness, for they had none, but simply of their marriage. Surely any marriage, however horrible, merits the envy of an old spinster of eighty-seven?

Especially when, as in this case, the marriage is based on the long-ago capture by one dear old friend of the other dear old friend's fiancé—a soldier-boy of the First World War he'd been then, very dashing and handsome in his khaki battle-dress, though you'd never have guessed it now. Emmeline remembered as if it was yesterday that blue-and-gold October afternoon, the last afternoon of his leave, when she had lost him.

"He says you're no good in bed!" Gladys had whispered gleefully, brushing the golden leaves from her skirt, all lit-up with having performed a forbidden act, spoken a forbidden phrase, and destroyed a friend's happiness all in one crowded afternoon. "He says . . ."

Details had followed: surprisingly intimate, perhaps, for that day and age, but unforgettable. Only lately, emboldened partly by old age and partly by a changing climate of opinion, had Emmeline found herself wondering, now and again, how "good in bed" Gladys herself had proved to be over the subsequent fifty-five years? Naturally, Emmeline had never asked, nor would Gladys ever have answered. But maybe Gladys's tight, bitter mouth, and the grey, defeated features of the once carefree soldier-boy were answer enough?

The visit on this particular Sunday had been more than usually exhausting. To start with, there had been seed-cake for tea instead of the usual scones, and the seeds had got in behind Emmeline's dentures, causing her excruciating embarrassment and discomfort: and on top of this, Gladys's budgerigar, who had been saying "Percy wants a grape!" at intervals of a minute and a half for the last eleven years, had died the previous Wednesday; and this left a gap in the conversation which it was hard to fill.

And so, what with the seed-cake, and the car-journey, and the boredom, and the actual physical effort of putting up with it all, Emmeline Fosdyke arrived back at the Sheltered Housing Unit in a state of complete exhaustion. She couldn't be bothered even to make herself a cup of tea, or turn on the television; she didn't feel up to anything more than sitting in her arm-chair waiting for it to be bed-time.

She hadn't meant to fall asleep. She'd learned long ago that when you are old, sleep has to be budgeted just as carefully as money: if you use up too much of it during the day, there'll be none left for the night. So she'd intended just to sit there, awake but thinking of nothing in particular, until the hands of her watch pointed to quarter to ten and it would be reasonable to start preparing for bed.

But it is hard to think of nothing in particular, after eighty-seven years. Out of all those jumbled decades heaped up behind, *something* will worm itself to the surface; and thus it was that as Emmeline's head sank further and further towards her chest, and her eyelids began to close, a formless, half-forgotten anxiety began nibbling and needling at the fringes of her brain: something from long, long ago, over and done with really, and yet still with the power to goad.

Must hurry, must hurry, must get out of here . . . this was the burden of the thing that nagged and prodded at her last wisps of consciousness. Urgency pounded behind her closed eyes . . . a sense of trains to catch, of doors to bolt, of decisions to be made . . . And now there seemed to be voices approaching . . . shouts . . . cars drawing up . . . luggage only half-packed . . . Slumped in her deep chair, Emmeline Fosdyke's sleeping limbs twitched ever so slightly in response to the ancient crisis; the slow blood pumped into her flaccid muscles a tiny extra supply of oxygen to carry them through the dream-chase along streets long-since bulldozed; her breath came infinitesimally quicker, her old lungs expanded to some minuscule degree at the need for running, running, running through a long-dead winter dawn. . . .

It was the telephone that woke her. Stunned by the suddenness of it, and by its stupefying clamour erupting into her dreams, Emmeline sat for a few moments in a state of total bewilderment. Who . . . ? Where . . . ? And then, gradually, it all came back to her.

It was all right. It was here. It was now. She, Emmeline Fosdyke, eighty-seven years old, sitting comfortably in her own chair in her own room on a peaceful Sunday evening. She was home. She was safe. Safe back from that awful outing to Gladys's, and with a full six weeks to go before she need think about going there again. There was nothing to worry about. Nothing at all. Nothing, certainly, to set her heart beating in this uncomfortable way, thundering in her ear-drums, pulsing behind her eyes.

Except, of course, the telephone, which was still ringing. Ringing,

ringing as if it would never stop. . . . Who could it possibly be telephoning
her on a Sunday evening as late as . . . as late as . . . Oh dear, what *was*
the time . . .? With eyes still blurred by sleep, Emmeline peered at her
watch, and saw, with a little sense of shock, that it was past midnight.

Midnight! She must have been dozing here for the best part of four
hours, then! That meant that even with a sleeping-pill, she'd never . . .

And still the telephone went on ringing; and now, her mind slowly
coming into focus, it dawned on Miss Fosdyke that she would have to
answer it.

"Hullo?" she half-whispered, her old voice husky and tremulous with
sleep. "This is 497 6402. Who . . .?"

There was no answer. Only the slow, measured sound of someone
breathing; breathing loudly, effortfully, and with deliberate intention: the
sounds pounded against her ear like the slow reverberation of the sea. In
. . . out. In . . . out. Aaah-eee. Aaah-eee.

For several seconds Miss Fosdyke simply sat there, speechless, the hand
that clutched the instrument growing slowly damp with sweat, and her
mind reeling with indecision. During her long decades of solitary bed-sitter
life, she'd naturally encountered calls of this nature quite a number of
times, and she knew very well that there was no infallible recipe for
dealing with them. If you simply hung up without a word, then they were
liable to ring again later in the night; if, on the other hand, you *did* speak
to them, then they were as likely as not to launch forth immediately into a
long, rambling monologue of obscene suggestions. It was a nerve-racking
situation for an old woman all on her own in an empty flat.

Miss Fosdyke decided to take the bull by the horns.

"Listen," she said, trying to speak quietly and control the quivering of
her voice. "Listen, I don't know who you are or why you're calling me,
but I think I ought to tell you that I'm . . ."

That I'm what? Eighty-seven years old? All on my own? Crippled with
arthritis? About to call the police?

That would be a laugh! Anyone who has been an elderly spinster for as
long as Emmeline Fosdyke knows well enough what to expect from
officialdom if she complains of sexual molestation. No, no policemen,
thank you. Not any more. Not ever again.

But no matter. Her decisive little speech seemed to have done the trick
this time. With a tiny click, the receiver at the other end was replaced
softly; and Emmeline leaned back with a sigh of relief—even with a
certain sense of pride, too, in what she had accomplished. Funny how
these sort of calls always came when you were least prepared for
them—late at night, like this one, or even in the small hours, rousing you

from your deepest sleep. Like that awful time—five years ago had it been, or six?—when she'd been living all on her own in that dark, dismal flat off the Holloway Road . . . even now she still trembled when she thought about that night, and how it might so nearly have ended. And then there was that other time, only a few years earlier, when she'd just moved into that bed-sitter in Wandsworth. There, too, the telephone had only recently been installed . . . just as it had been here . . .

Well, I *told* her, didn't I? That prissy, know-all little chit of a Welfare Worker—no one can say that I didn't warn her! I *told* her that a telephone was dangerous for a person like me, but of course she had to know better—she with her potty little three-year Training Course, which she thinks qualifies her to be right about everything for evermore! *Training Course* indeed!—as if life itself wasn't a training-course tougher and more exacting than anything the Welfare could think up, if it sat on its bloody committees yakketty-yakking for a thousand years!

Nearly one o'clock now. Emmeline still had not dared to undress, or to make any of her usual preparations for the night. Even though it was more than half an hour now since she'd hung up on her mysterious caller, she still could not relax. Naturally, it was more than possible that nothing further would happen: that the wretched fellow had given up, turned his attentions elsewhere. Still, you couldn't be sure. It was best to be prepared.

And so, her light switched off as an extra precaution, and a rug wrapped round her against the encroaching chill of the deepening night, Emmeline sat wide awake in the velvety darkness, waiting.

It was very quiet here in this great block of flats at this unaccustomed hour of the night. Not a footstep, not a cough, not so much as the creaking of a door. Even the wardens must be asleep by now, and the caretaker too, down in his boiler-room in the depths of the building. Emmeline had never been awake and listening at such an hour before; the silence hummed in her hearing-aid, and so insistent was its gentle buzzing that at first, when it grew a little louder, she paid no attention. Brr-rr. Brr-rr . . . only when the sounds grew sharper, more irregular, did Miss Fosdyke suddenly become alert, heaving her slumped body painfully upright, and leaning forward to listen.

A car! A car drawing up outside the building, its tyres crunching on the gravel; and then the soft slam of the driver's door.

So it was a man of substance this time? A car-owner, not some pathetic, drunken down-and-out? Even with her hearing-aid turned up full, Emmeline could not quite hear the light, furtive footfalls on the grass, nor the soft sigh of the swing-doors as they opened and closed. Nor, actually, did she manage to hear the cautious steps coming nearer along the quiet, carpeted corridor; but it was very nearly hearing: she could feel the throbbing, indefinable sense of expectation growing stronger, seeping in under the very door.

Emmeline was trembling now, from head to foot. She'd never get out of it this time, never! Ten years ago—even five—she'd at least been mobile; able to hide, to slip through a doorway; to get away from the house even, and if necessary stay away . . . for days . . . or even weeks. . . .

Not now, though. This time, she would be helpless, a sitting-duck . . . and even as this thought went through her mind, she became aware, through the humming of her hearing-aid, of a new sound; a sound quite distinct and unmistakable; the sharp click of the latch as her door-handle was being quietly turned.

Softly, expertly, making no noise at all, Emmeline Fosdyke reached into the darkness for the long, sharp carving-knife that lay in readiness.

It was a shame, really, having to do this to them, after having been so nice to them on the phone, giving them her address and everything, and encouraging them to think that her tense, husky whisper was the voice of a young girl. It was a real shame; but then, what else could she do?

In the deep darkness, the unknown male lips coarse and urgent against her own, she would have her brief moment of glory; a strange, miraculous moment when it really seemed that the anonymous, ill-smelling mackintosh of some stranger was indeed a khaki battle-dress of long ago; that the blind clutchings of lust in the darkness were indeed the tender caresses of first love, sixty years past. For these few wild, incredible seconds, in the meaningless grip of some greasy, grunting stranger, she would be young again, and loved again, under the poignant blueness of a war-time summer sky. During these mad, brief moments she could allow hard masculine fingers to fumble with her cardigan in the darkness, and with the buttons of her blouse, scrabbling their way nearer and nearer to those withered breasts which were already quivering with the joy of it, and the longing. . . . A shame it was, a crying shame, that at exactly this moment—just before the eager, questing fingers had discovered the sagging, empty loops of skin and had recoiled in horror—this was the moment when she had to stab the poor nameless fellow, if possible to the heart.

Had to. It was self-defence. Even the Law had agreed about this, on the rare occasions when the Law had caught up with her.

She'd *had* to do it; *had* to stab them all, swiftly and surely, before they had a chance to discover how old she was: and that she was no good.

THE SENSITIVE EARS OF MR SMALL

Julian Symons

THE KITCHEN DOOR closed with a slight, yet decisive and deliciously promising click. Mr Small moved smoothly into his daydream. He got up, went smiling out to the kitchen, discovered Marilyn there in the act of pulling up her stockings. She gave a small protesting but delighted gasp as his arms clasped her from behind. Beneath his hand he heard the soothing sound of fingers on silk . . .

Crunch. His wife's teeth as they bit into toast destroyed the dream. Crunch and crunch again, like a series of mortars exploding. It was a relief when she dipped a spoon into the pot for more marmalade, although the resultant *squelch* was still unpleasant. But then inevitably came another *crunch*, against which he rustled the morning paper in vain.

The attack quite drowned any sound that Marilyn was making in the kitchen. He felt himself unable to bear it. This was a very bad morning. He rose and said he must go. The touch of his lips on Lucy's cheek was the briefest possible contact. In the car on the way to the station he said aloud, "It can't go on."

The curious condition of his hearing had existed now for some four months. It had begun, if he liked to put a time to it, just after Marilyn came to work for them three mornings a week. It was as though he felt things through his sense of hearing rather than through his sense of touch; the result was that almost every movement Marilyn made gave him a thrill of pleasure while everything Lucy did, whether it was moving a chair or turning the pages of a magazine, jarred his nerves.

Apart from things done by Marilyn and Lucy his hearing was perfectly normal, which somehow did not make things any better. He tried to explain it to old Dr Bentham.

"When I become excited, you see, my hearing becomes very—very acute." It did not seem wise to mention Lucy and Marilyn.

Dr Bentham was old and red-faced. His hand shook a little and his breath smelled of whisky. He made a cursory examination and said, "Nervous strain. Overworking in the office. The pace we all live at nowadays. Need to slow down a bit. Give you some pills."

The pills had no effect, and within another few days it became clear to

Mr Small that pleasure was associated with Marilyn, pain with Lucy. One was as intense as the other. He began to indulge in daydreams in which the pleasure was accentuated and the pain did not exist . . .

Mr Small was rather small, although not diminutive. He was forty years old. Everybody liked him because he was almost always cheerful and placid. His name was Geoffrey, but most people called him Geoff. Friends and acquaintances felt rather sorry for him because Lucy, although a splendid manager and good cook, was inclined to lay down the law about everything and wait for him to agree.

As people said, it was a pity they had no children, although of course they got on terribly well. And at Truwell Hanslit, the firm of manufacturing chemists where Mr Small was the assistant accountant, he got on terribly well, too, enduring better than anyone else the schoolboy sarcasm of the general manager, Mr Best. Yes, everybody liked Geoff Small.

On the morning that he had said, "It can't go on," Mr Small had lunch in the executives' restaurant with Grady, the company's chief analytical chemist. Grady, an ebullient Irishman, liked to talk, and there was no better listener than Geoff Small. As a matter of fact, they'd had lunch together quite often in the past month. While Grady talked, Mr Small noticed that the ordinary restaurant noises did not bother him at all.

Truwell Hanslit manufactured dozens of different branded preparations, from a new cortisone ointment for rashes to a contraceptive pill that was said to have no side effects of any kind. Grady liked talking about these, but he talked rather more about the power held by analytical chemists in general and the importance of his own work in particular.

"Some of the things we work on and then give up, Geoff, you'd never believe. Talk about the power of life and death! You know what the Home Office analysts say."

"What do they say?" Mr Small inquired timidly.

"Well, they only whisper it, mind you, but everyone knows there are a hundred different laboratory ways of committing undetected murder."

"Poisons, you mean?"

"Not poisons, Geoff, compounds." Grady jabbed with his fork. "There are half a dozen compounds in the lab at this moment that would send somebody off to sleep for good. Experiments, you know, we shan't manufacture them." He gave a great belly laugh. "Next time you're in the lab—"

It happened that Mr Small had to go across to the laboratory that very afternoon, on a query which proved to be a mistake in the Accounting Department. Grady was delighted to see him and continue their conversation. At the end they made what was almost a conducted tour of the laboratory in which Grady cast a little light on his companion's ignorance. It has been said that Mr Small was a good listener, and he did not mention to Grady that long ago he had passed a physics examination which naturally included chemistry. His knowledge was haphazard but genuine.

On the way home that evening Mr Small made a few purchases at three different chemists. It would be pointless to say what they were, for each of the substances was harmless in itself. On the way back from the station in the car he repeated, "It can't go on."

Mr Small had always liked pottering about in the kitchen. He did nothing elaborate, but he baked bread, made teacakes, and always took up a bedtime drink to Lucy. On the evening after his conversation with Grady he pottered about, then took up not only a sleep-inducing drink but one of the little buns he had just made.

Lucy ate it, and burped. A sound like a shot went through Mr Small's body. "Too much baking powder," she said.

That night she felt ill. Not very ill, but Mr Small insisted on calling Dr Bentham. He came, bad-tempered and sleepy, diagnosed injudicious eating; and gave Lucy a sedative.

On the following morning Marilyn arrived to find Mr Small making breakfast for Lucy, who was still in bed. He explained that she had had a nasty turn.

"Oh ah." She was a blonde girl, whose parents had died a few years back. She had a slightly crooked smile and a way of looking sideways that was conspiratorial and attractively sly. As she took off her coat, standing close to him, there was a rustle like music.

It seemed the moment to turn the daydream into reality, and he put an arm around her. She seemed to move away, but somehow did not. For a moment his lips met hers, then she did move away.

"Now then." She gave that sideways glance. "What would *she* say?"

The tinkle of her charm bracelet rang through his ears, travelled all over his body. He gulped. "Would you come out one night? To, say, a little dinner?"

"What would *she* say?" Marilyn repeated.

Lucy got up later that day and felt much better. When Dr Bentham came in to look at her on Saturday morning, she said she was quite fit. The doctor had a couple of stiff whiskies and told her to be careful what she ate.

Mr Small saw the doctor out to his car and said he knew she was still in pain. The doctor said it was gastritis, but if it went on they'd have to do something about it.

On Sunday they had arranged that a couple of neighbours come in to dinner, and Lucy insisted they should not call it off. The Longleys remembered afterwards that Geoff had seemed anxious, and had tried to stop Lucy from having a second helping of roast duck. Marilyn had come in to wash up and she was in the kitchen when Geoff, as usual, made the coffee.

At midnight Lucy felt some pains and Mr Small went downstairs, as he said, to call the doctor. He was distressed about the pains—his chemical knowledge was limited, and he couldn't really be sure about the effects of the white powder that had been the product of his pottering. He had kept it in the kitchen in a small jar labelled *Powder for Wine Making*, which was reasonable enough, because he had previously made parsnip and elderberry wine. Now he locked up the powder in his desk drawer.

He didn't actually call the doctor until half-past one. During that period of an hour and a half he sat in the living room with the door closed and the radio playing so that he could not hear the sounds upstairs.

When Dr Bentham arrived he was angry, but when he came downstairs he looked grave. The usual unpleasant things were done, but without effect. Mr Small suggested getting a second medical opinion, but it proved too late for that. The cause of death was stated on the certificate to have been acute gastric inflammation.

Everybody was very sympathetic. Even Best at the office, sarcastic overbearing Best, said he was sorry. Quite a lot of people attended the funeral and several of them came back to the house. Mrs Longley had arranged a little buffet meal, and Marilyn was there to hand things round.

Mr Small did not say very much, but his friends said that you could see how he felt. In fact, he hardly heard what was said, because all the time the music of Marilyn's charm bracelet sounded in his ears a message of infinite promise.

After the visitors had gone he could not resist doing what he knew to be unwise. He went out to the kitchen where Marilyn was clearing up and planted a kiss on her neck. It was as soft as roses; in some strange way he did not merely feel the contact but first of all *heard* it. The sound was the most exciting he had ever known.

She half turned but did not disengage herself. "I don't know what you're thinking about," she said. "And her only just buried."

Mr Small's thoughts were inexpressible. He could only stammer her name. In the end she pushed him away. She said he ought to be ashamed of himself, but that sideways glance seemed to have a different message. Then, enunciating the words carefully, she said she thought it would be better if she did not come in any more. It wouldn't be right.

He could hardly believe what she said. "But I must—I must see you again."

The sound as she put a hand up to her disarranged hair was beautiful. "You'll be moving out anyway. To a flat."

"Oh, I don't think so. I like to have a house. My wife didn't make a will, you know, and she had a little money."

"Did you say something about taking me out to dinner?" As he moved toward her again she said coolly, "No. And I'm not coming in after the end of this week. It wouldn't be right."

She was as good, or as bad, as her word. He took her out, and saw her almost every evening, but she would not come to the house. Mr Small was no housekeeper, and the place began to look slovenly. That delightful magnification of every sound she made continued, so that in a way it was always a pleasure to be with her; but in another way he knew he was being cheated.

At the end of three weeks they were married by special licence, with witnesses brought in from the street. Immediately after the wedding they left for a honeymoon in Venice. There Mr Small experienced the joys he had contemplated, which proved after all not to be so very joyful. His sensual experiences seemed to be inextricably linked to the extreme sensitivity of his hearing, and after a few days in Marilyn's company her movements and gestures were less vividly heard. By the end of the honeymoon her voice, which was—what else could you call it?—common, had begun to grate on his ears.

When they moved back to the house she got rid of all Lucy's curtains and chair covers and some of the carpets. She said the place needed brightening up. The replacements were in various shades of tangerine and pink, with an occasional essay into burnt gold. Mr Small had not realized that the colours of furnishings could jar the whole nervous system, but this proved to be the case. He not only *saw* these horrid colours but *heard* them too, and he did not like the sounds.

And yet beyond this he had a deep sense of comfort when he thought about the powder in his desk drawer. Mr Small had not done many positive things in his life, and it was comforting to feel a kind of power.

He was distressed to find that his popularity had suddenly disappeared. The Longleys came in one evening for drinks, but it was not a success. After they had left, Marilyn said that they were a stuck-up lot round here, why didn't they move? Mr Small replied that he had no intention of moving.

After all, he had the money—it turned out that Lucy had a nest egg he knew nothing about—and it was a pleasure to dig his toes in. Marilyn shrugged, became sluttish, watched TV all evening, and ate box after box of chocolates. Mr Small refused to have anybody in to help with the housework, and more often than not it didn't get done.

At the office, too, life was not easy. Grady was still friendly, but Mr Small rather avoided contact with him, and Best had reverted to type and become his old intolerable self. He was always making references in execrable taste, saying that he hoped Mr Small got plenty of home comforts, and suggesting that he looked extremely tired mornings.

These remarks were often made in the presence of junior members of the staff who seemed to find them funny, and in the end Mr Small decided to act. He still did some home cooking and often brought in teacakes for the morning "break". One day he persuaded Best to have a teacake. There were two to choose from, and Best took the one intended for him.

Mr Small smiled a private smile when he learned that the general manager had gone home after lunch, feeling extremely unwell. He was away the next day and still looked greenish when he returned. Power had been exercised, honour satisfied. The jokes didn't hurt any more.

It was in the following week that Mr Small, passing through the typing pool, heard a sound that made a shiver of delight pass through his ears and vibrate like a gong in the region of his solar plexus. It recurred, and he identified its source as a new young typist. She was sniffling, and it was the most delicious sniffle he had ever heard.

He took her to lunch in the canteen and learned that her name was Jennifer. The sniffle appeared to be a natural asset, not the result of a cold. Mr Small felt that he could listen to it forever. He thought of asking her out for the evening, but decided against it.

He was not shocked or even surprised when, that evening, Marilyn took a chocolate from a box and he heard, with the magnification given by a stethoscope, the rustle of the paper which sounded as though somebody was tearing silk, and the _crunch_ of teeth on chocolate which was like a drill attacking rock.

"Why are you looking at me as though I am a freak?" she asked. "What's wrong with me?"

"Nothing," Mr Small said softly. "There's nothing wrong at all."

"Well, there is something wrong and I'll tell you what." What could her voice be compared to—a file screeching on metal? "There's nothing to do in this damned place! And we never go out now. I'm sick of it."

"I thought perhaps we might go on a holiday."

"A holiday?"

"Perhaps on a cruise."

She stared at him, with that sideways calculating look he had once found so attractive. "It would make a change. But can you get the time off?"

He said he could, although he knew very well he couldn't. He had taken his yearly holiday for their honeymoon and they had been married only six months. It would have been nice if what he thought of as "the event" could take place on a cruise, but it was really not important. Afterward it might be advisable to move from the neighbourhood. Perhaps Jennifer would like the idea of a flat?

He unlocked his desk and stared at the powder. He found that he was looking forward to "the event".

He had given up drinking coffee, but a couple of nights after their talk about the cruise he took Marilyn to the cinema and then made coffee for them both. In the night she felt ill, and he suggested getting Dr Bentham, but she said no. She was so vehement about hating doctors that he did nothing.

After all, it was not necessary for this trial run, as he thought of it. Grady had said that a post-mortem in the case of this compound would reveal nothing but symptoms of unsuspected cardiac trouble; on the other hand, it might be as well if the circumstances did not precisely repeat those in Lucy's case.

The following day something disconcerting happened. Jennifer said she was too busy to come to lunch; but then he passed her as she was going into the canteen with two other girls. After he had gone by he heard their laughter, like the cackle of monkeys. In the past such an incident would have embarrassed him, but now he felt the swell of anger. At some time little Jennifer would have to be taught a lesson; but that could wait.

When he got home Marilyn was on the sofa watching television. She said she felt better and was coy, almost kittenish, as she pulled him down beside her. Soon after their marriage he had bought her a pair of gold bangles, and now he winced as they clattered against each other.

"How about that cruise, Geoff?"

He felt every movement she made—the harsh touch of her thighs, the rub of her dress on the sofa, the shriek of her right-hand index finger as it rubbed his left-hand thumbnail. His ears were assaulted so violently that at first he could not reply. Then he said faintly that it was all settled, they would get the tickets next week.

He unlocked the drawer of his desk and took out the powder. It would have to be tonight.

He took the coffee in to the living room. Marilyn continued to be kittenish, saying now that she wanted brown and not white sugar. He fetched it for her. A sense of power and ease flowed through him as she raised the cup to her lips. Now it was a question of waiting, nothing more.

Later he lay in bed with the light out, staring up into the blackness. Marilyn was totally silent, yet with his wonderfully attuned ears he could hear the sibilation of her breath. Who had written something about hearing the press of an ant's foot on grass? He could have heard that too. He looked at his watch. The time was ten minutes after midnight.

"Are you all right?" he whispered, and the words came back immediately like an echo. "Are you?"

At these two innocuous whispered words he experienced a feeling that could not be identified exactly, a feeling that combined apprehension and discomfort. Her next words were also whispered. "I drank your coffee. You drank mine."

For a few moments the words were meaningless, then he understood them, and at the moment of understanding, the discomfort changed to a pain that gripped his body as though a giant crab had gripped his chest with one claw and his stomach with another. Electric lights struck at his eyes, and Marilyn was spitting at him like some great cat.

"Did you think I was fool enough to let you get rid of me the way you got rid of her?" He gasped something and tried to get out of bed, but his legs seemed made of soft plastic. "I was in the kitchen when you were making coffee that night. Do you think I didn't see what you were doing? *Powder for Wine Making.* You dirty little devil."

The words grated like a rake over gravel. He started to say something. Then the pain came again, and he stopped.

"I thought you'd spend money, not throw it about like a man with no hands. But I've been watching to see if you tried anything." She put on her dressing gown. "There's no will. So I'm your heir."

"Call the doctor." With a supreme effort he managed to swing his legs out of bed. She came and pushed him back.

"Not yet." She looked at her watch. "I reckon you waited more than an hour before you rang old Bentham. I'll make it two. And now I've got to wash up the dinner things. *And* the coffee cups." She held up something bright and shining in her hand. A key. "I don't think you'll be any trouble from the look of you, but better safe than sorry."

As she went out, a lightning stroke of pain—much worse than what he had experienced before—split his body; and at the same moment he heard, like a roll of thunder—terrible, decisive, final—the turning of the key in the lock.

CAPTAIN LEOPOLD INCOGNITO

Edward D. Hoch

I T W A S F L E T C H E R ' S case in the beginning, and oddly enough that was how it became Leopold's case. "He knows me too well," Lieutenant Fletcher said, taking a sip of coffee from his paper cup. "There's no way I could follow him up there undercover."

Connie Trent, full of department spirit after her recent promotion to sergeant, volunteered, "I could go in his place, Captain."

Leopold smiled. "To a men's health spa? I don't believe you'd stay undercover very long, Connie."

"Don't they have women there too?"

Fletcher shook his head. "Not in the spring. At Dr Rohmer's it's strictly men now. In the summer they have women's sessions and even co-ed ones, but now it's men only."

Connie thought about it. "What you need is a cop who looks like he could use a week at Dr Rohmer's Health Spa. Not some young guy with muscles. You need one who's middle-aged and overweight."

Captain Leopold smiled. "You've just described me, Connie."

"You!"

"Why not? I don't have any pending cases here, and best of all Walter Hazard is new to this city and doesn't know me. Call the spa and see if they'll take me without an advance reservation. I can go up there tomorrow. And contact the sheriff's office up there. I'll need them to make the actual arrest."

Fletcher wasn't happy. "It's my case, Captain. You shouldn't be taking the risk for me."

"It's the department's case, Fletcher."

The object of all this discussion, Walter Hazard, was a forty-one-year-old man with a long record of dealing in narcotics. He'd come to Leopold's city only recently, apparently intent on taking over the heroin trade from a man named Max Guttner, who controlled the drug traffic throughout southern New England.

Max Guttner had died ten days ago, shot twice in the head by a silenced .22-calibre target pistol. It was a weapon becoming more and more popular in criminal circles because it could be effectively silenced. And at close

range it was just as deadly as a .45. Fletcher was convinced Hazard had
killed Guttner to get control of the heroin traffic, but knowing it and
proving it were two different things. They needed the murder weapon.
And they needed proof that Hazard was now in charge of the Guttner
operation. Fletcher hoped to find that proof at Dr Rohmer's Health Spa.

The spa, located in northern Vermont near the Canadian border, had
long been rumoured as a way station in the narcotics pipeline from
Canada. Respectable businessmen, relaxing for a week in the Vermont
woods, returned with their suitcases full of heroin. "We could stop Hazard
on the way back," Connie suggested, but Fletcher vetoed it.

"He'd be clean. He knows all the tricks. He has to be taken at the
moment he gets the stuff in his hands. And the only way to do that is with
an undercover man. We can hold him on the drug charge and use it as
evidence he'd taken over Guttner's organization. That'll give us our
motive for the killing."

"All right," Leopold said. "I can use a week up there. What about this
man Rohmer who runs the place?"

"It seems he must be involved, though we've got nothing against him."

"Is Hazard there now?"

Fletcher nodded. "He went up last night."

"Today's Monday. If he's staying a full week, chances are the delivery
will be made on Thursday or Friday. But I'd better get up there tomorrow,
just in case."

"What name will you use?" Connie asked.

"I'll think of a good one."

Walter Hazard arose early on Tuesday morning for a brisk run in the
woods before breakfast. He was ready to admit there was something to
this health spa business, even after only one full day on the premises. A
combination of exercise, diet, and steam room had already shown results. It
was almost enough to make him forget the reason for his trip.

Hazard had driven up from Connecticut on Sunday night. Dr Rohmer
told him that most clients came by train, but Hazard would have a special
need for his car on the return trip. The plan was for a man named Kellogg
to cross the border with fifty pounds of uncut heroin on Thursday night.
He was expecting to meet Max Guttner, but the word had been passed to
him that he'd be meeting Walter Hazard instead.

Hazard was a man without morals, which he insisted was the only way
to get ahead in the modern world. He never thought about what happened
to the heroin after it left his hands, and he never thought about the men
he'd killed along the way to his present position. It hadn't bothered his

conscience a bit when he'd walked up behind Max Guttner and fired two bullets into his head at close range. It was the way of the world these days. Only the strong, the unscrupulous, survived.

Hazard had a woman named Margo who'd been with him for the past two years. She was beautiful and smart, and could have succeeded on her own in the business world. Somehow she preferred the uncertainties of Hazard's existence, and he never questioned that. He'd had to leave her behind on this trip, which depressed her, but he'd promised to phone.

In fact he was thinking of phoning her as he completed his run, coming up to the dining-room entrance at a trot. That was when he saw Dr Rohmer awaiting him. Rohmer was a slim, balding man who rarely smiled. At this moment he was looking especially unsmiling. "Can I see you in my office, Mr Hazard?"

"Now? Before breakfast?"

"Before breakfast."

Hazard wiped the sweat from his face and neck and followed the man inside. "What's up?" he asked when they were alone in the spa's main office. It was after eight and his stomach was growling with hunger.

"I just had a phone call from a friend at the sheriff's office."

"Oh?"

"Do you know a detective named Leopold? Captain Leopold?"

"I may have heard the name. What about him?"

"He notified the sheriff that he's coming here undercover as part of a murder investigation. He wants their help if an arrest needs to be made, since he's outside his own jurisdiction."

"Was my name mentioned?"

"No—but it's you he's after, isn't it? He knows you killed Max."

Hazard merely stared at Dr Rohmer. Finally he said, "That sort of talk can get you in big trouble, Doctor. When's this Leopold arriving?"

"Today."

"I'll be watching for him."

"I don't want him here, Hazard. Nor you either!"

"Don't worry. There won't be any trouble. How will he arrive—by car?"

"You're the only one this week who came by car. He'll take the train up from Montpelier like everyone else, to avoid attracting attention."

"How's he get here from the station?"

"Fellow from town named Gus brings up the mail every day. Any strays come along in his station wagon."

"Strays?"

"Those with reservations arrive on Sunday as you did. But there are always a few who turn up later in the week unannounced, and we try to accommodate them if there's room."

"What time does Gus get here?"

"Around eleven if the train's on time."

"All right," Hazard said. "Thanks for the warning."

"Are you clearing out?"

"No. I'm staying."

When Hazard saw the station wagon coming up the hill he left his exercise class and trotted over to the main building. A stocky man in soiled coveralls was unloading suitcases from the back of the vehicle. "Are you Gus?" Hazard asked.

The man straightened up. "That's right, mister."

"Where's the fellow you brought up from the train?"

"Fellow? I brought up three fellows. They're in at the desk, registering."

"Three?" Hazard hurried up the steps and into the lobby. There were indeed three men there—all middle-aged and overweight. Typical clients for Dr Rohmer. One was taller than the others, with white hair and a boyish face. He put out his hand as Hazard entered the lobby.

"Are you Dr Rohmer? I'm Ed Murray from Boston. I don't have a reservation but I was told on the phone it didn't matter."

Hazard shook hands and said, "Sorry, I'm not the doctor. Just a patient like yourself."

"Oh."

Gus deposited the luggage in the lobby and accepted tips from the men. Then he turned his station wagon around and headed back down the hill. Presently Dr Rohmer appeared, casting a glance in Hazard's direction, and welcomed the three men. "Our regular week at the $150 rate starts on Sunday. By the day it's $30. If you'll just sign in I'll have one of the boys show you to your rooms."

One of the two shorter men spoke up. "I'm Frank Gibbons, from Springfield. Could you make sure I get an air-conditioned room? I have a bit of an allergy problem, and—"

Dr Rohmer came close to smiling but didn't quite make it. "You're here to relax and get over things like that. A few sessions in the steam room and some good healthy food and you'll forget you ever had an allergy."

Hazard stole a glance at the registration cards. The third man, well built and probably still in his late forties, was named Sam Young. He gave his home as Providence, Rhode Island, and stood off to one side without speaking.

When they'd been led away to their rooms, Dr Rohmer came over to Hazard. "Did you look them over?"

"A little. Which one is Leopold?"

The doctor frowned. "I have no idea. I told you I want you out of here."

"Let's go in your office and talk it over."

"There's nothing to talk over." The doctor turned and stalked away.

Hazard watched him go, wondering just how serious he was. If Rohmer did anything to block the transfer of the heroin, he could ruin Hazard's takeover of the Guttner network. Without a leader they'd be selling the stuff on the streets for whatever the market would bring.

Hazard went up to his room and opened his suitcase. From the zipper pouch of toilet articles he extracted his .22-calibre target pistol, a box of cartridges, and the silencer. He went about his task with loving care, checking the weapon to make certain it was still well oiled. It was American intelligence agents who'd first discovered that such weapons were just about the only production handguns which could be effectively silenced. The information had taken years to seep through to the underworld, but now the pistol was being used with excellent results.

Hazard loaded the gun and attached the silencer. Then he carefully taped it to the skin of his calf, beneath his baggy sweatpants. He'd lose some hair off his leg when he pulled it free, but that was nothing. A brief bit of pain had never bothered him.

He went back outside, watching some of the early comers already heading for the dining room. It was just about noon, almost lunchtime, but he wasn't the least bit hungry. "Going to eat?" a voice behind him asked. It was the white-haired Ed Murray from Boston.

"Not quite yet," Hazard replied.

"Hurry up and I'll save you a seat at our table." Murray had changed into shorts and a sweatshirt and seemed ready to take on the world.

"Sure," Hazard said. "You do that."

He crossed the exercise field to the administration building and entered Rohmer's office through the side door. The doctor was at his desk, checking over a pile of bills from the morning mail. "What—? Oh, it's you again, Hazard. What now? I thought you'd be gone."

"I'm not going, Rohmer. I can't go till Kellogg gets here Thursday night with the stuff."

Dr Rohmer sighed and went back to checking the bills. "Kellogg won't be coming. I'm putting through a call to Montreal this afternoon, telling him to cancel the trip."

"I was afraid of that."

"Damn it, Hazard, I'm not going to let this business go down the drain for you! Max Guttner always paid me well, but he respected my position too! I can't have Kellogg coming across the border Thursday night with an undercover detective captain on the premises. Especially when I don't even know which one he is!"

"I'll find out."

"Don't bother—the deal's off. I'm phoning Kellogg."

"I'm sorry to hear that."

Hazard squatted as if to tie his sneaker, pulling the pistol free from under his pants leg. He felt the sudden flash of pain as the tape pulled away some hair. Then he straightened up, and without saying a word fired two bullets into Dr Rohmer's left temple.

There was almost no sound from the pistol, and very little blood from the two small wounds. Hazard quickly stepped to the door and bolted it. Then he lifted Rohmer's body from the chair and half dragged, half carried it across to a closet. It would have to remain there till after dark. He couldn't risk anyone finding it till after Thursday, when he completed his deal. Any hint of Rohmer's murder and Leopold would have the local police in immediately.

Hazard replaced the gun beneath his baggy sweatpants and jogged over to the dining room to join Ed Murray for lunch. The other two newcomers were at the table with him, and they'd saved a chair for Hazard. He wondered who'd had the idea of inviting him. "Sit right here," Murray said. "You come to this place often?"

"First time. How about you?"

"First time for all of us, I guess."

Gibbons, the man from Springfield, patted his bulging stomach. "I been going to these health spas for years, but they sure don't do much for me. This one's a picnic compared to some I've seen. There's a place in the Catskills that's run like a concentration camp, with enforced fasting. That'll take the pounds off!"

"Really?" Hazard sipped his vegetable juice. He turned to the silent Sam Young. "What about you? First visit here?"

"Yeah."

"You don't talk much."

"Nothing to say."

"Only reason I'm here is my wife," the white-haired Murray said. "She's always beefing about the shape I'm in, wanting me to lose weight."

Hazard glanced at Murray's left hand. There was no wedding ring, but that proved nothing. Many men didn't wear them. But Murray said he was from Boston and he talked more like a New Yorker. That might mean something. He tried to put himself in Leopold's place. Would he be more likely to pose as a devoted husband or a health nut like Gibbons or a silent stranger like Sam Young?

The trouble was, Hazard didn't know Leopold.

But someone must know him.

Someone back in Connecticut.

After lunch Hazard excused himself and went to his little room. He had two phone calls to make.

First he got an outside line and then dialled the number of Dr Rohmer's Health Spa. When the switchboard answered he asked for the front desk. Then, muffling his voice and trying to imitate Rohmer's monotone, he told the room clerk, "This is Dr Rohmer. I'm in town and something important has come up. I may have to go down to Burlington for a few days."

"Yes, sir," the clerk answered dutifully.

"Tell the staff to carry on as usual. I'll be back no later than Friday."

"Very good, sir."

Hazard hung up smiling. He knew Rohmer's car was in the garage at his nearby house, but that could be moved after dark, along with the body. Rohmer was separated from his wife, so there'd probably be no one to question his disappearance, at least till Friday. By that time Hazard would have finished his business.

Next he phoned his apartment in Connecticut, hoping Margo would be home. She was.

"How are you doing up there?" she asked. "Losing weight?"

"Some. Look, Margo, I want you to do something for me. I need a photograph of a man named Leopold, a detective captain down there."

"What's up?"

"He may be here. If he is, I need to identify him."

"If he's there, how do I get a picture of him?"

"Go down to the newspaper morgue—right now, this afternoon. If he's a captain he must have had his picture in the paper sometime. When he was promoted, if nothing else. Make a Xerox copy of the clipping. If they won't allow copies, steal the damn thing. Call me back when you've got it. I'll give you the number here."

"All right." She didn't ask any more questions. She knew what he wanted and how to get it. "Take care of yourself, Walter."

"Don't worry."

He hung up and went back outside. It was almost time for the steam room and massage.

The silent Sam Young was on the massage table next to Hazard, and he noticed the scar tissue on Young's side. "What's that from?" he asked. "Looks like a bullet grazed you."

Sam Young eyed him with interest. "That's what happened."

"Where?"

"Vietnam."

Young closed his eyes and said no more. Hazard rolled over on his stomach and studied the scar. There was no way of telling if it had been caused by a .50-calibre machine gun in the jungle or a .32-calibre handgun in an alley.

It was just before dinnertime when Margo called back. He could tell from the edge of excitement in her voice that she had what he needed. "You got it?"

"Sure, Walter. No problem. There were lots of clippings about him, and two pictures. I copied them both."

"What's he look like?"

"Middle-aged, a little overweight."

"I figured that much. Does he have white hair?"

"No, it looks dark in these pictures."

"How recent are they?"

"One's about three years old, but the other ran six months ago."

"Can you tell how tall he is?"

"Not from these pictures. They're head-and-shoulders."

"Anything in the articles that might help? Do they mention a bullet wound?"

"No, I don't remember anything like that."

Hazard was feeling frustrated. "What about his face? Anything unusual? Scars?"

"Nothing like that, Walter. It's just a face."

"What colour eyes?"

"These are black-and-white pictures, Walter. How the hell do I know what colour eyes? Not real light, though."

"All right," he said finally.

"Do you want me to drive up with these?"

"No, no—a woman up here this week would be too noticeable. Besides, it's a six-hour drive. Put them in the mail to me—but take the letter to the post office so you're sure it goes out tonight."

"You probably won't get it till Thursday morning."

"I know." He hated putting himself at the mercy of the mail, but maybe he'd get lucky in the meantime. He still held an advantage because Leopold couldn't know when the shipment from Canada was due—if he knew about it at all.

"Be careful, Walter."

"Don't worry. I'll see you the end of the week."

He hung up, wondering if the phone might be tapped, and then decided it wasn't. The line went through the switchboard. They couldn't have put a tap on it without Rohmer's knowledge.

After dinner he strolled and chatted with Ed Murray, inventing a mythical midwestern business he'd managed to counter Murray's stories about the business world of Boston. As they parted, Hazard reflected that at least Margo's information had cleared the white-haired Murray.

Unless, that is, Leopold had dyed his hair.

*　　*　　*

After dark Hazard went over to Dr Rohmer's house and opened the lock on the garage door, using a key from the doctor's pocket. He drove the big green limousine up to the rear entrance of the administration building, hoping no one was looking out a window. He could hear the TV sets blaring, and he knew that Murray and the other two were engaged in a three-handed pinochle game. With luck he'd be safe, but he carried the .22 pistol under his jacket just in case.

He pulled Rohmer's body from the closet, hoisted it over his shoulders, went out to the car, and put it in the boot. There was a large stain of blood on the closet floor that he covered with a little rug from the office. Then he smoothed out the marks of the dead man's heels on the office carpeting.

Hazard drove the big car slowly down the winding road toward the town. He remembered seeing an abandoned marble quarry on the drive up. It wasn't the perfect place to hide a car and a body, but it should serve for a few days.

He left the car deep in the quarry, placing a few wooden planks and tree branches around it to camouflage its appearance from a distance. Then he walked about a mile into town.

The first person he saw was Gus, standing by his station wagon near the train station. "What'll you charge to run me up the hill to the spa?" he asked.

The stocky man spit out some tobacco juice. "Two bucks."

"Good, let's go."

"You been out walkin'?"

"Exercise. Walked farther than I thought. It's easy downhill, but I guess I need a ride back up."

Gus grunted and opened his door. "Get that dust off your shoes. I try to keep my wagon clean."

"Sure," Hazard said.

In ten minutes he was back at the health spa. He paid Gus for the trip and went inside to watch the card game. No one seemed to have missed him.

In the morning, on his pre-breakfast run, Hazard was accompanied by Frank Gibbons. The man seemed to have overcome his worry over allergies, but he was still full of horror stories about the other spas he'd visited.

"One place out west," he told Hazard as they jogged along the wooded path, "they all kneel naked in the sun on a stone terrace overlooking the ocean. Men and women together! I tried it for an hour and was sunburned for two weeks!"

"They go for that stuff in California," Hazard agreed. "A bunch of oddballs, if you ask me."

"It cured my allergy though—I gotta admit that."

"How were the women out west?"

"Beautiful! But they were all into this meditation kick. It wasn't a health spa, it was a religion."

The mail arrived a little before noon and was quickly sorted into a row of slots, one for each letter of the alphabet. There was nothing in the H slot for Hazard, but he'd known it was too soon to receive Margo's letter and the pictures.

After lunch he tried to strike up another conversation with Sam Young, but without much luck. He'd just about ruled Young off his list of suspects—certainly Leopold would try harder to be friendly, if only to keep a close eye on him.

That evening he started to grow nervous. Maybe it was all this exercise that had tired his mind as well as his body. He started thinking of all the things that could go wrong, especially with this Leopold on the premises. He wished he knew the name of the person in the sheriff's office who'd tipped off Rohmer. But then he decided the name wouldn't be of much help. The man was obviously loyal to Rohmer, and the doctor was out of the picture now.

But what if Rohmer had lied to him?

What if he'd already phoned Kellogg before Hazard killed him?

He looked through the little notebook he'd taken from Max Guttner's body and found the phone number in Montreal where Kellogg could be reached. But this time he didn't risk using the phone in his room. He went outside and entered Dr Rohmer's office through the back door. Sitting at the desk where the doctor himself had last sat, he put in the call to Montreal.

There was some trouble reaching Kellogg, but finally he came on the line. Voices in the background suggested a party was in progress. "This is Hazard, at the spa."

"Oh, yeah."

"Will I see you tomorrow?"

"Sure. Why not?"

"Dr Rohmer had to go away suddenly. I was afraid there might have been a change in plan."

"Not on this end. I should get there before midnight."

"Fine."

"You have the money?"

"Don't you worry about that. It's right here."

"See you, then. By the big rock on the north path."

Hazard hung up, feeling better. All was going well. He was being nervous without the slightest cause.

At breakfast in the morning Ed Murray was talking about the roads. "Driving in this part of the country is murder. Don't you agree, Walter?"

Hazard was immediately on guard. Had Murray seen him in Rohmer's car on Tuesday night? "Oh, I don't know. I brought my car up."

"Over these roads? I don't know how you did it!"

"You took the train?"

"A bus, actually. The schedule was better."

Hazard studied the face across the table, trying to picture the man as a detective captain. It could be. It could easily be.

"Going to the lecture on mental health?" Murray asked.

"I suppose so," Hazard said. "Hope I don't fall asleep."

They sat together during the late-morning lecture, in which one of Dr Rohmer's assistants expounded on the importance of a correct attitude toward life. Yes, thought Hazard, that's one thing I've got—a right attitude toward life. And toward death too.

The room was only about half full, and he couldn't help noticing that both Gibbons and Young were among the missing. "I think Young was going for a run," Murray said in answer to Hazard's question. "And Frank Gibbons wanted a dip in the outside pool. This is the first really warm day we've had."

The lecture ended just before lunchtime, and Hazard hurried to the mail slots. The letter from Margo was there. He recognized her slim slanted handwriting at once.

He held his breath and tore it open.

Her note said simply: *Here it is*. He unfolded the clipping and stared at it.

The story was from a Boston newspaper, about a spring visit to the zoo. The picture accompanying it showed a large male gorilla pounding his chest.

Hazard sat down in the lobby, stunned. He knew Margo would never play a trick like this. Someone had got to the mail, removed the letter from its slot while he sat in that damned lecture!

He examined the gummed flap of the envelope. It had been steamed open and resealed with rubber cement. The picture of Leopold had been taken out and this foolish thing substituted. And only one person could have done it—Captain Leopold himself.

The two of them were circling each other like wildcats in the dark, each at a disadvantage. Hazard still didn't know Leopold's cover identity, and

Leopold still didn't know the Canadian heroin was arriving that night.

But maybe, just maybe, Leopold had overextended himself.

Because Hazard had been with Ed Murray all morning, sitting right next to him during the lecture, there was no way the white-haired man from Boston could have taken this letter out of the slot and substituted the clipping.

So Ed Murray wasn't Captain Leopold.

And that left just two of them—Gibbons the health nut and Sam Young the silent, with the bullet scar on his side.

One of them was Leopold.

Hazard bit his lip and thought about the gun back in his room. If necessary he could kill them both.

But it would be better just to kill the right one.

Gibbons or Young?

Gibbons' mail slot, the G, would be right next to Hazard's. Gibbons could have taken the letter and returned it later without much risk. And that damned picture of the gorilla! Wasn't a gibbon an ape of some sort? Leopold could be giving him a hint.

But why would he do that? Wouldn't he be more likely to cast suspicion on someone else, on the wrong man?

And why had he left this foolish clipping in the first place?

Of course he had to remove the real picture once he found it, and doing that much was enough to tip his hand. A clipping from a handy Boston paper could do no further harm—and in Leopold's view it might even force Hazard's hand. Sam Young might even have left the ape picture to point suspicion at the Gibbons name.

Hazard went back to his room after lunch and got out the .22 pistol. He'd carry it taped to his leg from now on, until he met Kellogg just before midnight. If Gibbons or Young tried to stop him, he'd kill either as he had Dr Rohmer.

Hazard's car was in a small parking area down the hill from the swimming pool. He was in the habit of checking it each afternoon, though it wasn't likely anyone would try to steal it. He checked it now, making certain no one was blocking him from a quick exit that night, and then he returned to the pool.

Sam Young pulled himself out of the water as Hazard approached, and began drying himself with a towel. "Beautiful day," Hazard remarked.

"Yeah."

He found his eyes drawn again to the scar on the man's side. "You come to these places often?"

"First time."

"Where do you work in Providence?"

"I'm with the city."

"Oh?"

Young finished drying himself and walked away, leaving Hazard standing there. He watched the man go, thinking in that moment that he'd like to kill him whether or not he proved to be Captain Leopold.

He sat by the pool for a time, until the start of the afternoon callisthenics. Then as he was getting up, something made him glance down the hill at his car. It seemed to be at an odd angle, with the rear end lower than the front. He strolled down for a closer look.

Both of his rear tyres were flat.

He glanced quickly in all directions, but no one was around. Yet he was sure the tyres had been perfectly all right thirty minutes earlier.

Leopold again—who else?

He tried to decide whether Young could have got dressed and out the other door in time to deflate his tyres. Probably not, and that only left Gibbons.

Gibbons was Leopold. He was almost certain of it now. All that talk of allergies and health spas was part of his cover.

But why deflate his tyres? What did Leopold hope to gain?

He wanted to prevent Hazard's escape, obviously. If Hazard called attention to the flat tyres, or tried to get them changed or inflated in a hurry, it would be a tipoff that he planned an early departure.

No, better to leave the car as it was and find another way out of there. He could always steal a car if necessary.

As he was passing through the lobby a better idea struck him. That man from town had his card tacked up on the notice board. *Gus's Taxi Service—Day & Night.*

He went to a pay phone and called the number. Gus wasn't in, the woman said. This was the drug store, and should she have Gus call back? No, Hazard told her. He'd call back.

All through dinner he kept his eyes on Frank Gibbons. The man ate heartily, speaking of the appetite he'd worked up. At one point in the conversation he wondered where Dr Rohmer was, and Ed Murray said, "I hear he's away for a few days."

After dinner Hazard phoned the taxi driver again. This time the woman put him on and Hazard said, "Gus? This is the man you brought up to the health spa the other night. Remember?"

"Yeah, I remember."

"Could you come get me tonight, around midnight?"

"I guess so."

"Don't honk your horn and disturb people. I'll walk down the road to the signpost and meet you there. At midnight. If I'm a few minutes late, wait for me."

"I'll be there."

Hazard hung up and relaxed. For the first time all day he felt some of the tension draining away. It was going to work. In spite of Leopold and his damned gorilla, it was going to come off.

There was one more thing to do and he'd be reasonably safe. He took Dr Rohmer's keys—his car keys and house keys—from their hiding place in his room and slipped them into the envelope with the money for Kellogg. If the Canadian was caught, or if he tried to double-cross Hazard, he could be blamed for Rohmer's murder. Perhaps he'd have an alibi for the past few days, but it would take time to prove.

Then Hazard opened his toilet kit and took out a bottle of sleeping capsules. He emptied the powder from three capsules into a little fold of paper and tucked this in his pocket. Just in case.

The evening pinochle game hadn't yet begun, though most of the regulars were assembled in the card room. Hazard sought out Frank Gibbons and suggested they have a little wine. It was the only alcoholic beverage to be found on the premises, so there wasn't a great deal of choice. Hazard poured from the decanter, slipping the sleeping powder into the glass intended for Gibbons. They sat on the terrace, drinking and chatting, and Gibbons passed up his game with the others.

"A fine night," Hazard said.

Gibbons agreed. "Look at that moon! Makes you want to run through the woods!"

After a time Hazard saw the sleeping powder beginning to take effect. "Why did you come here?" he asked Gibbons. "To trap me?"

"W—what?" His head dipped forward on to his chest.

Hazard smiled and stood up. "Sweet dreams, Captain Leopold."

He came off the terrace and strolled toward the woods. He'd have an hour or more to wait, but he liked to be early. He crouched and pulled the tape from his leg again, feeling the cool steel of the gun in his hand. Then he moved deeper into the woods, and presently when he'd found the meeting place he sat down on a rock and lit a cigarette.

Kellogg came up the path a few minutes after eleven, giving the bird call that was his signal. "Are you Hazard?" he asked.

"That's right."

"What happened to old Max?"

"He had an accident."

The Canadian nodded. "Those things happen. You got the money?"

"In this envelope."

Kellogg lit a match to count it. "What are these keys?"

"Do me a favour and throw them away in the woods."

"Huh?"

"Do you have the stuff?"

Kellogg unstrapped a knapsack from his shoulders. "Fifty pounds, uncut."

"Good." Hazard did a quick test with the tip of his tongue. It seemed like the real thing.

"When do you want some more?"

"I'll be in touch. Goodbye for now."

He watched the Canadian hurry back down the trail. They hadn't shaken hands because Hazard was holding the silenced pistol in his right hand. The Canadian must have seen it, but in this business such actions weren't that unusual. Hazard glanced at his watch. He had plenty of time to get his suitcase and meet the station wagon.

He hurried back to the spa, where most of the lights were out now, and entered his room. The knapsack went into his suitcase but the pistol stayed in his hand. He was going out the door, weighted down with the heavy luggage, when someone grabbed him in the dark.

He saw the white hair and knew it was Ed Murray.

"Not so fast, mister. I saw you putting something into Frank's drink and he passed out! What's your game, anyway?"

Hazard growled an obscenity and tried to break free, but Murray held him tight. Hazard's right hand came up, unable to get the long-barrelled pistol into firing position. Instead, he brought it up and over in an arc, catching Murray across the back of the head. The man's knees buckled and Hazard hit him again.

Then he pointed the weapon at the fallen figure. It was all coming apart—Gibbons and now Murray! Were they both Captain Leopold? But that was crazy.

He realized the silencer had come off the weapon when it hit Murray's skull. He couldn't find it in the dark and he couldn't risk a shot without it. He left Murray lying there and hurried out.

He was panting when he reached the signpost down the road. Gus's station wagon was already there. "You're out of breath," the stocky man told him. "Let me help you with that suitcase."

Hazard brought up the gun. "Don't touch it. Just get in and drive." He slid the suitcase on to the seat ahead of him.

"Sure, mister."

Then, before Hazard realized what was happening, the car door hit his hand holding the gun. He screamed in pain and dropped the weapon, then looked up at the gun in Gus's hand. "Sure, mister," the man said, "I'm driving us right to jail. I'm Captain Leopold."

*   *   *

It was the following afternoon before Leopold was back in his office with Lieutenant Fletcher and Connie Trent. "I saved you some work and our local taxpayers some money," he told Fletcher. "Hazard will be tried in Vermont for killing Dr Rohmer and we won't have to extradite him unless he beats that rap. Luckily the man he hit on the head wasn't badly hurt."

Fletcher merely shook his head. "I've got so many questions I don't know where to begin."

"Suppose I just tell you what happened," Leopold said. "I had every intention of going to the spa as a guest until I met this man Gus and saw that he was stocky like me. I paid him to let me take his place for a few days, and he filled me in on the layout of the spa and the daily rounds with the mail and such. The story to the townspeople was that Gus was ill and I was his cousin, filling in for a few days. Hazard took me by surprise on Tuesday and asked if I was Gus, so I said I was, and stuck to that story with him. I told the desk clerk the cousin story. Rohmer, who'd know I wasn't Gus, was killed before he ever saw me."

"How'd you know Hazard killed him?" Connie asked.

"On Tuesday night he came into town on foot, looking for a ride back to the spa. There was marble dust on his shoes, from the quarry outside of town. I got somebody to show me the place the next morning and I found Rohmer's car with his body in the boot. Rohmer had a stooge in the sheriff's office, but once his body was found that guy just wanted to save his own skin. He admitted tipping off Rohmer that I was coming, so I figured Hazard knew it too. When I saw a letter arrive for him yesterday, I steamed it open and found my picture inside. I substituted a newspaper clipping about the Boston zoo, which properly unnerved Hazard."

Fletcher scowled at Leopold. "Opening mail without a warrant?"

"We won't tell the postal authorities that part. Actually, Hazard was so busy suspecting the other guests of being me that he never thought of the most likely person to tamper with the mail—the person who delivered it every day."

"What about the Canadian?"

"They picked him up trying to recross the border."

"How'd you know Hazard would phone you for a ride last night?" Connie asked.

"Well, I'd given him a ride Tuesday night, and I figured if I let the air out of his tyres he might decide to call on me again. If he hadn't, I'd have been waiting for him anyway."

"You let the air out of his tyres?"

Captain Leopold grinned. "There's something about this undercover work that brings out the worst in a cop. But for people like Walter Hazard, the worst is none too bad."

SUB-PLOT

Jean McConnell

"Yes, we're burying her tomorrow morning," said Belfrage.

"Were you very close to her?"

I was only making conversation. Or rather extending it. Nobody could say Belfrage was a scintillating talker, but I valued these brief chats.

"Oh no. She wasn't that well liked. Mind you, the family converged near the end."

"That was decent."

"She had a bob or two."

"Ah well—"

"You what? You never saw wrangling like it."

"Nothing divides a family like a common sorrow."

Maggie, behind the bar, shot me a glance. Belfrage flowed on.

"Would you believe we can't find the old girl's Will?"

"Oh dear."

"Had the place upside down. Solicitors don't have it. Wife's there now, having another search. She was her favourite niece. She says."

"Frustrating."

"You're right. Maggie! Same again, love. I'd like there to be something. Not for myself, you know. But it would be nice for the wife. She never complains, bless her."

Maggie served us. "Perhaps she has nothing to complain about," she remarked.

Belfrage acknowledged this as a compliment.

Maggie pushed me my glass. "And how is *your* wife, Mr Norton?"

On certain days, Maggie enjoyed knifing the wounds of husbands who were only too aware they had made a bad choice. She had comprehended my situation within a couple of weeks of my moving into the neighbourhood. Perhaps I had given signals. Such as when there was talk of closing the Feathers for repairs and I had protested so strongly. Or when she'd caught me checking my watch so frequently as it drew near eight o'clock.

Belfrage had paused only to take a pull at his beer.

"How are they getting on with the grave then?"

I was startled.

"You came across the churchyard, didn't you? Have they finished it? You'd not miss it. Family plot. Seddon. Right by the pathway. Have they done it?"

"Ah! Yes. There was one. Rusty had a scratch there. Oh, sorry!"

"Don't fret, lad. Aunt Mercy loved animals. Mice anyroad. House was full of them."

We all laughed.

"Time I was off." I tugged at Rusty's lead.

"Doesn't want to go home," said Belfrage, then stopped abruptly and stooped down to tousle the dog's head.

"See you tomorrow," said Maggie. Her mood had softened to normal.

"Same time. Same place," quipped Belfrage.

"Yes. Goodnight all."

I left him silhouetted against the rosy glow of the bar.

Only twenty-three hours to get through.

Seddon. I shone my torch on the headstones. Amelia Seddon. William Seddon. Grace Seddon. Nearby, a freshly-dug trench with planks across it.

William Seddon's tomb was topped with an urn. Moss clung to the crumbling stone. Beautiful. Anne had loved old churchyards. We had strolled in many, reading the quaint words, puzzling out the Latin, touched by the tiny graves. We never found them mournful.

I had buried Anne in a hallowed acre by the shore. It was far away. Time and ivy must by now have softened the lines of her stone.

When a man has been happy in marriage, he is vulnerable. When a man is convalescing from an illness, he is doubly so. And when a man is believed to be well-off, he should take care.

I knew all this now. But at the time, the attentions of Ellen seemed such a balm to the spirit. Filled such a terrible vacuum.

It had taken such a short time to go wrong. Perhaps only as long as it took me to recover from my emotional and physical shocks. And for Ellen to discover that my financial position was only modest.

At first, it had been mere misgivings. I had thought it natural enough when the house was changed throughout. Then, this done, and every trace of Anne disposed of, the demand to move to the southern end of the country. It had meant taking an early retirement for me, but that did not seem important if Ellen would be happy. Indeed, Anne and I had often thought of Brighton in this respect. But where Anne had seen cast-iron balconies, Ellen saw only candy floss.

So we had settled in a quiet, respectable village in Kent. Leaving my friends had been less of a wrench than it might have been, because Ellen had not cared for them, and ties had already been broken.

But slowly it came home to me that Ellen was one whom there was no pleasing. The friends were not replaced. Acquaintances might be made, but always Ellen would ferret out some Achilles heel, and expose it. She could not expect to be loved for this, and she wasn't. "If people can't stand the truth," she would say, in reply to my protests.

We seemed to spend more and more of our time alone together, while emotionally we grew further and further apart.

With Ellen the act of love was clinical as a diagram in a sex manual. I am one who finds no pleasure if the woman is not satisfied. With Anne, we had constantly delighted each other afresh. Anne, so sweetly flushed, who would lie calm in my arms. Ellen, who made straight for the bathroom, as if to wash all trace of me from her body. Did I not assuage her? Perhaps I simply aroused her without fulfilment, so that she needed to comfort herself alone. But she denied this. And the question no longer arose, since all manifestations of love had ceased between us.

It was ironic that although Ellen seemed to find me increasingly aggravating in everything I did, yet she insisted that I stay near, and was only in some measure content when I was doing repairs about the place under her supervision.

Perhaps I am somewhat inept as a handyman. All I know is that Anne's encouragement and aid from the bottom of a ladder had been more productive than Ellen's relentless criticism. And if the job required a craftsman, so much the worse. This invariably lead to unpleasant situations. Ellen treated everyone with suspicion and distrust, while she herself was capable of a sharpness that bordered on dishonesty.

I am not a man who loses his temper easily—at least on the outside. Perhaps I should have done. I should have stopped Ellen's nonsense long ago. Maybe it was a challenge, stemming from insecurity. A completely unjustified insecurity. How had she misread my character so completely? I suppose she needed a firm hand. But all I had to offer was a gentle touch. It had been all that Anne had wanted.

God knows I am not insensitive. I had been willing to bury the dead and live for the living. But in one matter I had stood firm. Rusty. He had not been Anne's dog especially, but Ellen lumped him together with my first marriage and had made every effort to get rid of him. This I would not allow. And in time I was more than glad I had not given in. His trusting eye and affectionate presence had become almost my sole joy in the home. And his need for exercise served as a valid reason for me leaving the house twice a day alone.

Rusty's morning run on the common did not arouse great comment since Ellen was still in bed at that time. But my evening walk, though it was simply down the garden, out of the gate, across the churchyard and along the lane to the pub, where I stayed no more than an hour then returned, was the subject of many a bad scene.

What Ellen imagined I was up to in that quiet country hostelry, I had no idea. It seemed enough that it was a pleasure to me. Pleasure was not really the word. Haven.

Rusty was no youngster and took his time about most things these days. My torch rested on him. He was ankle-deep in the soft earth of Aunt Mercy's pit, kicking up a shower of clods with his back legs.

It was a chilly night, and he slipped past me when we reached home, dodged through the kitchen and into the sitting room. He left a track of pawmarks all the way to the fireplace.

It was this that started the night's row. But if not, there would have been something else. Ellen appeared in the doorway, a half-eaten jellycube in her fingers. She took one a day to strengthen her nails—part of the newest of her endless health diets.

Immediately she began screaming at the dog and at me. As she advanced on him, Rusty backed into the corner, cowering away from her in confusion.

Perhaps it was the contrast of those quiet moments amongst the old gravestones and this hysterical display that made me rise in unaccustomed revolt. I ordered her to calm down.

She turned on me in a fury.

"This is the last time that dog enters this house!"

"No, Ellen. Let's have no more of that. Don't worry about the carpet. I'll clean it."

"You didn't hear me! For the last time, I said, I'm getting rid of that animal!"

"The dog stays."

"Correction! He goes! And for good!"

At a peak of passion, she seized the heavy poker from the fireside and swung at Rusty. With all her force she brought the weapon down on his head.

The dog dropped to his side and lay still as death.

The gravesoil still darkened his feet. Rusty. All I had left of the happy times. There was blood on the precious carpet now.

Ellen raised the poker again, higher this time. As she did, I grasped it from behind her. And brought it straight down again—on her burnished, herbalised, permanently-perfect head. Again and again. As she sank to her knees, the blows grew harder. All my disappointment in the marriage—all my pent-up resentment was channelled into my arm.

I am not an especially muscular man—a fact which Ellen had often dwelt on with some scorn. But she had no cause for complaint this time.

It seemed the most natural thing in the world.

How long the silence was afterwards I couldn't tell. Aeons later, it seemed, Rusty stirred and sat up.

Ellen didn't.

I bathed the dog's head and found it was not a deep wound. I gave him half an aspirin in warm milk. This done, I went to the telephone. Ellen was dead. I supposed it was the police I should ring.

We should have parted. She should have left me long since. What force of nature had kept us on this collision course? Now I had destroyed her. And by this she would destroy me. I lifted the receiver. Ellen would have the last word again.

I paused. It had been a very satisfying experience to defeat Ellen for once. It was unfortunate that it had involved killing her. I tried to feel some remorse. But there was nothing but a lightness within me. The whole house seemed airier, sweeter.

Rusty whined to be let out. I strolled down the garden with him. The stars glittered. Over the fence the pleasing grave ornaments were outlined against the dark yews. An owl called. I brushed against the rosemary bush. And the lavender. A moth fluttered up.

The night was alive with soft sounds. Creatures hunting. Killing. Being killed. And in the undergrowth small carcasses being eaten, drawn down, buried, tidied away. No panic. No retribution.

I got the wheelbarrow out of the shed, and a spade. I left the spade by the gate and took the barrow in through the back door.

Chocolate brown blankets had been a recent addition to the bedroom. Ellen had thought them smart. I had thought them rather depressing. "And they're a practical colour," she had argued. She was right, again. One was enough for my purpose. Ellen had never allowed an ounce of spare flesh to settle on her. I could appreciate that now.

As I wrapped her up and got her settled into the wheelbarrow, my thoughts raced ahead. I could see advantages at last in Ellen's inability to keep friends. Who would notice her absence? Or if they did, who would be greatly concerned? Her parents were long dead. And there were no relatives who kept in touch.

Now I would clean the carpet. There was time enough. Cold water for the blood stains. A cookery book yielded this useful tip. The pawmarks might do better left till they dried. They would brush off easily enough in the morning.

Two hours later, I shut Rusty in the house and wheeled the barrow down the path. At the gate I picked up the spade and balanced it on top of my load.

The night was blacker now. I found Aunt Mercy's plot with quick flashes of my torch. I would ration the beams to essentials. In any case my eyes were already adjusting to the dark. I must work as fast as I could.

I lifted out the swathed bundle, laid it nearby in the long grass, and wheeled the barrow several yards away. Then I removed the planks and lowered myself into the grave.

It took me longer than I had expected to dig down about a foot. The minimum I required. It would have to serve. There already seemed a hint of dawn in the distance.

I planted the body and firmed it down, then shovelled a sprinkling of soil over the top. The depth seemed much the same as it had before. There were, perhaps, no more than three inches of earth covering the body, but the grave must not appear to be any shallower than it had been. True, any slight disturbance would bring the hiding place to light, but who would need to touch it? The grave was finished. Tomorrow the coffin would be lowered gently to the bottom by its webs. And Aunt Mercy would conceal Ellen for the rest of time. Or long enough for me to—to what?

I returned the wheelbarrow and spade to the shed and went indoors to wash my hands. There were plans to be made. I repaired the fire and sat down. Rusty's head lay on my foot.

By daylight I had decided that if all went well I would emigrate to Australia and make a new life. I had money enough, and old friends there. I went to bed, set the alarm clock for eight, and slept.

Since I did not know the time of the funeral, I was obliged to keep look-out from the bedroom window for two hours before I saw the cortège arriving. I trained my binoculars on the site and watched.

I could make out Belfrage with his wife leaning on his arm. There seemed a great show of mourners for one who had not been liked. When they gathered round the graveside my view was obscured. But I saw the coffin carried over, and no sign came that anything other than a normal burial service was taking place.

At last the group began to stir. Gradually everyone moved off, helping each other to pick their way back to the cars. The white figure of the clergyman remained a short while, then also departed.

A gravedigger appeared with a shovel and rolled up his sleeves. God. Not long now. The man completed his task with the speed of a professional.

It was all over. And not even lunchtime.

Rusty had yet to have his morning walk. The cut had crusted over cleanly.

I took him across the common. I dearly longed to call in for a drink, but my pattern of behaviour must not be changed yet.

But I did go that evening.

I walked through the churchyard and passed Aunt Mercy's mound, now neatly packed over and covered with wreaths. It suddenly occurred to me what a blessing it had not rained. The slightest subsidence of the meagre covering of earth over Ellen's body would certainly have revealed the blanket and aroused suspicion. Such a possibility had not entered my mind at the time. I had put my faith in the slenderest chance. In the light of day I realised it was a small miracle. Anne must have been watching over me. Maybe she and Ellen had squabbled over my fate. Well, Anne had won.

Belfrage was already in the bar when I entered.

"Ah, Norton! You're two minutes late."

There was general laughter—of a friendly nature.

Had I been so routine-bound that people told the time by me? That was all in the past now. I was finished with the ten-to-eight teas-made, the five-to-one hand-washing, the two-thirty-to-four silence, the four-five kettle-whistle, the ten-thirty clock-winding and cheerless twin-bedding.

"What's Rusty done to his head then?" asked Maggie. She missed nothing.

"He knocked over the ironing-board," I said. "Got the flatiron right on his bonce."

"Poor old chap. Give him a crisp."

"How did the funeral go, Belfrage?"

I saw no harm in asking. Just touch on the subject.

"Oh very well. Not too chilly, thank God. Good turn-out. All hoping we'd got news of the Will, I suppose. Hard cheese!"

"I noticed the flowers as I came through. Very nice."

"Mm. What a price these days, eh? And the headstone's costing a bomb. I told them, I said we'll have to club together on it."

"That seems fair."

Should I ask him to chip Ellen's name on the bottom?

I hadn't felt so impish for years. Not since Anne died. Anne and I could laugh at such little things. There was so much happiness it spilt out very easily.

"My round, Belfrage. Maggie! Same, please."

I wanted her close, to hear my next remarks.

"Nip in the air today. I hope the weather holds. My wife's flying off to Australia tomorrow."

"Is that so?"

"Yes. She's got a cousin out there who's been in a bit of an accident. We got a telegram. Ellen's going off at once. I'll sort things out, then follow on. Reckon we'll stay out there for a spell. See the cousin all right, then make it a holiday, you know."

"Good idea. Summer over there, isn't it?"

"Flying off to the sun. How lovely," said Maggie.

It had registered. Splendid.

Now I could leave in a week or two, and later on when I was settled, I'd write to a local estate agent and get them to dispose of the house. I'd fade from the minds of these acquaintances in due course, and if I never showed up again they wouldn't be likely to query it. Maybe I'd drop them a postcard in a month or so. Just the one.

Belfrage lifted his glass.

"Here's to poor old Aunt Mercy," he said. "May she rest in peace."

I drank to that.

The next day I went up to London to make arrangements about my flight. And to enquire about a booking for Rusty. First, I went to Australia House to check up on what inoculations both of us would need. Then I went to the airline office.

It seemed Rusty would be crated up and travel in the freight compartment of the same plane as me. If I gave a diet sheet he would be watered and fed in his usual way during flight. The airplane staff would know he was aboard and inlets would be opened so that he could enjoy warmth and fresh air.

My booking was accepted for three weeks ahead. This would give me time to clear up my affairs without suspicious haste. And time to adjust to my role, and to circulate my story in a casual way. To be seen in a normal state of mind. And to be sure, my state of mind was more normal than it had been these several years past. My main task was not to appear abnormally untroubled. The mirror showed me a face where the furrows were fast disappearing—like a ploughed field planed by a duststorm.

I continued to make my nightly visits to the Feathers, regretting only that I was obliged to leave at a reasonably early hour. It must not seem that I took too much advantage of Ellen's absence. I had to be wary of Maggie. I caught her regarding me keenly from time to time. Whether this was the speculative eye of a warm woman who knows your wife is away, or the female sixth sense of something amiss, I could not be sure.

I had one bad moment, and this was when Belfrage, feeding a peanut to Rusty, enquired innocently, "What's going to happen to this old lad, then?"

It was on the tip of my tongue to say, "He'll come too, of course." I realized just in time the mistake this would be.

"Kennels," I said. Adding quickly. "Very good ones. He's been there before." To scotch any possibility of Belfrage offering Rusty accommodation.

"Oh. Only if you hadn't, I was going to say—"

Another hurdle over. It had to appear at this stage that I had no intention of staying in Australia. Once I had gone, then the decision to remain would be much more acceptable. I was not so well established in this area, and God knows not so fascinating a person for folk seriously to be concerned about my movements and motivations. How many of us are, when it comes down to it. But simple precaution was required.

As the days went by, my life took on such a calm and pleasant tenor that I sometimes looked at the tickets for Australia with regret. Then I would walk through the graveyard and know that although I had at last got the better of Ellen, she would continue to jostle with Anne for a place in my mind as long as Aunt Mercy lay nearby as a reminder. No, it was best to go far away. Anne would not blame me for leaving her earthly remains alone on that northern seashore. Her memory was alive in my heart.

The day arrived for our departure. I presented myself at the freight department with Rusty. He was to be sedated so as not to be upset by the flying. He greeted the airline staff in his trusting, friendly way and they received him with a caring attitude which gave me every confidence in his welfare. This was an even greater comfort by reason of the fact that he was to travel one flight ahead of me. It would not involve him in a long wait at the other end, but I was sorry to think he was not on the same plane. There had been an unfortunate overbooking. However, I would touch down in Sydney only a few hours after he did, and he would, I knew, be well looked after. The airline had a good reputation for transporting animals.

I chatted to the official as he consigned Rusty on his load sheet and I stayed by the dog as long as possible. Then I went home. I would use the last few hours to make sure all my arrangements were complete.

But I had dealt with matters so efficiently that there was time on my hands. I needed to check in at the terminal at eleven p.m. A last drink at the Feathers? I felt I needed to say goodbye. For one thing I wanted to. And it would seem natural.

I bought myself a double and one for Maggie. Belfrage had not yet arrived. Time went by and I began to wonder about him. A creature of habit was Belfrage. Not, as I had been, on limited parole.

Soon I would have to go. I intended to be at the airport in good time.

The door flew open and Belfrage came rushing in. He was flushed and his eyes shone.

"Thought you might be here," he said. "Glad I didn't miss saying cheerio. Wanted you to know my news. I'm in the money! Drinks all round, Mag."

Maggie hastened to serve Belfrage and me, herself and an ancient person in the corner.

"What's happened?" I asked.

"Aunt Mercy's Will. We found it. Slipped behind a drawer in the bureau. If there hadn't been such a load of junk everywhere—Anyway, who's a lucky girl then—? My wife! Bulk of it to her. Odd bits elsewhere. Enough to keep them all quiet. How about that?"

He looked so happy, I realised that it was possible this windfall would be a godsend.

"I'm very pleased. Really pleased for you."

I shook his hand and Maggie leaned over and gave him a peck on the cheek.

It was a good moment. In an hour or two I would be starting a new life. Behind me I was leaving a man—just an acquaintance perhaps—but a decent man who was equally enjoying a fortunate turn of circumstances.

"Maggie," said Belfrage. "Since I've bent your ear on the subject of my aunt these three months, here's a little present in compensation." Belfrage produced a large box of chocolates from the depths of his raincoat.

The atmosphere was euphoric.

"I must go now," I announced, at last.

"One for the road. Or should I say for the sky?" said Belfrage.

"To Aunt Mercy," I said, raising my glass high.

"Aunt Mercy!" echoed Belfrage. "Poor old soul. You'd never guess. In her Will she said she wanted to be cremated!"

A pain shot through my chest.

"Oh Lord," said Maggie. "And you buried her!" She giggled.

"Well, I ask you, who'd have thought?" said Belfrage. "With the family plot and all that."

"What will you do?" The voice didn't sound like mine.

"No choice," said Belfrage. "They're digging her up tonight."

THE VICTIM

P. D. James

Y OU KNOW PRINCESS Ilsa Mancelli, of course. I mean by that that
you must have seen her on the cinema screen; on television; pictured in
newspapers arriving at airports with her latest husband; relaxing on their
yacht; be-jewelled at first nights, gala nights, at any night and in any place
where it is obligatory for the rich and successful to show themselves. Even
if, like me, you have nothing but bored contempt for what I believe is
called the international jet set, you can hardly live in the modern world
and not know Ilsa Mancelli. And you can't fail to have picked up some
scraps about her past. The brief and not particularly successful screen
career, when even her heart-stopping beauty couldn't quite compensate
for the paucity of talent; the succession of marriages, first to the producer
who made her first film and who broke a twenty-year-old marriage to get
her; then to a Texan millionaire; lastly to a prince. About two months ago
I saw a nauseatingly sentimental picture of her with her two-day-old son
in a Rome nursing home. So it looks as if this marriage, sanctified as it is
by wealth, a title and maternity may be intended as her final adventure.

The husband before the film producer is, I notice, no longer mentioned.
Perhaps her publicity agent fears that a violent death in the family,
particularly an unsolved violent death, might tarnish her bright image.
Blood and beauty. In the early stages of her career they hadn't been able
to resist that cheap, vicarious thrill. But not now. Nowadays her early
history, before she married the film producer, has become a little obscure,
although there is a suggestion of poor but decent parentage and early
struggles suitably rewarded. I am the most obscure part of that obscurity.
Whatever you know, or think you know, of Ilsa Mancelli, you won't have
heard about me. The publicity machine has decreed that I be nameless,
faceless, unremembered, that I no longer exist. Ironically, the machine is
right; in any real sense, I don't.

I married her when she was Elsie Bowman, aged seventeen. I was assistant librarian at our local branch library and fifteen years older, a
thirty-two-year-old virgin, a scholar *manqué*, thin faced, a little stooping,
my meagre hair already thinning. She worked on the cosmetic counter of

our High Street store. She was beautiful then, but with a delicate, tentative, unsophisticated loveliness which gave little promise of the polished mature beauty which is hers today. Our story was very ordinary. She returned a book to the library one evening when I was on counter duty. We chatted. She asked my advice about novels for her mother. I spent as long as I dared finding suitable romances for her on the shelves. I tried to interest her in the books I liked. I asked her about herself, her life, her ambitions. She was the only woman I had been able to talk to. I was enchanted by her, totally and completely besotted.

I used to take my lunch early and make surreptitious visits to the store, watching her from the shadow of a neighbouring pillar. There is one picture which even now seems to stop my heart. She had dabbed her wrist with scent and was holding out a bare arm over the counter so that a prospective customer could smell the perfume. She was totally absorbed, her young face gravely preoccupied. I watched her, silently, and felt the tears smarting my eyes.

It was a miracle when she agreed to marry me. Her mother (she had no father) was reconciled if not enthusiastic about the match. She didn't, as she made it abundantly plain, consider me much of a catch. But I had a good job with prospects; I was educated; I was steady and reliable; I spoke with a grammar school accent which, while she affected to deride it, raised my status in her eyes. Besides, any marriage for Elsie was better than none. I was dimly aware when I bothered to think about Elsie in relation to anyone but myself that she and her mother didn't get on.

Mrs Bowman made, as she described it, a splash. There was a full choir and a peal of bells. The church hall was hired and a sit-down meal, ostentatiously unsuitable and badly cooked, was served to eighty guests. Between the pangs of nervousness and indigestion I was conscious of smirking waiters in short white jackets, a couple of giggling bridesmaids from the store, their freckled arms bulging from pink taffeta sleeves, hearty male relatives, red faced and with buttonholes of carnation and waving fern, who made indelicate jokes and clapped me painfully between the shoulders. There were speeches and warm champagne. And, in the middle of it all, Elsie my Elsie, like a white rose.

I suppose that it was stupid of me to imagine that I could hold her. The mere sight of our morning faces, smiling at each other's reflection in the bedroom mirror, should have warned me that it couldn't last. But, poor deluded fool, I never dreamed that I might lose her except by death. Her death I dared not contemplate, and I was afraid for the first time of my own. Happiness had made a coward of me. We moved into a new bunga-low, chosen by Elsie, sat in new chairs chosen by Elsie, slept in a befrilled bed chosen by Elsie. I was so happy that it was like passing into a new phase of existence, breathing a different air, seeing the most ordinary things as if they were newly created. One isn't necessarily humble when greatly in love. Is it so unreasonable to recognize the value of a love like mine, to believe that the beloved is equally sustained and transformed by it?

She said that she wasn't ready to start a baby and, without her job, she was easily bored. She took a brief training in shorthand and typing at our local Technical College and found herself a position as shorthand typist at the firm of Collingford and Major. That, at least, was how the job started. Shorthand typist, then secretary to Mr Rodney Collingford, then personal secretary, then confidential personal secretary; in my bemused state of uxorious bliss I only half registered her progress from occasionally taking his dictation when his then secretary was absent to flaunting his gifts of jewellery and sharing his bed.

He was everything I wasn't. Rich (his father had made a fortune from plastics shortly after the war and had left the factory to his only son), coarsely handsome in a swarthy fashion, big muscled, confident, attractive to women. He prided himself on taking what he wanted. Elsie must have been one of his easiest pickings.

Why, I still wonder, did he want to marry her? I thought at the time that he couldn't resist depriving a pathetic, under-privileged, unattractive husband of a prize which neither looks nor talent had qualified him to deserve. I've noticed that about the rich and successful. They can't bear to see the undeserving prosper. I thought that half the satisfaction for him was in taking her away from me. That was partly why I knew that I had to kill him. But now I'm not so sure. I may have done him an injustice. It may have been both simpler and more complicated than that. She was, you see—she still is—so very beautiful.

I understand her better now. She was capable of kindness, good humour, generosity even, provided she was getting what she wanted. At the time we married, and perhaps eighteen months afterwards, she wanted me. Neither her egoism nor her curiosity had been able to resist such a flattering, overwhelming love. But for her, marriage wasn't permanency. It was the first and necessary step towards the kind of life she wanted and meant to have. She was kind to me, in bed and out, while I was what she wanted. But when she wanted someone else, then my need of her, my jealousy, my bitterness, she saw as a cruel and wilful denial of her basic right, the right to have what she wanted. After all, I'd had her for nearly three years. It was two years more than I had any right to expect. She thought so. Her darling Rodney thought so. When my acquaintances at the library learnt of the divorce I could see in their eyes that they thought so too. And she couldn't see what I was so bitter about. Rodney was perfectly happy to be the guilty party; they weren't, she pointed out caustically, expecting me to behave like a gentleman. I wouldn't have to pay for the divorce. Rodney would see to that. I wasn't being asked to provide her with alimony. Rodney had more than enough. At one point she came close to bribing me with Rodney's money to let her go without fuss. And yet—was it really as simple as that? She had loved me, or at least needed me, for a time. Had she perhaps seen in me the father that she had lost at five years old?

During the divorce, through which I was, as it were, gently processed by highly paid legal experts as if I were an embarrassing but expendable nuisance to be got rid of with decent speed, I was only able to keep sane by the knowledge that I was going to kill Collingford. I knew that I couldn't go on living in a world where he breathed the same air. My mind fed voraciously on the thought of his death, savoured it, began systemmatically and with dreadful pleasure to plan it.

A successful murder depends on knowing your victim, his character, his daily routine, his weaknesses, those unalterable and betraying habits which make up the core of personality. I knew quite a lot about Rodney Collingford. I knew facts which Elsie had let fall in her first weeks with the firm, typing pool gossip. I knew the fuller and rather more intimate facts which she had disclosed in those early days of her enchantment with him, when neither prudence nor kindness had been able to conceal her obsessive preoccupation with her new boss. I should have been warned then. I knew, none better, the need to talk about the absent lover.

What did I know about him? I knew the facts that were common knowledge, of course. That he was wealthy; aged thirty; a notable amateur golfer; that he lived in an ostentatious mock-Georgian house on the banks of the Thames looked after by over-paid but non-resident staff; that he owned a cabin cruiser; that he was just over six feet tall; that he was a good business man but reputedly close-fisted; that he was methodical in his habits. I knew a miscellaneous and unrelated set of facts about him, some of which would be useful, some important, some of which I couldn't use. I knew—and this was rather surprising—that he was good with his hands and liked making things in metal and wood. He had built an expensively-equipped and large workroom in the grounds of his house and spent every Thursday evening working there alone. He was a man addicted to routine. This creativity, however mundane and trivial, I found intriguing, but I didn't let myself dwell on it. I was interested in him only so far as his personality and habits were relevant to his death. I never thought of him as a human being. He had no existence for me apart from my hate. He was Rodney Collingford, my victim.

First I decided on the weapon. A gun would have been the most certain,

I supposed, but I didn't know how to get one and was only too well aware that I wouldn't know how to load or use it if I did. Besides, I was reading a number of books about murder at the time and I realized that guns, however cunningly obtained, were easy to trace. And there was another thing. A gun was too impersonal, too remote. I wanted to make physical contact at the moment of death. I wanted to get close enough to see that final look of incredulity and horror as he recognized, simultaneously, me and his death. I wanted to drive a knife into his throat.

I bought it two days after the divorce. I was in no hurry to kill Collingford. I knew that I must take my time, must be patient, if I were to act in safety. One day, perhaps when we were old, I might tell Elsie. But I didn't intend to be found out. This was to be the perfect murder. And that meant taking my time. He would be allowed to live for a full year. But I knew that the earlier I bought the knife the more difficult it would be, twelve months later, to trace the purchase. I didn't buy it locally. I went one Saturday morning by train and bus to a north-east suburb and found a busy ironmongers and general store just off the High Street. There was a variety of knives on display. The blade of the one I selected was about six inches long and was made of strong steel screwed into a plain wooden handle. I think it was probably meant for cutting lino. In the shop its razor-sharp edge was protected by a strong cardboard sheath. It felt good and right in my hand. I stood in a small queue at the pay desk and the cashier didn't even glance up as he took my notes and pushed the change towards me.

But the most satisfying part of my planning was the second stage. I wanted Collingford to suffer. I wanted him to know that he was going to die. It wasn't enough that he should realise it in a last second before I drove in the knife or in that final second before he ceased to know anything for ever. Two seconds of agony, however horrible, weren't an adequate return for what he had done to me. I wanted him to know that he was a condemned man, to know it with increasing certainty, to wonder every morning whether this might be his last day. What if this knowledge did make him cautious, put him on his guard? In this country, he couldn't go armed. He couldn't carry on his business with a hired protector always at his side. He couldn't bribe the police to watch him every second of the day. Besides, he wouldn't want to be thought a coward. I guessed that he would carry on, ostentatiously normal, as if the threats were unreal or derisory, something to laugh about with his drinking cronies. He was the sort to laugh at danger. But he would never be sure. And, by the end, his nerve and confidence would be broken. Elsie wouldn't know him for the man she had married.

I would have liked to have telephoned him but that, I knew, was impracticable. Calls could be traced; he might refuse to talk to me; I wasn't confident that I could disguise my voice. So the sentence of death would have to be sent by post. Obviously, I couldn't write the notes or the envelopes myself. My studies in murder had shown me how difficult it was to disguise handwriting and the method of cutting out and sticking together letters from a newspaper seemed messy, very time consuming and difficult to manage wearing gloves. I knew, too, that it would be fatal to use my own small portable typewriter or one of the machines at the library. The forensic experts could identify a machine.

And then I hit on my plan. I began to spend my Saturdays and occasional half days journeying round London and visiting shops where they sold secondhand typewriters. I expect you know the kind of shop; a variety of machines of different ages, some practically obsolete, others hardly used, arranged on tables where the prospective purchaser may try them out. There were new machines too, and the proprietor was usually employed in demonstrating their merits or discussing hire purchase terms. The customers wandered desultorily around, inspecting the machines, stopping occasionally to type out an exploratory passage. There were little pads of rough paper stacked ready for use. I didn't, of course, use the scrap paper provided. I came supplied with my own writing materials, a well-known brand sold in every stationer's and on every railway bookstall. I bought a small supply of paper and envelopes once every two months and never from the same shop. Always, when handling them, I wore a thin pair of gloves, slipping them on as soon as my typing was complete. If someone were near, I would tap out the usual drivel about the sharp brown fox or all good men coming to the aid of the party. But if I were quite alone I would type something very different.

"This is the first comunication, Collingford. You'll be getting them regularly from now on. They're just to let you know that I'm going to kill you."

"You can't escape me, Collingford. Don't bother to inform the police. They can't help you."

"I'm getting nearer, Collingford. Have you made your will?"

"Not long now, Collingford. What does it feel like to be under sentence of death?"

The warnings weren't particularly elegant. As a librarian I could think of a number of apt quotations, which would have added a touch of individuality or style, perhaps even of sardonic humour, to the bald sentence of death. But I dared not risk originality. The notes had to be ordinary, the kind of threat which anyone of his enemies, a worker, a competitor, a cuckolded husband, might have sent.

Sometimes I had a lucky day. The shop would be large, well supplied, nearly empty. I would be able to move from typewriter to typewriter and leave with perhaps a dozen or so notes and addressed envelopes ready to send. I always carried a folded newspaper in which I could conceal my writing pad and envelopes and into which I could quickly slip my little stock of typed messages.

It was quite a job to keep myself supplied with notes and I discovered interesting parts of London and fascinating shops. I particularly enjoyed this part of my plan. I wanted Collingford to get two notes a week, one posted on Sunday and one on Thursday. I wanted him to come to dread Friday and Monday mornings when the familiar typed envelope would drop on his mat. I wanted him to believe the threat was real. And why should he not believe it? How could the force of my hate and resolution not transmit itself through paper and typescript to his gradually comprehending brain?

I wanted to keep an eye on my victim. It shouldn't have been difficult; we lived in the same town. But our lives were worlds apart. He was a hard and sociable drinker. I never went inside a public house, and would have been particularly ill at ease in the kind of public house he frequented. But, from time to time, I would see him in the town. Usually he would be parking his Jaguar, and I would watch his quick, almost furtive, look to left and right before he returned to lock the door. Was it my imagination that he looked older, that some of the confidence had drained out of him?

Once, when walking by the river on a Sunday in early spring, I saw him manoeuvring his boat through Teddington Lock. Ilsa—she had, I knew, changed her name after her marriage—was with him. She was wearing a white trouser suit, her flowing hair was bound by a red scarf. There was a party. I could see two more men and a couple of girls and hear high female squeals of laughter. I turned quickly and slouched away as if I were the guilty one. But not before I had seen Collingford's face. This time I couldn't be mistaken. It wasn't, surely, the tedious job of getting his boat unscratched through the lock that made his face look so grey and strained.

The third phase of my planning meant moving house. I wasn't sorry to go. The bungalow, feminine, chintzy, smelling of fresh paint and the new shoddy furniture which she had chosen, was Elsie's home not mine. Her scent still lingered in cupboards and on pillows. In these inappropriate surroundings I had known greater happiness than I was ever to know again. But now I paced restlessly from room to empty room, fretting to be gone.

It took me four months to find the house I wanted. It had to be on or very near to the river within two or three miles upstream of Collingford's house. It had to be small and reasonably cheap. Money wasn't too much of a difficulty. It was a time of rising house prices and the modern bungalow sold at three hundred pounds more than I had paid for it. I could get another mortgage without difficulty if I didn't ask for too much, but I thought it likely that, for what I wanted, I should have to pay cash.

The house agents perfectly understood that a man on his own found a three-bedroom bungalow too large for him and, even if they found me rather vague about my new requirements and irritatingly imprecise about the reasons for rejecting their offerings, they still sent me orders to view. And then, suddenly on an afternoon in April, I found exactly what I was looking for. It actually stood on the river, separated from it only by a narrow tow path. It was a one-bedroom shack-like wooden bungalow with a tiled roof, set in a small neglected plot of sodden grass and overgrown flower beds. There had once been a wooden landing stage but now the two remaining planks, festooned with weeds and tags of rotted rope, were half submerged beneath the slime of the river. The paint on the small veranda had long ago flaked away. The wallpaper of twined roses in the sitting room was blotched and faded. The previous owner had left two old cane chairs and a ramshackle table. The kitchen was pokey and ill-equipped. Everywhere there hung a damp miasma of depression and decay. In summer, when the neighbouring shacks and bungalows were occupied by holidaymakers and weekenders it would, no doubt, be cheerful enough. But in October, when I planned to kill Collingford, it would be as deserted and isolated as a disused morgue. I bought it and paid cash. I was even able to knock two hundred pounds off the asking price.

My life that summer was almost happy. I did my job at the library adequately. I lived alone in the shack, looking after myself as I had before my marriage. I spent my evenings watching television. The images flickered in front of my eyes almost unregarded, a monochrome background to my bloody and obsessive thoughts.

I practised with the knife until it was as familiar in my hand as an eating utensil. Collingford was taller than I by six inches. The thrust then would have to be upward. It made a difference to the way I held the knife and I experimented to find the most comfortable and effective grip. I hung a bolster on a hook in the bedroom door and lunged at a marked spot for hours at a time. Of course, I didn't actually insert the knife; nothing must dull the sharpness of its blade. Once a week, a special treat, I sharpened it to an even keener edge.

Two days after moving into the bungalow I bought a dark blue untrimmed track suit and a pair of light running shoes. Throughout the summer I spent an occasional evening running on the tow path. The people who owned the neighbouring chalets, when they were there which was infrequently, got used to the sound of my television through the closed curtains and the sight of my figure jogging past their windows. I kept apart from them and from everyone and summer passed into autumn. The shutters were put up on all the chalets except mine. The tow path became mushy with falling leaves. Dusk fell early, and the summer sights and sounds died on the river. And it was October.

He was due to die on Thursday October 17th, the anniversary of the final decree of divorce. It had to be a Thursday, the evening which he spent by custom alone in his workshop, but it was a particularly happy augury that the anniversary should fall on a Thursday. I knew that he would be there. Every Thursday for nearly a year I had padded along the two and a half miles of the footpath in the evening dusk and had stood briefly watching the squares of light from his windows and the dark bulk of the house behind.

It was a warm evening. There had been a light drizzle for most of the day but, by dusk, the skies had cleared. There was a thin white sliver of moon and it cast a trembling ribbon of light across the river. I left the library at my usual time, said my usual good-nights. I knew that I had been my normal self during the day, solitary, occasionally a little sarcastic, conscientious, betraying no hint of the inner tumult.

I wasn't hungry when I got home but I made myself eat an omelette and drink two cups of coffee. I put on my swimming trunks and hung around my neck a plastic toilet bag containing the knife. Over the trunks I put on my track suit, slipping a pair of thin rubber gloves into the pocket. Then, at about quarter past seven, I left the shack and began my customary gentle trot along the tow path.

When I got to the chosen spot opposite to Collingford's house I could see at once that all was well. The house was in darkness but there were the customary lighted windows of his workshop. I saw that the cabin cruiser was moored against the boathouse. I stood very still and listened. There was no sound. Even the light breeze had died and the yellowing leaves on the riverside elms hung motionless. The tow path was completely deserted. I slipped into the shadow of the hedge where the trees grew thickest and found the place I had already selected. I put on the rubber gloves, slipped out of the track suit, and left it folded around my running shoes in the shadow of the hedge. Then, still watching carefully to left and right, I made my way to the river.

I knew just where I must enter and leave the water. I had selected a place where the bank curved gently, where the water was shallow and the bottom was firm and comparatively free of mud. The water struck very cold, but I expected that. Every night during that autumn I had bathed in cold water to accustom my body to the shock. I swam across the river with my methodical but quiet breast stroke, hardly disturbing the dark surface of the water. I tried to keep out of the path of moonlight but, from time to time, I swam into its silver gleam and saw my red gloved hands parting in front of me as if they were already stained with blood.

I used Collingford's landing stage to clamber out the other side. Again I stood still and listened. There was no sound except for the constant moaning of the river and the solitary cry of a night bird. I made my way silently over the grass. Outside the door of his workroom, I paused again. I could hear the noise of some kind of machinery. I wondered whether the door would be locked, but it opened easily when I turned the handle. I moved into a blaze of light.

I knew exactly what I had to do. I was perfectly calm. It was over in about four seconds. I don't think he really had a chance. He was absorbed in what he had been doing, bending over a lathe, and the sight of an almost naked man, walking purposely towards him, left him literally impotent with surprise. But, after that first paralysing second, he knew me. Oh yes, he knew me! Then I drew my right hand from behind my back and struck. The knife went in as sweetly as if the flesh had been butter. He staggered and fell. I had expected that and I let myself go loose and fell on top of him. His eyes were glazed, his mouth opened and there was a gush of dark red blood. I twisted the knife viciously in the wound, relishing the sound of tearing sinews. Then I waited. I counted five deliberately, then raised myself from his prone figure and crouched behind him before withdrawing the knife. When I withdrew it there was a fountain of sweet smelling blood which curved from his throat like an arch. There is one thing I shall never forget. The blood must have been red, what other colour could it have been? But, at the time and for ever afterwards, I saw it as a golden stream.

I checked my body for blood stains before I left the workshop and rinsed my arms under the cold tap at his sink. My bare feet made no marks on the wooden block flooring. I closed the door quietly after me and, once again, stood listening. Still no sound. The house was dark and empty.

The return journey was more exhausting than I had thought possible. The river seemed to have widened and I thought that I should never reach my home shore. I was glad I had chosen a shallow part of the stream and that the bank was firm. I doubt whether I could have drawn myself up through a welter of mud and slime. I was shivering violently as I zipped-up my track suit and it took me precious seconds to get on my running shoes. After I had run about a mile down the tow path I weighted the toilet bag containing the knife with stones from the path and hurled it into the middle of the river. I guessed that they would drag part of the Thames for the weapon but they could hardly search the whole stream. And, even if they did, the toilet bag was one sold at the local chain store which anyone might have bought, and I was confident that the knife could never be traced to me. Half an hour later I was back in my shack. I had left the television on and the news was just ending. I made myself a cup of hot cocoa and sat to watch it. I felt drained of thought and energy as if I had just made love. I was conscious of nothing but my tiredness, my body's coldness gradually returning to life in the warmth of the electric fire, and a great peace.

He must have had quite a lot of enemies. It was nearly a fortnight before the police got round to interviewing me. Two officers came, a Detective Inspector and a Sergeant, both in plain clothes. The Sergeant did most of the talking; the other just sat, looking round at the sitting room, glancing out at the river, looking at the two of us from time to time from cold grey eyes as if the whole investigation were a necessary bore. The Sergeant said the usual reassuring platitudes about just a few questions. I was nervous, but that didn't worry me. They would expect me to be nervous. I told myself that, whatever I did, I mustn't try to be clever. I mustn't talk too much. I had decided to tell them that I spent the whole evening watching television, confident that no one would be able to refute this. I knew that no friends would have called on me. I doubted whether my colleagues at the library even knew where I lived. And I had no telephone so I need not fear that a caller's ring had gone unanswered during that crucial hour and a half.

On the whole it was easier than I had expected. Only once did I feel myself at risk. That was when the Inspector suddenly intervened. He said in a harsh voice:

"He married your wife didn't he? Took her away from you, some people might say. Nice piece of goods, too, by the look of her. Didn't you feel any grievance? Or was it all nice and friendly? You take her, old chap. No ill feelings. That kind of thing?"

It was hard to accept the contempt in his voice but if he hoped to provoke me he didn't succeed. I had been expecting this question. I was prepared. I looked down at my hands and waited a few seconds before I spoke. I knew exactly what I would say.

"I could have killed Collingford myself when she first told me about him. But I had to come to terms with it. She went for the money you see. And if that's the kind of wife you have, well she's going to leave you sooner or later. Better sooner than when you have a family. You tell yourself 'good riddance'. I don't mean I felt that at first, of course. But I did feel it in the end. Sooner than I expected, really."

That was all I said about Elsie then or ever. They came back three times. They asked if they could look round my shack. They looked round it. They took away two of my suits and the track suit for examination. Two weeks later they returned them without comment. I never knew what they suspected, or even if they did suspect. Each time they came I said less, not more. I never varied my story. I never allowed them to provoke me into discussing my marriage or speculating about the crime. I just sat there, telling them the same thing over and over again. I never felt in any real danger. I knew that they had dragged some lengths of the river but that they hadn't found the weapon. In the end they gave up. I always had the feeling that I was pretty low on their list of suspects and that, by the end, their visits were merely a matter of form.

It was three months before Elsie came to me. I was glad that it wasn't earlier. It might have looked suspicious if she had arrived at the shack when the police were with me. After Collingford's death I hadn't seen her. There were pictures of her in the national and local newspapers, fragile in sombre furs and black hat at the inquest, bravely controlled at the crematorium, sitting in her drawing room in afternoon dress and pearls with her husband's dog at her feet, the personification of loneliness and grief.

"I can't think who could have done it. He must have been a madman. Rodney hadn't an enemy in the world."

That statement caused some ribald comment at the library. One of the assistants said:

"He's left her a fortune I hear. Lucky for her she had an alibi. She was at a London theatre all the evening, watching *Macbeth*. Otherwise, from what I've heard of our Rodney Collingford, people might have started to get ideas about his fetching little widow."

Then he gave me a sudden embarrassed glance, remembering who the widow was.

And so one Friday evening, she came. She drove herself and was alone. The dark green Saab drove up at my ramshackle gate. She came into the sitting room and looked around in a kind of puzzled contempt. After a moment, still not speaking, she sat in one of the fireside chairs and crossed her legs, moving one caressingly against the other. I hadn't seen her sitting like that before. She looked up at me. I was standing stiffly in front of her chair, my lips dry. When I spoke I couldn't recognize my own voice.

"So you've come back?" I said.

She stared at me, incredulous, and then she laughed:

"To you? Back for keeps? Don't be silly, darling! I've just come to pay a visit. Besides, I wouldn't dare to come back, would I? I might be frightened that you'd stick a knife into my throat."

I couldn't speak. I stared at her, feeling the blood drain from my face. Then I heard her high, rather childish voice. It sounded almost kind.

"Don't worry, I shan't tell. You were right about him, darling, you really were. He wasn't at all nice really. And mean! I didn't care so much about your meanness. After all, you don't earn so very much do you? But he had half a million! Think of it, darling. I've been left half a million! And he was so mean that he expected me to go on working as his secretary even after we were married. I typed all his letters! I really did! All that he sent from home, anyway. And I had to open his post every morning unless the envelopes had a secret little sign on them he'd told his friends about to show that they were private."

I said through bloodless lips:

"So all my notes—"

"He never saw them, darling. Well, I didn't want to worry him, did I? And I knew they were from you. I knew when the first one arrived. You never could spell communication, could you? I noticed that when you used to write to the house agents and the solicitor before we were married. It made me laugh considering that you're an educated librarian and I was only a shop assistant."

"So you knew all the time. You knew that it was going to happen."

"Well, I thought that it might. But he really was horrible, darling. You can't imagine. And now I've got half a million! Isn't it lucky that I have an alibi? I thought you might come on that Thursday. And Rodney never did enjoy a serious play."

After that brief visit I never saw or spoke to her again. I stayed in the shack, but life became pointless after Collingford's death. Planning his murder had been an interest, after all. Without Elsie and without my victim there seemed little point in living. And, about a year after his death, I began to dream. I still dream, always on a Monday and Friday. I live through it all again: the noiseless run along the tow path over the mush of damp leaves; the quiet swim across the river; the silent opening of his door; the upward thrust of the knife; the vicious turn in the wound; the animal sound of tearing tissues; the curving stream of golden blood. Only the homeward swim is different. In my dream the river is no longer a cleansing stream, luminous under the sickle moon, but a cloying, impenetrable, slow moving bog of viscous blood through which I struggle in impotent panic towards a steadily receding shore.

I know about the significance of the dream. I've read all about the psychology of guilt. Since I lost Elsie I've done all my living through books. But it doesn't help. And I no longer know who I am. I know who I used to be, our local Assistant Librarian, gentle, scholarly, timid, Elsie's husband. But then I killed Collingford. The man I was couldn't have done that. He wasn't that kind of person. So who am I? It isn't really surprising, I suppose, that the Library Committee suggested so tactfully that I ought to look for a less exacting job. A less exacting job than the post of

Assistant Librarian? But you can't blame them. No one can be efficient and keep his mind on the job when he doesn't know who he is.

Sometimes, when I'm in a public house—and I seem to spend most of my time there nowadays since I've been out of work—I'll look over someone's shoulder at a newspaper photograph of Elsie and say:

"That's the beautiful Ilsa Mancelli. I was her first husband."

I've got used to the way people sidle away from me, the ubiquitous pub bore, their eyes averted, their voices suddenly hearty. But sometimes, perhaps because they've been lucky with the horses and feel a spasm of pity for a poor deluded sod, they push a few coins over the counter to the barman before making their way to the door, and buy me a drink.

DEERGLEN QUEEN

Bill Knox

MARY-ANNE RANSOME, unmarried at thirty-seven and resigned to it, found the air-mail letter waiting when she got back to her tiny apartment at the end of a day's typewriter jockeying.

The British stamps and Edinburgh postmark puzzled her. Mary-Anne didn't know anyone over there. In fact, the only time she'd been outside of the States was the time she'd tried a week's skiing vacation in Canada. She'd twisted her ankle the first day and caught a cold by the second.

Habit took her through to the kitchen, and she switched on the coffeepot before opening the envelope. The letter inside ran to two typewritten sheets, and she frowned as she began reading. Then the frown died and her mouth fell open a little.

Still clutching the letter, Mary-Anne switched off the coffeepot with slightly trembling fingers. Then she opened the larder cupboard, brought out the bottle of gin she kept for visitors, and took the first straight slug of liquor she'd ever tasted.

She felt she needed it. When you're red-haired and rawboned and the description "homely" means too big a nose and too small a mouth, it comes as a shock to discover you're an heiress.

Or, to be exact, that a great-uncle you've never heard of has gone and died and left you his whisky distillery over in Scotland.

But there it was in cold print under the Edinburgh law firm's old-fashioned letterheading.

" . . . sole heir and legatee under the will of the late Alasdair MacKenzie, proprietor of Deerglen Distillery and certain other property in the parish of Deerglen in the County of Ross-shire, Scotland."

Well, her mother had been born in Scotland, and all the rest of the family detail given, including her own birthdate, fitted.

It must be true.

"Glory, hallelujah!" said Mary-Anne Ransome. And had the second straight gin of her life.

Five days later the midmorning mail-bus from Inverness topped a final rise on the bumpy, single-track road which was the main traffic artery for its particular corner of the Scottish West Highlands. Up front, the last passenger remaining aboard, Mary-Anne leaned forward for her first glimpse of Deerglen parish. She saw a long, narrow valley, a fringe of cloud-capped hills which were stained purple with heather and a small village in the distance.

She still wondered if she were crazy. But after an exchange of cables with the Edinburgh law firm, she'd thrown up her job, blown her savings on a transatlantic air ticket, and had waved good-bye to the girls of the Friday Lunch Club.

All of it seemed a world away as the mail-bus coasted down the gradient into the Highland glen. Sheep were grazing on the rough moorland, and the wheels of the bus rumbled as it crossed a bridge over a rushing, tumbling burn. A distance from the road and close to the start of the hills was what looked like an old, ruined castle. But Mary-Anne was more interested in what she saw on ahead, beyond the village—a concentration of low, modern, warehouse-style units.

She fought back a grin, remembering what Mr Sinclair, the ancient but sharp-eyed old lawyer in Edinburgh, had said when she'd visited his office.

"A valuable property, Miss Ransome. With a purchaser already anxious to meet you. His name is Harris, the offer is one hundred thousand pounds sterling, which is nicely over the book value of the distillery and its stocks. Go up, look around—then let me know."

Suddenly the bus stopped. The driver swung from his seat, reached Mary-Anne's suitcase down from the rack, and beckoned. Puzzled, she followed him out. Then, as the man laid the case on the roadside grass, she made a protesting noise.

"I wanted the distillery."

"Aye," nodded the driver. "You're at it. Over yonder on the right."

He climbed back in, and the mail-bus growled off.

Mary-Anne Ransome looked where he'd indicated, looked again, and swallowed hard. A dirt track led from the road toward the old ruin. Except it wasn't any kind of castle. Now she could see the stacked whisky casks lying under the shadow of its dilapidated walls. Smoke was gently wisping from a medium-sized chimney at the rear.

Pursing her lips, Mary-Anne picked up the suitcase and began walking. High heels sinking in the soft earth, it wasn't easy going. And as she drew close, her heart sank.

A battered sign nailed over the main door said "Deerglen Whisky Company". Like the woodwork around, its paint was blistered and faded. The grey slate roof of the building had a large patch of rusty corrugated iron covering most of one corner.

"Not much to look at, eh?" said a chuckling voice behind her. "Still, welcome to Deerglen."

She spun round, saw an elderly gnome-like figure in a well-worn tweed jacket, wondered exactly where he'd sprung from, and drew a deep breath. "Hello. I'm—"

"Wi' that nose, lassie, it's easy to guess." The man, who looked around sixty, grinned cheerfully. "It's the twin o' the one old Alasdair MacKenzie had. You're his kin all right." He came nearer. "I'm Fergie Ross, the distillery manager. Sinclair, the lawyer, phoned to say you'd be arriving."

Taking the suitcase, he led the way into the building. They walked down a short, stone-flagged corridor, then Mary-Anne was waved into a small, untidy cubbyhole of a room.

"This was his office. I've been using it." Fergie Ross cleared a chair by the simple expedient of dumping a pile of correspondence on the floor. The chair creaked alarmingly as Mary-Anne sat down, and his eyes twinkled. "All the way from America—aye, it's a fair journey. You'll be ready to sample the product, eh?"

Mary-Anne hesitated, then decided she'd better conform. "Thanks—I'd like it long and cool. With lemonade."

Fergie Ross's smile died. "Miss Ransome, you've a thing or two to learn. Up here the custom is to take our whisky as nature intended it." His mouth tightened. "There are some who would count it a sacrilege to mention Deerglen Triple Run and—and your lemonade in the same breath."

"Sorry," apologized Mary-Anne. "Would water be all right?"

"Let's say it would be just acceptable." Ross crossed to the door and raised his voice in a bellow. "Katie—"

A moment later an attractive, dark-haired girl of around twenty looked in.

"My daughter Katie," introduced the distillery manager. "She helps keep the books and makes herself useful." He waited just long enough for Mary-Anne and the girl to exchange a formal smile. "Katie, the new proprietor would like some water with her Deerglen."

"Water, father?" The girl pronounced the first word carefully to make sure there was no mistake.

"Aye," said Fergie Ross sadly.

By the time his daughter returned with a water jug, he'd produced a bottle and two glasses from the office filing cabinet. Solemnly, Fergie Ross poured a king-sized measure of amber gold into each glass, and handed one to Mary-Anne. He watched in silence while she topped it up with the water.

"Drowned," muttered Ross under his breath. Sighing, he lifted his own glass. "*Slainch* . . . your good health."

"Cheers," said Mary-Anne. And sipped.

A bomb seemed to explode at the back of her throat, then changed to liquid fire. She fought down a sudden need to cough, while a strange wailing sound began ringing in her ears.

"Good stuff, eh?" demanded Fergie Ross.

"Very . . . nice." She managed to nod.

"Like the kiss of morning dew," said Ross proudly.

Bottled dynamite might have been a better description, thought Mary-Anne. But that strange noise was persisting, might almost have been an attempt at music.

"That sound—"

Katie laughed. "Just bagpipes, Miss Ransome. Most of the village pipe band work here. That sounds like Angus Mathieson. He's having trouble with his pibroch."

Whatever that meant, it sounded painful. But as the bagpipes skirled on, Ross glanced at his daughter and gestured toward the door. She left them, and once more he raised his glass.

"Mary-Anne Ransome, I'll drink a toast of my own," he said quietly. "To the day you sample Deerglen's pride—the Quadruple Run." He took a long swallow from the glass.

"That sounds like something special," said Mary-Anne.

"It is." Fergie Ross said it proudly. "There will be just the one bottle made. That's the tradition, always has been. The last Quadruple Run was for Old Alasdair when he was still called Young Alasdair. The Quadruple Run is for the day the next proprietor of the family line proves worthy of the experience of drinking it."

"I—" Mary-Anne hesitated. Well, my plans aren't final."

Frowning, Fergie Ross set his glass down. "Meaning you might be selling the place?"

As if on cue, the bagpipe music wailed to a stop outside. Mary-Anne nodded awkwardly. "There are taxes to be paid, things like that. The offer that's been made is a good one."

"From Matthew Harris. Aye, I know." Fergie Ross closed his eyes in pain. "Old Alasdair must be birling in his grave. Your mother never talked of him?"

"No." Mary-Anne's face clouded a little. Both her parents had died when she was in her twenties, and she'd been an only child. "Look, if I've got a good offer, what's wrong with taking it?"

"Because of Harris," grated Fergie Ross, with a flash of anger. "Damn the man. Deerglen Distillery has been in the one family for almost 300 years." He saw Mary-Anne's expression and twisted a grin. "I know, the place looks it, too—looks ready to fall about our ears. But there's good reason. How much do you know about whisky?"

"Nothing," said Mary-Anne truthfully.

Fergie Ross took a deep breath. "Then this is a good time to start learning. Come on."

It was a guided tour of sights, sounds and smells. Of seeing men at work on malting floors. Of things called mash tuns and wash backs, of mashes, low wines and draffs. Of the fragrance of peat as it was fed to the furnaces and the sweet-sour odour of the still-house, where a great, gleaming copper bowl sat like a giant teakettle topped by a delicate swan-neck spout.

There were other places. The cooper's shed, with its casks. The spirit vat—and finally the store-sheds where the casked whisky lay maturing for the full ten years which had to pass before a drop of Deerglen Triple Run was allowed to leave for the outside world.

At last, thankfully, Mary-Anne found herself led back to the little office. Where a stranger was waiting. A big, ugly man in a baggy blue suit. A man who, when he shook hands, did it with something resembling a bear paw.

"Here's your mystery piper," said Fergie Ross. "Angus Mathieson—Angus the Revenue we call him. He works here, but for the Government, not us."

Angus the Revenue grinned, and his craggy face softened considerably in the process. "Customs and Excise collect a lot of tax from a bottle o' whisky, so each distillery has a resident Revenue man—just to make sure we get our share."

"When he says resident, he means it," grumbled Ross. "He has a cottage on the hill at the back and keys for every door in this place—sometimes the only keys."

"Och, I don't cause too much trouble," assured Angus. Then he glanced at Ross. "But, mentioning trouble, Katie asked me to tell you there's been a phone call from Matthew Harris. He's coming over, wanting to meet Miss Ransome."

"When?" demanded Ross.

"About now." The Revenue man strolled over to the window and glanced out. "In fact, I can see his car heading up the road."

Fergie Ross moistened his lips and spoke quickly. "Mary-Anne, I'm going to ask a favour. Harris will try to get an answer to his offer. But tell him you want to think about it. Give me a chance to talk to you before you sign anything. Will you do that?"

She saw the anguish on his wrinkled, gnome-like face, and nodded.

Three men climbed out of the long, grey limousine which stopped in the yard. Moments later, a coldly polite Fergie Ross brought them into the office.

Matthew Harris was tall, thin, smartly dressed, and sharp-eyed. He laid down his briefcase and strode over to Mary-Anne.

"A pleasure to meet you, Miss Ransome," he declared briskly, taking her hand. "A genuine pleasure." Then, glancing briefly over his shoulder. "These are my—ah—business associates, Mr Green and Mr Ellis."

The two men stayed in the background, dull-faced and silent, giving only the shortest of nods. Smiling around, Harris chatted easily for a moment or two, then got down to business.

"What I have in mind is a private talk, Miss Ransome. Between principals, just you and I."

The office emptied. Harris closed the door, offered Mary-Anne a cigarette, lit it for her, and took one himself. Then, sitting opposite her, he leaned forward.

"I'll be direct. You know I want to buy this place. But"—deliberately he drew a finger along the desk-top, held it up, and showed the resultant dirt smear on his fingertip—"probably you're wondering why."

"The place could use some organizing," admitted Mary-Anne cautiously.

"Organizing?" Harris gave a long laugh. "It needs to be rebuilt from the ground up. It needs modern production methods, backed by decent marketing and advertising. Given that, sales could be increased five, maybe six times over." He tapped the desk. "But that requires money and patience. About two hundred thousand of the first—pounds, not dollars. And anything up to ten years of the second.

"Have you got that kind of money or patience, Miss Ransome?"

She shook her head. Sinclair, the Edinburgh lawyer, had been explicit. Once death duties and the rest had taken their whack, Old Alasdair MacKenzie's distillery was going to be distinctly short of ready cash.

Outside, in the courtyard, a sudden wailing note heralded Angus Mathieson returning to his bagpipe practice. Harris winced visibly, but picked up his briefcase, brought out a thick envelope, and handed it to her.

"That's a fully prepared contract of sale. You know the offer—one hundred thousand pounds, near enough a quarter million dollars."

A quarter million . . . Mary-Anne had a sudden dream of a big, open-plan house on Long Island, of a private swimming pool, of inviting the girls of the Friday Club for long weekends. But a deep-down streak of ancestral caution took command.

"I'm not sure—"

"From our viewpoint, it is a long-term investment, Miss Ransome. Believe me, you won't get a better offer."

Outside, the piping changed to a new, fast, ear-drilling tempo. Harris swore under his breath, and put a hand to his forehead.

"Something wrong?" asked Mary-Anne.

"That din," gritted Harris. "I'd ban every damned bagpipe in existence—I can't stand them." Face beginning to pale, he dragged out a pen. "Well, there's the contract, I've a certified cheque in my pocket, and all you've got to do is sign—"

Somehow Mary-Anne kept her fingers from the pen. Somehow she managed to shake her head.

"I—I'd like to call the lawyer first. Maybe after that . . ."

Harris smiled with an effort and glanced at his watch. "Take your time. Let's say till this afternoon. I'll come back at three o'clock." Rising, he scowled as the pipes shrilled on. "Maybe things will be quieter then."

Once he'd gone and the car had driven off, Fergie Ross came back into the office.

"Well?" he asked hopefully.

"I stalled him like you asked. Till this afternoon."

"Good." The little distillery manager showed his relief. "Did you like his pals?"

She grimaced. "They weren't exactly talkative."

"That's not their line," he said stonily. "Folks reckon they're a couple of low-grade hired thugs."

Outside, the piping died with a final squeal. Mary-Anne stared at him. "I'd better hear the rest."

"You will," agreed Ross, settling in a chair. "But first I'm going to tell you something about whisky and this place. We make a single-malt whisky, one o' the best. We don't make much of it, and we couldn't. Whisky's like a woman—it keeps its secrets, and if you try to force things, you're in trouble."

"What's a single-malt?"

"It means what we bottle comes from this distillery and nowhere else. There aren't many single-malts nowadays—most o' the big-time commercial whiskies are blended." He scrubbed a hand across his chin. "That means different whiskies from any number o' different distilleries put together in some big warehouse. Wi' any reputable firm that's fine. But wi' a few the result is rubbish—cheap, bulk, low-grade liquor just dumped together and sold to folk who don't know any better."

She nodded her understanding, and he grunted.

"Right. And Deerglen Triple Run has a reputation for quality, even if few folk get to drink it. But remember, this whole parish, this valley, is called Deerglen. That's why just about a year ago Matthew Harris appeared from Glasgow wi' plenty of money behind him and an idea for making more.

"He straight away built a big blending warehouse near the village—"

Mary-Anne snapped her fingers. "I saw it in the distance when I was on the mail-bus!"

"Aye, you would," said Fergie Ross grimly. "The idea was to turn out a cheap, rot-gut whisky—one they could call blended at Deerglen and cash in on our reputation. Except that Old Alasdair stopped them short. He took them to court, claimed Deerglen as a registered brand, and won."

"Good for him," said Mary-Anne proudly.

"That's as maybe," frowned Ross. "You see, he held a wee party to celebrate winning. Halfway through it he tried to dance a Highland Fling on the table." He sighed at the memory. "At ninety-three he was a bit old for that kind o' caper. He dropped dead halfway through."

"And now?"

"If you say no, Harris will play rough," warned the distillery manager. "It's not your fault you're a woman."

"I'm also Old Alasdair's great-niece," reminded Mary-Anne firmly, stroking a suddenly proud finger along the length of her nose. Her mind was made up. "Fergie, I feel like another sample of the product."

"You mean it?" Beaming, he jumped to his feet. "I'll fetch some water—"

"Who needs water?" asked Mary-Anne.

Matthew Harris returned promptly on three. He came alone and confident, saw the account books lying on Mary-Anne's desk, and nodded wisely.

"Been checking on the situation?"

"As far as I can," she agreed.

"And found everything I said was true," purred Harris. "You'll sell?"

"No." She said it calmly.

He pursed his lips. "We might up the offer a little—"

"I'm not interested," Mary-Anne told him crisply. "Now get out of my distillery, Mr Harris. Don't bother to come back."

Matthew Harris swallowed hard, retreated to the door, then glared at her.

"Make it difficult if you want," he snarled. "But you'll sell before long and be glad to do it."

A whole week passed without incident. Mary-Anne took up residence in what had been Old Alasdair's living quarters above the office. Each lunch hour the outbursts of piping in the yard grew noisier. And Fergie Ross subjected her to regular lectures on the finer points of whisky production.

The piping was easily explained. Deerglen Parish Band would hold its annual village *ceilidh* at the end of the month. Angus Mathieson was pipe major and was keeping his team up to scratch.

Fergie Ross's lectures often left her dazed. But one did help explain the distillery's ramshackle condition.

"Lassie, you could have a whole damned row o' identical distilleries working side-by-side—and still find only one producing a decent, drinkable whisky," he told her gravely. "There's been plenty o' money spent trying to find out why, but it is still a mystery—even to me. So, when a distillery gives something really good, you daren't change anything.

"Looks don't matter." He thumbed across the yard. "We've needed a new pot-still for years, and the one we've got is damned near as thin as paper in places wi' sheer old age. But it will be a real crisis when we're forced to change it. And the still-maker knows he'll have to make one next best thing to identical, right down to the dents—just in case."

He saw her expression, and grinned. "It sounds daft. But, when you've caught a mystery, you're terrified o' losing it."

Angus Mathieson came round, too. Partly to check the Excise records, partly to talk. His bulky frame filling the tiny office, he suddenly told her, "Mary-Anne, it is good having you here."

For the first time in years Mary-Anne blushed. "Meaning?"

He waved a paw in a vague gesture. "That I'd hate to see Deerglen go to a character like Matthew Harris."

"Oh." Her smile died.

"Yes, I like it here," mused Angus. "You know, being a Revenue man doesn't exactly make for popularity in the Highlands. Folk see the tax on whisky as midway between sacrilege and moral outrage. Still"—the heavy features crinkled—"nobody has hit me on the head so far."

Two nights later someone did.

A frantic pounding on her bedroom door wakened Mary-Anne at 1 a.m. When she opened it, still pulling on a dressing gown, an agitated, breathless Katie Ross practically fell into the room.

"A fire, Mary-Anne—a bad one. It's at the ten-year shed. My father's there . . ."

Mary-Anne Ransome forgot her bare feet, the cream plastered on her nose, even the curlers in her red hair, and went running out into the yard.

An eerie, wavering glow lit the whole distillery. She turned a corner, reached the storage area, and saw the end shed was already a blazing fury. The crackle of flames was punctuated by fresh gouts of blue-tinged fire as liquor casks exploded.

Heat beating against her, sparks and smoke everywhere, she tried to get nearer—then Fergie Ross appeared, coughing and swearing as he waved her back.

"No use," he croaked. "Katie's phoned for help, and we can stop it spreading. But that's all."

They found a dazed Angus Mathieson sitting nursing his head near the entrance. On his way back from a late-night piping practice in the village—plus, he admitted, a few drams—he'd seen someone moving in the courtyard. He'd gone closer, heard a sound behind him, then the world had burst inside his head as he was clubbed.

His head wasn't his main concern. Still rubbing it, he pointed at the ground beside him.

"The damned vandals—"

His precious bagpipes lay smashed and broken, the bag slashed open by a knife.

"I'll get you another set," said Mary-Anne, listening to the noisy, bell-ringing approach of the village fire engine. "That's a promise."

He twisted an expression of thanks. "Och, I've a spare set. But I'll tell you this. There's only one man in the whole county would do a thing like that—and he must have a heart as black as the Earl of Hell's waistcoat."

She thought he meant the fire, then realized differently.

"Harris can't stand the pipes," grated the Revenue man. "That figure I saw in the yard—aye, it could have been one o' those tame thugs of his."

But, as MacLeod, the village constable, pointed out when he at last arrived on his bicycle, that was no kind of proof for anything.

In the morning, as the distillery crew cleared up the charred ruin of the ten-year shed, Mary-Anne did some calculating. They'd lost 15,000 gallons of almost matured whisky, whisky which could have been marketed in a matter of weeks . . . whisky which would have paid most of Deerglen's immediate bills. And Old Alasdair's idea of insurance cover, though it would meet some of the loss, couldn't be called impressive.

She knew the telephone would ring eventually, and it did, in the late afternoon.

"Hard luck about your fire," said Matthew Harris's smooth voice over the wire. "Well, I'm prepared to be generous. The offer still stands."

"Go to hell," said Mary-Anne, and hung up.

That night they began a shotgun patrol. Six of the largest distillery workers volunteered for the rota, patrolling in pairs from dusk till dawn. As all six were in the pipe band, it caused a near crisis at the village practice sessions.

But Mary-Anne had other problems, the cash variety. As she explained to Fergie Ross on a grey, rain-swept morning, none of the local banks showed any great enthusiasm to her suggestion of an overdraft.

"Maybe we could release the next shed of whisky early," she said hopefully. "It would be ready in three months anyway."

Grimly, stubbornly, the distillery manager shook his head. "You can't.

Deerglen Triple Run is ten years matured, every drop—we've always guaranteed it."

"Who'd know the difference, just this once?" she protested.

Fergie Ross raised his eyes significantly toward the ceiling. "Old Alasdair would, for one."

"Damn your Old Alasdair," snapped Mary-Anne. Then gasped and grabbed her desk in alarm as a loud blast shook the office like instant retribution.

Fergie recovered first. "The drying kiln—come on!"

When they reached it, there was a gaping hole where the kiln floor had been. The furnace room below resembled so much scrap metal. The white-faced furnace stoker, miraculously unhurt, could hardly speak until he'd swallowed a large-sized dram.

"Man, I was lucky," he said shakily. "There I was, shovellin' on more peat to top up the furnace. Then one big lump breaks open as it goes in, and I saw what was inside it. I know what a stick of dynamite looks like—I got out fast!"

Mary-Anne groaned. The main peat fuel store was an open shed outside the distillery walls. Anyone could have got at it, anytime.

Once more MacLeod, the constable, came cycling up from the village. He took statements, scratched his head, and went away again—while all other work at the distillery came to a halt and every available man helped try to repair the damage.

The following afternoon Matthew Harris drove his grey limousine into the courtyard, got out cautiously, waited until his two henchmen were positioned one on either side, then marched into the office. Mary-Anne and Fergie were there, with Angus Mathieson hovering angrily in the background.

"You'd another unfortunate accident, I hear," said Harris, his thin face expressionless. "I thought I'd look in and say how sorry I am."

Fergie Ross took a step forward and described Harris's family tree in a bitter five-word outburst. If what he claimed was possible, it would have wrecked the Darwinian theory.

Harris laughed. Fergie took another step forward, then had sense enough to halt as their visitor's bodyguards executed a smart pincer movement.

"Feel like selling?" asked Harris.

Mary-Anne threw the ink bottle at him—and missed. It smashed against the wall, and ink spattered Angus Mathieson from head to foot.

Harris laughed again.

"Next time you'll say yes," he promised, and went out. His henchmen grinned, and followed.

Mary-Anne sat down, put her head in her hands, and wept with rage. A tear went trickling down the length of her nose, then suddenly a large, tobacco-smelling handkerchief was wiping it away.

"Easy, Mary-Anne," said Angus Mathieson awkwardly.

"Easy?" She looked up at his ink-spotted face and bawled this time. "Damn Harris, damn the distillery, damn everything," she wailed. "I wish I'd never left the States. Who—who the hell needs whisky anyway?"

"Look, Mary-Anne"—the Revenue man shifted awkwardly on his large feet—"maybe what you need is cheering up. How about coming down to the village tonight?"

She gulped and sniffed hard. "You mean with you?"

"No, with the band. We're having our concert and *ceilidh* tonight. Fergie is going to watch the distillery till we get back."

"Is he?" Mary-Anne's tears began pouring again. "Well, I can manage without being dated by a pipe band, thanks very much. In fact—in fact, you and your bagpipes can go jump in the ocean. Just leave me alone!"

Angus Mathieson shrugged unhappily, sighed, and left.

"He meant well," said Fergie Ross, after a moment. "Now listen, Mary-Anne—"

She cut him short, still snuffling. "No, you listen for a change. All I've inherited so far is a nightmare—a nightmare run by a bunch of idiots. And I've had enough. I can still go back to my nice, dull job and my nice, dull apartment—and salvage a nice fat bank balance to go with them."

Fergie Ross stared at her, aghast. "You mean you'll sell?"

Mary-Anne raised her head with an attempt at dignity. "If I do, it's none of your damned business."

Only Katie was around for the evening meal. Her father, she explained cautiously, had decided to go down to the village for a little while.

Mary-Anne looked at her through red, still-swollen eyes. "You mean he's gone to get drunk," she accused.

"I wouldn't say that, exactly," said Katie uneasily, beginning to gather up the dishes and tidy around. "It's just that—well, with the *ceilidh* on in the village and him maybe late coming back, there's only you and I left here. And—" she stopped, undecided.

"And you want to go out?" said Mary-Anne, guessing the rest with a touch of envy. "Do I know the boy?"

Katie shook her head. "He's from a farm in the next glen. But—"

"You go out," said Mary-Anne firmly. "Enjoy yourself—you should while you can. Believe me, I know."

An hour later, as darkness fell, Mary-Anne watched Katie vanish into the night on the pillion seat of a motorcycle. Mini-skirt high on her firm young thighs, her arms were tight round the rider's waist.

Mary-Anne suddenly felt very lonely, very far from home, and every last minute of her thirty-seven years. She went down to the office, collected Fergie Ross's shotgun, checked it was loaded, and on an impulse helped herself to a bottle of Deerglen Triple Run from the filing cabinet.

Back in her room, Mary-Anne grimaced at her face in the mirror. She tried combing her hair, freshening her lipstick, and even changed into her best dress—but still felt miserable.

She poured herself a drink, sipped, then pushed the glass away. With a long sigh, she switched off the light and lay back on the bed, glad of the night darkness.

Heck, there was no need to be stuck in this crazy backwoods glen. All she had to do was sign that piece of paper, then laugh all the way to the bank. If she got up right now, went over to the office, and phoned Harris, then it needn't even wait till morning.

Mary-Anne rose from the bed and was reaching for the light switch when she heard a noise from outside. She froze, and it came again, the sharp clink of metal on metal. Quietly, she crossed the darkened room and looked out.

In the yard below two shadowy figures were working on the door of the pot-still building. A third man stood nearby, acting as lookout.

Trembling a little, Mary-Anne found the shotgun, held it tight, and wondered what to do.

With the distillery in darkness and the *ceilidh* well under way in the village, the men below must think they had the place to themselves. Well, she could try to get to the telephone and summon help. But that would take time.

A sound louder than the previous ones came from outside, and she quickly returned to the window. The pot-still building's door was wide open. The two men were going inside.

To the precious pot-still.

Mary-Anne Ransome took a deep breath, gripped the shotgun even tighter, and headed downstairs. Reaching the outside door, she eased it open a fraction. The lookout man was standing a few feet away, his back to her, his eyes on the road to the village.

Mary-Anne crept across the gap, shifted her grip on the shotgun, and brought the butt down hard on his head.

He crumpled and lay motionless.

Hurrying now, she crossed to the pot-still building and peeped in. Matthew Harris and the second of his thugs were standing beside the vast copper bowl of the still. Harris had a torch in his hand, and his companion was carrying a heavy hammer. A few blows of that hammer against the old, thin shell . . .

The main light switch was just inside the door. Mary-Anne snapped it down. As the men spun round, startled by the sudden glare, she trained the shotgun from her hip.

"Drop the hammer. Then both of you come out—slowly."

The hammer dropped. Matthew Harris swallowed and tried to speak.

"Out," said Mary-Anne, moving the shotgun a fraction.

They came.

"March." She brought them over to where the lookout was just beginning to groan. "Pick him up. Then we start walking."

"You've no witnesses," said Harris with a desperate attempt at optimism. "It'll be our word against yours. Maybe . . . maybe we could still do some kind of deal—"

"No. Pick him up," said Mary-Anne resolutely. "We're walking to the village."

Harris's companion grunted his alarm. "Look, lady, that's a good couple of miles!"

"Good exercise," she told him crisply. "And I'll be right behind you."

The little procession was almost halfway to the village when an old truck came rattling toward them. It braked as its headlamps shone on Harris and the two musclemen, Mary-Anne strolling blithely at the rear with her shotgun.

Then it was her turn to be surprised. A flurry of kilts and sporrans erupted from the truck. Angus Mathieson and the pipe band swarmed around her.

"Och, I didn't feel right about you not coming," said the Revenue man, after her swift explanation. "Then, when I found that old devil Fergie had left you up there on your own—"

"My fault, all my fault—an' I'm sorry, Mary-Anne." Fergie Ross came forward miserably. "It's just that I felt a bit low. Angus has given me a dozen different kinds of hell already. Well, now it's your turn."

"Forget it," she told him turning back to Angus. "Go on, Angus."

He twisted a grin. "Well, when I found out, I told the lads that if we couldn't get you to the *ceilidh*, then we should damned well take a wee bit of it to you." He glanced at Harris and the two men. "A good thing we came. What will we do with them?"

The big drummer came forward, reached ponderously into his sporran, and took out a notebook and pencil. Mary-Anne recognized MacLeod, the constable, for the first time, and found herself quivering on the brink of hysterics.

"There'll be charges," said MacLeod solemnly.

"Let's not rush things." She pursed her lips thoughtfully for a moment. "I'd like to go back to the distillery first."

They bundled Harris and his companions aboard the truck, climbed up after them, and the vehicle made short work of the distance. Once it had halted in the distillery yard Mary-Anne took control again.

"Can someone take care of the hired help?"

MacLeod the constable produced a pair of handcuffs from his sporran and anchored the two thugs to a length of railing.

"Now for Mr Harris," said Mary-Anne sweetly. "We know he doesn't like bagpipes. But I wonder how he'd react to a full band at close quarters—inside a place like the still-house!"

Pale face going several shades whiter, Matthew Harris began loud, protesting noises. But they shoved him into the small, high-roofed building.

"Sit," ordered Mary-Anne, prodding with the shotgun.

He gulped and squatted on the floor under the squat, glinting still.

"We'll start wi' a march, lads . . . 'The Black Bear'," decided Angus Mathieson proudly.

Bags were puffed, drones tuned, then the discord changed and the tune howled out from a dozen sets of pipes, and MacLeod, the constable, began thundering his drum.

"Oh my God," moaned Matthew Harris, and put his hands to his ears.

"Oh, no," said Mary-Anne, tickling his nose with the shotgun.

The wild music of the pipes vibrated through the still-room, echoed off the great copper globe, bounced around the stone walls. Pibrochs followed reels, strathspeys took over from marches. In the background, Fergie Ross moved from man to man with a bottle and glasses.

Face gradually tightening in agony, Matthew Harris crouched lower and lower. Beside him, Mary-Anne felt her head begin to throb.

"Angus"—she had to shout at the top of her voice, though the Revenue man was beside her—"how long can they keep this up?"

Angus Mathieson stopped playing and beamed. "Och, if Fergie keeps our throats moist, we'll be getting into our stride in an hour or two. We played for three days when MacLeod's daughter got married."

The strathspey ended, and the pipers paused, gathering in a circle while Fergie hurried round with a fresh bottle.

"Three days!" Mary-Anne considered the Revenue man with awe.

"Three I remember," qualified Angus, tucking a thumb in the waistband of his kilt. "After that there's a wee doubt in our minds. Eh . . . would you like 'Highland Laddie' next? That's one o' our favourites."

"I'll ask our guest," said Mary-Anne dryly. "What about it, Mr Harris?"

A haggard, woebegone Matthew Harris bit a quivering lip. "I . . . I'm going out of my mind. What do you want, anyway?"

"For a start, a full, written confession," she told him.

"And sign myself to jail?" He managed to shake his head.

"I wasn't finished," said Mary-Anne. "You'll also sign over that blending warehouse as compensation in full for damage caused. We can use it—it's time we expanded. Oh, and I want a new set of bagpipes for Angus. In Mathieson tartan with all the trimmings."

"You're crazy," croaked Harris.

"Maybe," shrugged Mary-Anne. "But my part of the bargain would be a guarantee of no prosecution."

Angus Mathieson signalled. The circle of pipers began puffing into their bags, and the first drones began to wail.

"A pen," groaned Harris. "You win."

The wailing died, the pipers grinned.

Watching the man write, Mary-Anne felt both tired and happy. She'd saved her distillery—and with the warehouse they could run a new quality blend along with the single-malt.

Suddenly, Fergie Ross came toward her with a small, cut-crystal glass in his hand and a look of solemn purpose on his wrinkled face.

"This is for you, lassie," he said with a great dignity. "The proprietor's whisky."

Mary-Anne took a deep breath, hoping. "The Quadruple Run?"

"Aye," agreed Fergie Ross proudly. "It's been ready, waiting. With a new name—Deerglen Queen."

There wasn't much more than a thimbleful of almost colourless liquor in the bottom of the glass. She drained it at a gulp.

"That's what I'd call beautiful," said Mary-Anne some ten seconds later. She wasn't quite sure what had happened to her. But she was looking straight at Angus Mathieson. He had the most wonderfully hairy legs under that kilt.

Angus winked.

And Mary-Anne Ransome knew she'd come home.

MRS CRAGGS AND A
CERTAIN LADY'S TOWN HOUSE

H.R.F. Keating

WITH ONE LADY in London, for whom Mrs Craggs worked briefly,
she had to sign a piece of paper, very thick and creamy and printed in big
black lettering, before she could start the job at all. In it she promised she
would never divulge any information she might learn in the course of her
employment under pain of various fearsome penalties.

Mrs Craggs hesitated about signing because one of the reasons she was
thinking of taking the job was so as she could tell some inside details to
her friend Mrs Milhorne, who at that time was in such a state of dis-
tress (owing to the sudden departure, once again, of Mr Milhorne) that she
felt herself unable so much as to put duster to furniture for
anybody—"What'd do her most good," said Mrs Craggs, "is polish a nice
big stretch o' lino, nothing like bringing up a good shine on lino to get you
over the 'ump"—but she reckoned in any case that just to tell her friend she
had noticed the lady out in the morning walking her corgi dogs or
something like that could do nobody any harm. And she was not even going to get into the place itself, just into the gardens.

The job which there was all the fuss about was only a temporary one,
providing extra help on certain days when there were garden parties. The
parties the lady gave were easily the biggest in London, "and posh," said
Mrs Craggs afterwards, "they were so posh that how any of 'em could
ever have swallered down a good hot cuppa an' a nice piece o' cake is more
nor I could say."

So, although she hesitated, in the end Mrs Craggs signed the paper, and
with a good conscience. But before the job was done, and it lasted only
one day—she never went back—she had learnt a dreadful secret indeed,
one which she was to take very good care that Mrs Milhorne never got
even the slightest hint of. It would have had her up off the old couch in
her front room—"the chaise-longoo" Mrs Milhorne was accustomed to
call it—and away to Fleet Street before you could say "Miracle cure".

Mrs Craggs hadn't been in the gardens there half an hour when she got
her first inkling that everything in those gardens was not as lovely as it
should be, despite many assurances from Mrs Milhorne. She had been
busy sweeping the wooden floor of the first of the huge marquees to be

erected, and incidentally had already collected enough gossip from her fellow workers to keep Mrs Milhorne happy on her chaise-longoo for a twelvemonth, if she felt on consideration it was proper to pass it on.

All them corgis 'aving to be rounded up first thing and kep' out o' the way in case they bite a guest, she thought, now is that something I could be sent to prison for, or ain't it?

Then a single small snag occurred in the smooth running of the preparations. A signboard proclaiming "Royal Tea Tent", which had just been taken from the box in which it had rested ever since the final garden party of the year before, was found to be smeared with a great smudge of sticky black mud. Where that had come from no one could say. But, more urgently, at this stage of the proceedings, there was no handy supply of water with which to wash it off.

"See to it, would you, Mrs—er," said the tenting manager, and away he went before any awkward questions could be asked.

Mrs Craggs knew that to go indoors and hunt about till she found a sink, though it would no doubt be easy enough, was simply not to be done. So she took a good look all round her and in a minute spotted, through a clump of trees, the gleam of water.

A pond or a stream or a lake even, she thought to herself. And, securely gripping the elegantly painted sign, off she went.

Sure enough, just beyond a big clump of a plant which Mrs Craggs recognised with a start of pleasure in these exalted surroundings as being a homely growth known to her mother before her as Devil's Snitchbane and very handy for putting a branch or two of in places where it ponged a bit, there was a lake. It was long and narrow, with a pretty looking low bridge across it, just like in the country, and three or four long-legged pink flamingoes pecking about, beautiful as a picture. Mrs Craggs gave a sigh of relief. It seemed her difficult little task would soon be neatly completed. Until she saw the soldier.

And what a soldier he was. No ordinary bloke in a khaki uniform whom Mrs Craggs might have felt she could go up to and confide her problem in, but a magnificent creature—more like a statue, painted, Mrs Craggs thought, not a chap as'd want ter 'ave a good scratch every now an' again—dressed in a faultless scarlet jacket, immaculately creased and immensely long black trousers, with a belt pipeclayed to a whiteness more dazzling than snow and brass buttons shining more brightly than the sun overhead, and above all crowned by a towering, softly gleaming, beautiful black bearskin. He was standing just on the far side of the little bridge, sternly regarding alternately the elegant pink-breasted flamingoes near him and the distant high brick wall which surrounded the whole gardens.

On guard. On duty. Important. Not to be spoken to. Or even smiled at. Much, much less, asked if it was all right to wash a signboard in the lake over which, ramrod stiff, he was presiding.

Mrs Craggs stood, just in the shadow of the big clump of Devil's Snitchbane, and looked at him and wondered what she was going to do now.

And then two quite unexpected things happened. First, the statue soldier suddenly seemed to slump to only about three-quarters of his previously imposing height and take a quick—and, yes, furtive—glance all round about him before in one swift movement he plucked off his magnificent bearskin, laid it on the ground just behind him, pulled out a handkerchief from under his scarlet jacket and gave a good mop to the sweat which must have collected on his scalp and forehead under the heat of the already brilliant sun. And, second, from out of a dense bush of purple-spiked buddleia nearby, at just that moment, there emerged, almost as startling as the sight of the guardsman's sudden alteration, what was plainly nothing other than a corgi dog.

And, worse, hardly had Mrs Craggs had time to reflect that almost certainly it would be a betrayal of that solemn piece of thick and creamy paper to tell Mrs Milhorne that even the most august canine arrangements sometimes went astray, when the little dog took one good sniff at the bearskin lying on the ground just in front of him and then lifted his leg and . . .

Mrs Craggs rushed forward from the shadow of the clump of Snitchbane.

"Hey! Stop! Stop that, you little brute," she yelled.

The little brute may have been accustomed to receiving orders from very much higher up in the social scale, but perhaps he had not before had any given him quite so vigorously. Because he took one quick look at Mrs Craggs, coming tearing over a verdant sward towards him, and he vanished.

Mrs Craggs went up to the soldier.

"Well, 'ere's a how-d'ye-do," she said. "Messed your titfer up right proper, 'e 'as, the little bleeder."

"What am I going to do?"

The soldier, for all his scarlet jacket, bright-shining brass and dazzling pipeclayed belt, was no longer a figure of untouchable statue-prestige. He was something Mrs Craggs recognized very well: a small boy in a stew.

"Well, we could dip it in the water," she suggested cheerfully, giving the polluted bearskin an appraising look.

"And ruin it?" gasped the soldier. "I'd be in the glasshouse as long as I lived."

"We could try giving it a bit of a brush wi' some grass or something."

"But it'd smell," the guardsman objected. "I'm not going to be stuck out here all day keeping an eye on a lot of blooming flamingoes. I got to go and direct guests out the front first thing this afternoon!"

"Yeh," said Mrs Craggs, unable to keep back a bit of a grin, "you'd direct 'em just about the wrong way, whiffing like that."

"It ain't no laughing matter," the soldier retorted, a look of real agony on his martial visage. "I'm done for. I'm up the creek. I'm down the pan."

"Oh, no, you ain't," Mrs Craggs said, half sharply, half cheeringly.

"But I must be. On parade and ponging like the back-end of nowhere."

"But you won't pong," said Mrs Craggs. "Not with a nice leaf or two o' Devil's Snitchbane under your 'at, you won't."

"Devil's Snitchbane? What the devil's that?"

So Mrs Craggs explained. And the plant—what reverberating Latin name it bore to the lady's many gardeners heaven only knew—was duly ransacked for a good bunch of its subtly aromatic leaves and these were quickly stuffed into the guardsman's tall and desecrated bearskin and before another five minutes had passed Mrs Craggs, sniffing the air round about him like a vacuum-cleaner, pronounced that no particular odour was any longer noticeable.

And then, with the soldier's help, she washed the mud-smeared sign and set off back.

But even trotting along towards the huge smooth lawns where the tea tents were, Mrs Craggs found that life inside the high brick surrounding walls was still flecked in its outward smoothness by little untoward incidents. Like the policeman burrowing in the bushes.

Mrs Craggs spotted him as she was approaching a small summerhouse with a nice thatched roof to it—"Why, I might be miles away in the country," she had just murmured to herself—and the policeman was crouching in the bushes at the back of the building seemingly poking into a small hole below the floor level. Of course, he might have been only making sure there were no bombs under the little building. But Mrs Craggs was pretty sure he was doing nothing of the kind. She had seen too many coppers on the beat at night tucking away their packets of fags or their bits of a snack somewhere convenient to have any doubts about that.

And, just to have a little bet with herself, as soon as the constable had strolled off, looking every inch the dignified bobby—I expect they picks 'em special, Mrs Craggs thought—and perhaps adding an extra touch of stateliness by proving to have, when he could be fully seen, a magnificent and well-trimmed red beard, she trotted up to the bushes and poked her hand into the hole under the little summerhouse.

Yes, fags.

Mrs Craggs smiled. But had that thick and creamy sheet of paper stopped her telling Mrs Milhorne about this?

"Well, you've been long enough," the tenting manager greeted her as she handed over the board. But as it was solemnly hoisted to its proper place Mrs Craggs answered not a word. Instead she went back to sweeping the floor of the huge marquee, making as good a job of it as she knew how.

But, though she was a great believer in a spot of hard work helping you to make up your mind about any problem, big or small, for all the care and vigour with which she wielded her broom no answer came to her about the question the surreptitious policeman had posed. She wanted to tell Mrs Milhorne—and all the more so because she knew telling her this would help her not to say anything about how one of the household corgis had defied even the best of arrangements—but she was not at all sure how far she could trust her friend.

As it happened, her mind was made up for her in quite a different way.

She had barely coaxed the last grains of dust from the floor into her dustpan when from just the other side of the marquee's canvas there came a yell of such volume and excruciating pain that everybody inside was frozen into stillness. Mrs Craggs, indeed, was the first to come to life. She rose from her knees, caught hold of the edge of a join in the canvas close beside her and with one heave opened a good big aperture in the tent's side.

And there, plain for all to see, was the very same red-bearded constable Mrs Craggs had been thinking of when the terrible yell had so startled them all. And, plain cause of the yell, there with its stout little jaws firmly clamped on to the blue of the policeman's trousers was the same little corgi who had already once this morning committed an outrage, on the guardsman's bearskin.

"Why, you—" shouted Mrs Craggs.

And at the sound of that by now familiar voice once again the little dog vanished from sight.

Which, since it was soon evident that the heavy cloth of the constable's trousers was still intact despite the corgi's best efforts, should have been the end of the incident. And it would have been, except for the constable's red beard.

Because for once at least popular belief proved true, and it turned out that the red-bearded policeman had a flaming temper. And, worse than that, it turned out his innermost political beliefs were of a rousing red character to match both temper and beard.

Terrible penalties were going to be exacted from the supposed owner of the offending canine. And the whole Press of the free world was, a trifle illogically perhaps and certainly in defiance of any papers signed, going to be enlisted in the cause of proclaiming the crime to the skies. It would have quite spoilt the garden party. Except that Mrs Craggs found an opportunity before very long to have a quiet word in the enraged ear above the flaming beard. The phrases "little thatched hut, ever so pretty" and "a packet o' fags and who's to blame?" might have been heard, and then all of a sudden the red-bearded policeman was the soul of sweetness and the incident of the incisive corgi no more than a passing joke.

And the garden party, far from being spoilt, was a great success. The sun shone. The guests glittered. The tea was excellent, the cakes more than excellent. The bands were of a jolly oompahness not to be beaten and the hostess gracious beyond belief, if perhaps as some observers noted—Mrs Craggs from behind a cloud of fragrant steamy washing-up water among them—looking occasionally just a little tired and in need of a few moments' respite as though she had spent unexpectedly a number of frustrating and ill-spared minutes early in the day engaged in some slightly unpleasant duty like calling and calling in vain to a particularly recalcitrant pet dog, or something of that sort. But this was less than a little cloud to mar the universal joy.

Something which could not have been said of the discovery which Mrs Craggs learnt of towards the end of the affair, though not so near it that the matter could safely be ignored. It was her friend of earlier in the day, the guardsman with the miraculously deodorized bearskin, who told her about it.

She had her head down in her washing-up bowl when a sudden hissing voice penetrated her cloud of steam.

"Hey, missus, he's done it again."

She looked up, recognized her friend and therefore knew at once who "he" was.

"That bleeding little corgi?" she said. "What now?"

"Worse than anything. Worse than my bearskin, worse than that copper's leg, silly idiot."

"What? What's the little perisher done? Don't jabber, lad. Speak up."

"It's a flamingo. One of them special flamingoes, given her by the Indian Ambassador or something, it was part of my orders to keep a particular eye on."

"Bitten one o' them, has he?"

"Worse."

Mrs Craggs thought like a spin-dryer.

"The corpse," she said, reaching to the heart of the matter at once. "Where's the corpse? If any o' the guests . . ."

"That's it, that's just it. It's down by the lake there, where it all happened, and I can't think of no way of doing anything about it."

"You wouldn't," said Mrs Craggs, with scorn.

And she set herself to meet the challenge as she had set herself to meet any challenge that had come along in the course of a longish old life not without its crises.

It took her hardly any time, not long enough for her washing-up water to have cooled even.

Then she removed her hands from the bowl, gave them a good wipe on the edge of her flowered apron and turned to go.

"Come on," she said to the soldier.

"Where to?"

"To get the body, o' course."

"But what'll we do with it?"

"Hide it, lad. What else?"

"But where? Where?"

"Where the policeman hid his fags, boy. Under the floor o' that nice little thatched summerhouse they got."

"Yeah," said the guardsman, enlightenment dawning. "Yeah, I know it. Seen it when I was patrolling. Yeah, just the place. Only."

"Only what, lad? Speak up."

"Only, well, the niff like."

"From the body? You're right about that, lad, but you ought to know what we can do there."

"What then?" The guardsman had as much faith in Mrs Craggs by now as he had in his Regimental Sergeant Major.

"Easy, lad. Devil's Snitchbane. Much as we can grab of it."

Mrs Craggs carried the feet and the guardsman the snake-like and drooping neck, Mrs Craggs considering that this was no less than a soldier should do. It did not take them as much as two minutes to hurry with their unseeable burden round to the back of the summerhouse, seizing on the way three stout branches from the fast diminishing clump of Snitchbane. And, though in among the bushes some difficulties presented themselves—largely to do with the size of the hole in the boards—their task was all but finished inside a six-minute limit.

Until a female voice from the small curtained window directly above coldly addressed them.

"Just what are you two doing there?"

Mrs Cragg's first thought, as she looked up from her crouching position, was that there was no way in which, on her knees, she could make even an attempt at a curtsey. Then she thought of all the circumstances that had brought about this unexpected meeting. Next, for half an instant she remembered Mrs Milhorne and the creamy sheet of paper. And finally a favourite old saying of hers planted itself firmly above the temporary confusion in her mind. "When there ain't no 'elp fer it, there ain't nothing like the plain old truth."

So she told it.

"But I never thought as 'ow you'd be in there, ma'am, straight I didn't," she concluded.

"I use it to come and freshen up if things get a bit too hectic out there," the owner of the house (and gardens) said.

"Well, an' if I 'ad any idea I wouldn't never 'ave dreamt o' stuffing that old bird underneath," Mrs Craggs replied. "I'm right sorry, ma'am, that I am."

"No," said the lady of the house. "No need to be sorry at all. The last thing any of us wants is for what little Joey has done to get out. So the sooner we all forget all about it the better, isn't it?"

"Well, yes," said Mrs Craggs. And she was so surprised and delighted by the suggestion that she added: "Yes, it bloody well is."

But she did not forget about it, not for as long as she lived, though she never ever gave a solitary soul so much as a hint of it all. Mrs Craggs knows how to keep a secret, pieces of creamy paper or no pieces of creamy paper.

"TO THE EDITOR, DEAR SIR—"

Michael Gilbert

It was seven o'clock on a misty November evening when the convoy reached the corner of Jamaica Road and Tunstal Passage. The corner block was the building belonging to Merriams, who are manufacturers of anchors, cables and other massive maritime iron-work. First came a police car, then the articulated lorry carrying the new cable press, a squat piece of machinery weighing about five tons, then Mr Fawke, the managing director of Merriams, in his private car. He spotted that there was some sort of hold-up ahead and jumped out to investigate.

The doors of Messrs Merriams' private goods hoist were at the side of the building and opened on to Tunstal Passage. Above them there jutted out a short fixed overhead crane. The plan had been to use this crane to lift the press off the lorry and draw it into the hoist, which would then take it up to the second storey, where a gang of men waited with rollers to coax it into its final resting place. The whole plan, including a modification in the width of the press to enable it to get into the hoist, had been worked out with meticulous care.

"Wonderful, isn't it," said the driver of the lorry. Right in front of the entrance to the hoist a private car was parked.

Mr Fawke glared at it. It was not only obstructing the doors of the hoist. It was blocking the narrow width of Tunstal Passage and so preventing the lorry from backing down it.

"I suppose it's locked."

The car, which was a newish dark blue four-door Austin saloon, was securely locked.

"You've got keys and things, haven't you?" said Mr Fawke to the police driver. "You use them to drive away parked cars."

"I haven't got anything with me, not personally," said the driver.

"What about a break-down van? There's one at Simmons Garage."

"The thing is, are you entitled to move it?"

"For God's sake! It's blocking my own hoist."

"We got twenty cars behind us now," said the driver of the lorry helpfully.

"Must you use your hoist?" said the constable. "What about taking it in the front entrance?"

"And up two flights of stairs?" said Mr Fawke. "Talk sense."

Down Jamaica Road horns were beginning to sound in the mist.

"Must do something," said the constable. "If you can't get it in, you'll have to move on."

One of the men said, "What we might do, is lift the car up with the hoist. Then we could swing it out of the way, see."

Mr Fawke said, "Good idea. Let's try it. And if it hurts the car it serves the owner bloody well right for leaving it in such a bloody stupid place. Fix the hook on the front bumper, Jim."

"I don't know as you ought," began the constable.

A figure was approaching up the passage.

"Some trouble here?" said the newcomer pleasantly. "Oh, my car in the way? If you'll ask your man to clear the entrance I'll back it out. Thank you. Thank you. Sorry to have been a nuisance. Urgent call."

They saw now that the car had a sticker on the wind-screen. "Doctor. On duty."

It was only after the car had gone that it occurred to the constable, who was busy clearing the traffic block in Jamaica Road, that he had failed to get the doctor's name. He had, however, made a note of the number of his car. UGC 368W.

Detective Sergeant Milo Roughead brought in a sheaf of papers and laid them on Chief Inspector Petrella's desk with all the decorum of a butler bringing the morning mail to a ducal breakfast table. Beside the papers he placed a copy of the *Stockwell and Clapham Courier*.

Milo Roughead was a newcomer to Patton Street. When he had first arrived Petrella, who had noted from his Details of Education and Previous Service that he was an Etonian, had been prepared to dislike him, but had found him entirely disarming.

"What's this little lot about?" he said.

"Most of it's routine stuff, sir," said Milo. "There's a letter from a Mr Raby."

"Yes, we know Mr Raby," said Petrella.

"Then there's a copy for information of a report from the boys in blue—"

"From the uniformed branch."

"I mean, sir, from the uniformed branch," agreed Milo unabashed. "It's about an incident in Tunstal Passage last night. It looked like being a bit of a box-up, but it came out all right in the end. Oh, and Inspector Blaikie from Junction wants a word with you."

"What's in that newspaper?"

"I thought you might like to see that. It's another letter from Mr Mayflower."

"About us?"

"About us," agreed Milo.

Mr Mayflower was an untiring writer to the Press. He acted as a local ombudsman, drawing attention to matters which he thought required airing. He seemed to devote a good part of his time to the police.

> It is a source of amazement to me [wrote Mr Mayflower], that the police who, as we are constantly assured, are undermanned and overworked do not concentrate their attention on the more serious crimes. Nine-tenths of their energies appear to be dissipated in pursuing misdemeanours of no conceivable importance. Trivial offenders against parking regulations, shop opening hours and licensing laws are pursued with untiring zeal. Hours and days of police time are wasted, not only in the detection of these earth-shattering matters but in subsequent attendance at court—

It was an old complaint. And Petrella recognized that there was an element of truth in it. Particularly the bit about attendance at court. But Mr Mayflower had chosen the wrong whipping boy. The fault did not lie with the police. They could not pick and choose which offenders they pursued. A more rational system of law and administration—

"Was there anything else, sir?" said Milo politely.

"You'd better tell Blaikie to come up. We don't want to keep him hanging about."

Inspector Blaikie was a railway policeman. Most of his work was concerned with pilfering from the two big depots in Petrella's manor. They had done a lot of jobs together, and Petrella liked the dry little man who saved the railways around twenty times his own salary every year of his working life and got few thanks for it. This time, however, it was something else.

"My man was coming back himself from the terminal at Grain," he said. "You know they travel in mufti sometimes to pick up ticket bilkers. Well, he noticed this man, who got on at Graystone Halt—that's a little station on the marsh between Cooling and Cliffe. When they reached London Bridge they both got out, and our chap heard this man say to the ticket collector, 'I'm sorry I hadn't time to buy a ticket. I got on at Gravesend.' So he intervenes, and says, 'I think you're mistaken, sir. I happen to know you got on at Graystone Halt.' Without batting an eyelid the man says, 'Exactly, that's what I said. Graystone.' "

"It would be easy to mishear it," said Petrella.

"Certainly. But they're both absolutely certain they didn't. They swear he said Gravesend, and said it distinctly. The upshot of it was, they took his name and address and reported it to me."

"What sort of man?"

"He was a doctor. Doctor Lovibond. He lives in your part of the world."

Petrella said, "Yes. I think I can place him. About sixty. Reddish brown face. Bushy grey eyebrows, grey moustache. Has done service in India."

"That's the man. Respectable citizen. Perfectly clean record."

"If your chap had waited a bit before he butted in and let him pay for a ticket from Gravesend you might have had a case. As it is, I don't believe you'll get anywhere with it."

"That's my view," said Blaikie. "We'd better drop it." He sounded relieved.

When he had gone, Petrella started on the various dockets and reports. The officious Mr Raby, until his retirement the manager of one of the local banks, reported that a shop called Blooms Antiques in Tooley Street was selling replicas in gold of the medallion struck to commemorate the recovery of King Edward VII from appendicitis.

"It appears to me," wrote Mr Raby in the neat handwriting which had refused a thousand overdrafts, "that unless Blooms is an authorised dealer in bullion, which I beg leave to doubt, he is acting in contravention of Section 2 of the Exchange Control Act 1947. The objects relate to an incident which took place in 1901, they cannot be described, in the words of Statutory Instrument No. 48 of 1966 as coins or objects of numismatic value more than one hundred years old."

Petrella took the report and placed it firmly at the bottom of his pending tray. He felt a growing sympathy with the views expressed by Mr Mayflower in the *Stockwell and Clapham Courier.*

The last report concerned what Sergeant Roughead had described as the box-up in Tunstal Passage. Petrella read it rapidly and was on the point of throwing it into the out-basket for filing when something struck him.

Petrella was blessed, or cursed, with visual memory. It was the sort of memory which enabled him to recall telephone numbers, dates on documents and details of that sort, usually quite unimportant. And he was certain that he had seen the number plate UGC 368W somewhere recently. He concentrated for a moment on the problem. A newish dark blue four-door Austin saloon. He saw it, in his mind's eye, parked outside a house. A house not far from his own. A house in Craven Road. A doctor's house. That was right. The car belonged to Doctor Lovibond. The man who had made a mistake about his railway ticket.

It was a mild coincidence. The sort of thing that was always happening in real life. If Petrella had had more to do that morning he would have dismissed the matter from his mind entirely. In the end the action which he did take was to extract Mr Raby's letter from the bottom of his pending tray, and send for Sergeant Roughead. He said, "Go and see Blooms Antiques. It's a respectable little shop, as far as I know, run by a man called Friar. Find out what this is all about."

"Loosen him up a bit?"

"Certainly not," said Petrella. "You're not playing the wall game now. Just ask him where he got these medallion things from."

When Milo had departed Petrella put on his hat and coat and walked down to have a look at Tunstal Passage. Something was worrying him.

Tunstal Passage runs sharply downhill from its junction with Jamaica Road, between the flanks of two large buildings. One was Merriams' iron foundry. The other was a furniture repository. There were side doors to the yards of both these buildings, after that a length of blank wall, then a pair of wooden gates which blocked the end of the passage. On the gates, in faded white lettering, Petrella could make out, "Waterside Properties Limited".

He got one foot on to a bollard, hoisted himself up, and looked over. Immediately in front of him was a row of shacks, the biggest being a Nissen hut, the smallest no larger than a toolshed. None of them looked habitable or inhabited. Beyond them he could see an expanse of grey flecked with flashes of white where Father Thames ran by in full flood.

Petrella came down off his perch and walked slowly back up the passage. What he was trying to work out was which of his patients Doctor Lovibond could have been calling on at seven o'clock in the evening in Tunstal Passage.

"I thought it funny myself," said Mr Friar, "but I didn't see anything illegal in it. This lady brought along six of them in a case. Said her great-uncle used to collect them. Heavy great things. Solid gold, no fooling. I've got the last one here."

He unlocked his wall safe and brought out the medallion.

"Weighs just over five ounces. Six of them. Two pounds of gold. Worth something these days, eh?"

Sergeant Roughead examined the medallion curiously. On one side was a conventional representation of the head of Edward VII, Hanoverian nose jutting defiantly over rakish beard. On the other side the date 1901 and the words "*Pacis Amator*".

"I took one of them along to Francks," said Mr Friar. "They looked it up for me in their catalogues. It's genuine all right. See what it says on the back. Lover of Peace. That's what they thought of him. My old father used to sing a song about that." Mr Friar threw back his head and croaked out, "There never was a King like Good King Edward: Peace with Honour was his motter: God Save the King."

Milo was enchanted. He said, "Do you know any more verses?"

"There was one about mothers and babies. I don't recall exactly how it went."

Milo recollected that he was there on duty and said, as sternly as he could, "You realise you're not supposed to deal in gold?"

"These are antiques."

"Nothing's antique until it's a hundred years old. You'd better not sell this one until I've found out what the form is. I mean, until I've made a report."

"I suppose," said Petrella, "that one of them could be genuine and the other five could be modern copies of it. They wouldn't be difficult to make. And there's no way of dating gold. It's the only metal that doesn't age in any way at all."

"What would be the point?" said Milo. "Friar was simply selling them for their weight in gold."

"The point," said Petrella, "is that he was able to sell them at all. And that someone was able to sell them to him. If you went along to a shop with a bar of gold weighing two pounds and tried to flog it, you'd have a lot of questions to answer, wouldn't you? But take along a set of six medals, in a nice case, property of your late great-uncle, and nobody bothers. I suppose, by the way, you found out who did sell them to him."

"It was a Mrs Smith. She gave her address as 92 Maple Avenue."

"There's no street called Maple Avenue in this district."

"The same thing struck Mr Friar. When she left, he sent his boy after her. She had a car parked out of sight round the corner. And he got its number: UGC 368W."

It was at this point that Petrella decided to devote some real attention to the case.

He said, "Go down to Graystone Halt. It's the station beyond Cooling on the Isle of Grain branch line. Doctor Lovibond was there two days ago. To hide the fact that he'd been there he told a stupid lie and risked getting into trouble. I'd like to know what he was up to."

"If I disguised myself as a tramp—"

"Wear your old Etonian tie," said Petrella. "No one will mistake you for a policeman."

"It's an odd sort of locality," said Milo. "Flat as your hat. Cabbages and cattle. Ditches between all the fields, running down to the river. You have to pick your way. There's several places you can go in up to your waist."

"Did you?"

"No. I had a guide. A chap who's got a big house down there. He's a stockbroker, but he's mad about birds. The ones with wings and beaks I mean. He spends his time out on the marshes watching them through field glasses."

"And who did you tell him you were? A fellow ornithologist?"

"As a matter of fact I used to be his fag. I thought it was time he did something for me for a change. He gave me a damned good lunch. And we walked over the fields down to the river. He spotted a pair of goosanders—"

"It sounds lovely," said Petrella. "I suppose you remembered what you went down there for?"

"Certainly. This chap's going to be very useful. He knows all the local characters. Pays them to report the arrival of any rare birds. It's a funny part of the world. Very cliquish, if you know what I mean. There aren't many strangers, and any that come along get noticed. It used to be a great place for smuggling. The ships came up the river by night and the stuff was floated ashore and picked up at Cassibon Inlet or Egypt Bay. If there was any trouble, they used to hide it in the church at Cooling. Under the pulpit, actually. My friend's going to pass the word round. Give people the number of the car. If that doctor's up to anything they'll soon ferret it out."

Petrella said, "That sounds quite a good arrangement." It had the feel of a nice little gold smuggling racket. As soon as they got some more information they could act on it. Meanwhile other more urgent matters occupied his time.

It was on a dark day at the beginning of December, a day of drizzle which could turn later into fog, that a further instalment of Mr Mayflower's letter-writing arrived on Petrella's desk. On this occasion he had abandoned the police and turned the searchlight of his attention on to the Immigration Service. It seemed that they were being very slow in answering enquiries from anxious relatives in India and Pakistan.

Did his readers know that there were cases where men had come to England and their families had not heard from them for eighteen months or even two years?

As he read it, a very faint prickle of alarm stirred in Petrella's mind. It was an instinctive reaction, born of experience, sharpened by the habit of joining together apparently unassociated scraps of information, which is the basis of all good police work. Somewhere, months before, he had read a report—From where, and about what? He could see himself sitting back in his chair and reading it. The hot tarry diesel-fumed smell of Patton

Street had been coming in through the wide-open window. So it must have been July or August. He had thought the report worth keeping and he had filed it. Interpol. That was right. It was a routine report from Interpol.

Petrella unearthed it, and read it a second time, with the murk of December swirling down Patton Street and the sounds of life coming muffled through the tight-shut window.

A French revenue cutter, patrolling in the early morning mist, had hit a small outboard motor boat which was running without lights. By the time the cutter had succeeded in turning round and getting back to the scene of the collision the boat had sunk, but the crew of two, who were wearing life-jackets, had been rescued without much trouble. They turned out to be local fishermen. They had offered no satisfactory explanation of what they were doing, and the look-out on the cutter asserted that, just before the crash, he had seen a third man in the small craft. The two fishermen had been released after questioning as there seemed to be nothing specific they could be charged with. A fortnight later a body was recovered. It had been swept by the current into the rocks at the foot of the Nez de Joburg and wedged there. It appeared to be an Indian, in early middle age, dressed in what had, before its immersion, been a respectable suit of clothes. Under the coat, in a webbing belt worn round the waist, were twelve four-ounce tablets of gold.

Petrella sent for Sergeant Roughead and was irritated to find that he was out on an enquiry. He spent some time after that on the telephone to the managing director of Waterside Properties.

It was four o'clock, and the drizzle of the morning had turned into a thick mist, when Milo arrived back. Petrella said, "There's been a development in the gold-running business. Do you think you could get on to your pal down at Cooling and see if he's got anything to report?"

"I've had three reports from him already," said Milo smugly.

"You've had *what?*"

"Three reports. The last one was two days ago. I don't suppose—"

Petrella said, "Are you trying to tell me that you've had three reports and sat on them?"

"They weren't very conclusive—"

"Do you want to continue in the police force?" The anger in his voice was so sharp that Milo went scarlet. He found nothing to say. "There is one use and one use only for information. You share it. You don't hoard it. Or decide what's important and what isn't. Or wait till you've got everything complete and wrapped up so that you can spring it on us as a nice surprise. Do you understand?"

"Yes, sir," said Sergeant Roughead, in a very small voice.

"Then let's have it."

"The doctor has been seen down there three times. Twice he came by car and once by train to Graystone Halt, and was picked up by his wife. She'd come down earlier by car. She didn't meet him at the station actually. She waited a short distance away and he walked to the car. They've got an old farm house on the marshes. It's down a track, leading off the main road."

"Don't explain it. Just show me."

Petrella had a one-inch Ordnance Survey map spread on his desk and Sergeant Roughead put his finger on a dotted line which led out over the marshes and stopped just short of the river. A building was marked at the end of it.

"It's called Barrows Piece," said Sergeant Roughead. He seemed to have recovered some of his spirits. "A farmer called Barrow built it, and commited suicide in the barn. It's pretty lonely. The Lovibonds seem to use it as a weekend cottage."

Petrella had picked up the telephone and dialled a number. Before he could speak, a recorded voice at the other end said, "Doctor Lovibond will not be available until Monday morning. If you have a message would you speak it slowly, beginning now."

Petrella replaced the receiver and looked out of the window. The mist was thickening into fog. He said, "Tell Anderson I shall want his car, with him driving it. He'd better have a set of chains with him. I shan't be starting before ten o'clock."

Milo said, "Right sir, Anderson plus car chains at twenty-two hundred hours." He looked like a dog who is not certain if he is going to be taken for a walk or not.

"All right," said Petrella. "You too."

As the car crept through the fog Petrella said, "The main outline's clear enough. Dr Lovibond had a medical practice in Pakistan. A lot of wealthy clients and a lot of contacts. He was just the man to run this end of a high-class illegal immigration service. When a rich Pakistani is taken on—one at a time probably—he's told to bring most of his portable wealth with him in gold. He comes overland to the north coast of France and is run out by the fishermen to a small cargo boat, which times its run to arrive off Tilbury in the early hours of the morning. At some point before they reach Tilbury the passenger is put ashore near Barrows Piece. The pay-off is in gold. We've found out that the doctor has a small workshop on that Waterside Properties lot. That's where he turns the gold into different saleable objects. Then his wife disposes of them for him. We've traced three of her outlets besides Blooms Antiques. When we get down to it we shall probably find a lot more."

"What did he do with the Pakistanis after he got them to Barrows Piece?" said Sergeant Roughead.

Petrella said to the driver, "You fork left here, Andy. Just before you get to the bridge." And to Sergeant Roughead, "That's what we may be going to find out. The doctor's down there and a fog like this is just the job for them."

It was past midnight when they reached the track, and drove slowly up it, chains churning the mud. It twisted and turned, between high hedges of thorn, going downhill all the time. Then they were out in the open, with nothing ahead of them but a wall of white mist.

"It can't be too far now," said Sergeant Roughead who had a torch on the map and his nose down over it.

"All right. We'll leave the car here," said Petrella. "See if you can turn it without getting bogged, Andy. You come with me, Sergeant."

A hundred yards, and the house loomed ahead of them. At first they thought it was deserted, but as they came nearer they could see that there was a chink of light in one of the downstairs windows. Petrella touched Sergeant Roughead on the arm and went forward alone. His feet grated on a gravel path and he stood very still. But the window ahead was tightly shut and now he could hear, through it, the sound of music.

He crept forward again, treading through a flowerbed, and peered through the gap in the curtains at a scene of innocent domesticity. Doctor Lovibond was sitting in one wicker chair in front of the fire, smoking a cheroot and reading a newspaper. His wife, in the other chair, was sewing. The portable wireless set on the table stopped giving out music and a voice made an announcement. The doctor lumbered to his feet and left the room. Petrella heard a door opening on the far side of the house. He wondered exactly what he was going to say if the doctor came round with a torch and found him kneeling in his rose-bed.

After a few minutes the doctor came back again. Whatever he was waiting for, it had been a false alarm. Petrella crept back to Sergeant Roughead. He said, "They wouldn't be sitting about at one o'clock on a winter morning for fun. They're waiting for something all right. We'll get back to the car and wait there. It's got a heater."

Sergeant Roughead said, "G-g-good."

It was nearly four o'clock when they heard it. The moan of a foghorn and the thump-thump of a diesel engine. A small, single-screw boat, Petrella guessed, coming up slowly against the stream. They climbed out of the car. During the time they had been sitting there a light wind had got up and was starting to roll away the fog.

When Petrella reached the window he saw that Mrs Lovibond was alone. She had her back to him and was doing something with a bottle and glasses at the sideboard. The beat of the engine was quickening again as the boat picked up speed. The woman half turned her head to listen, and Petrella saw her face for the first time. Piled grey hair, a beak of a nose, a deep cleft down each side of an unsmiling mouth, a strong firm chin. It was a face that had built empires. A face that had ruled a thousand Indian servants. The face of a pukka mem-sahib. The back door banged and Dr Lovibond came in, carrying a heavy portmanteau in one hand, his other hand on the arm of a tall, thin Indian, enveloped in a greatcoat, the astrakhan collar turned up to his ears, a woollen cap pulled down over his head.

The doctor prodded the fire into a blaze, whilst his wife helped the newcomer to take off coat and cap and sat him down in one of the chairs in front of the fire. Doctor Lovibond produced some dry socks and a pair of slippers which the man put on. Mrs Lovibond had gone across to the sideboard, where three glasses stood ready. She selected one of them carefully, brought it back, and handed it to their guest. The smile which she switched on as she did so raised her lips away from her teeth.

Petrella put one shoulder to the flimsy casement, which broke inwards with a splintering of wood and glass. As he got one knee on to the sill to climb through, he said, "I don't think I should drink that."

The first to move was the woman. She put down the glass on the table, took a quick step back to the sideboard, snatched up one of the bottles standing there, and aimed a blow at Petrella's head. Petrella ducked. The bottle missed his head, flew out of her hand and hit the wall just beside Sergeant Roughead who was climbing through the window. Petrella got his arms round the woman, who was screaming at the top of her voice. They rolled on to the floor together. The two men had hardly moved. The newcomer seemed paralysed with shock. The doctor looked, without any expression on his face at all, at his wife, rolling on the floor, at Sergeant Roughead, at the police driver who was climbing through the shattered window. Then, before they guessed what he was going to do, he picked up the glass on the table and swallowed the contents. As his body jack-knifed forwards on to the floor, the woman started howling.

"Strychnine," said the police doctor. "I suppose the whisky would have disguised the taste long enough for the visitor to have got some of it down. One mouthful would have finished him. Your face could do with a bit of patching."

It was nine o'clock and the sun was shining over a landscape which had turned white with frost. Petrella said, "It was her nails."

They had taken away Nora Lovibond, strapped to a stretcher. Through the gap in the window Petrella saw the Chief Constable and went out to have a word with him.

He said, "We've found the place. It's just behind the barn. They're opening it up now."

The digging was being done by a constable and Sergeant Roughhead. They were uncovering a pit. A dapper figure, in a neat fawn coat, watching the operation was Dr Summerson, the Home Office Pathologist. He said, "Careful now. It would be better to take the last earth away with your hands." He looked doubtfully at Milo whose face was grey. "That is, if you don't mind. Perhaps I'd better get my coat off and give you a hand."

"That's all right," said Milo. He got down into the pit and started to scrape away the last of the earth.

There were six bodies, each wrapped in a coat, seeming to huddle together in their earthen bed as if to make room for more.

"Peace with Honour," said Milo. He climbed out of the pit, turned away and was sick.

THE DEATH OF MR X

Herbert Harris

READERS OF THE *Burrowfield Gazette*, serving a largely agricultural community in Southern England, found on their front pages one morning a photograph of a clean-shaven, fair-haired, carefully groomed man, and, above the photograph, a heading that asked them: "DO YOU KNOW THIS MAN?"

One week later the picture was published for a second time, and this time beneath the words: "STILL UNIDENTIFIED—THE MYSTERIOUS MR X."

Some of the more squeamish of the *Burrowfield Gazette* readers would have been entitled to shudder slightly if they had been told (and, of course, they were not) that the picture had been taken by a police photographer *after* the man's death.

The more perceptive might have remarked upon the strange expressionless stiffness of the face, the hint of post-mortem rictus, the lifelessness of the staring eyes, and probably thought that the mysterious Mr X, whoever he might be, must have been a pretty cold-looking fish.

That bastion of the Burrowfield Criminal Investigation Department, Detective Inspector Anderson, kept the photograph permanently on his desk. So, in fact, did his principal assistant, Detective Sergeant Phelps.

Anderson looked upon it as a challenge. He thoroughly disliked mysteries that did not appear to make sense and which had to be left lying about unsolved. It offended his strong sense of tidiness. Besides, Anderson was comparatively new to Burrowfield, and he was anxious to prove his ability beyond all shadow of doubt.

"I just can't make any confounded sense out of it, and that's a fact!" he declared irritably, storming into the office and flinging his hat like a quoit at the hat-stand. He missed it, and Sergeant Phelps always regarded this as a bad sign. "Flummoxed, that's what, flummoxed," he added, collapsing into his swivel chair.

The young detective sergeant, who had been idly doodling with a pencil when his superior burst in so suddenly, quickly thrust the offending doodle out of sight and dragged his mind reluctantly away from dream-fantasies involving Woman Detective Constable Dorothy Whatmough.

"Sir . . . ?"—Phelps's brow creased enquiringly.

"That fellow they found lying just behind the hedge in Braddock's bottom field!" the Inspector elaborated crossly.

"Ah, that one, sir."

"You must admit it's damned funny, Phelps. Not *one* perishing individual in this district recognizes him. Nobody can even guess where the heck he came from—or, for that matter, what the heck he did with himself while he was here." He shook his head. "They even took his fingerprints, as you know, but there's nothing in Records to show who the blighter was."

"Yes, it *is* pretty odd, sir," Phelps agreed. "And it doesn't appear that the chap was a tramp or a gipsy or anything like that."

"He was anything but that! Much too decently clothed, appearance too well looked after. *And* a quite well-fed and healthy looking specimen into the bargain."

"Not a sign of foul play either, sir."

"Well, there were certainly no injuries." Inspector Anderson was rapt in thought for a few moments. "Mark you, the doctor did think that the cyanosis was a bit strange. . . ."

"The what, sir?"

"Cyanosis, Phelps. That's a slight blue discoloration of the skin, you know. Of course, ordinary heart failure can often cause it. But so—on the other hand—can suffocation."

"You mean, sir, something like a pillow held over the victim's face?"

"That's right. Mind you, there isn't anything to go on, nothing at all. There very seldom is in a case like this. But who can ever really say for certain that a person found dead in a field died from natural causes?"

"That's true enough, sir. I wonder why nobody has reported him missing, though?"

The Inspector regarded his junior keenly. "That's exactly what I keep on wondering myself. I mean, when a chap like that—reasonably well clothed, well groomed, well fed—is found dead, and not a soul claims him, the chances are that somebody wanted him out of the way. You agree, Phelps?"

"Certainly, sir. But I suppose there is just the odd chance that he *could* have been a vagrant?"

"If he *was*," Anderson suggested, "then I think it unlikely that the chap would have walked right past the Hospice of Saint Theresa."

"That charity place where they dish out the grub to passing tramps?"

"The very place, Phelps. It's my opinion the fellow would have called in for his bread-and-cheese and cider, or whatever it is they dish out there. They say that most vagrants know the place well and make a bee-line for it."

The Inspector sat rubbing his chin thoughtfully. Then he said, "I think I'll go up there and have another little chat with the Marchants."

Anderson had been exactly right in his description of the Hospice's charitable fare.

The Hospice of Saint Theresa, a former Cistercian priory which was now preserved and maintained under some ancient-buildings trust, bore an historic notice on its gate promising hospitality to all weary and footsore travellers. By a firmly established tradition of charity, centuries old, the nomad of the highways and byways was provided with free shelter, bread-and-cheese and cider.

At the time of the "Mr X" case, the caretaker-tenants of the old Hospice were a couple called James and Sheila Marchant. They were rather younger than Anderson had expected rural caretaker-tenants to be.

When Anderson returned to pay them a further visit, James Marchant was busy sawing up some logs in the orchard lying to one side of the priory. He was a sturdily-built dark-haired man with a fairly heavy moustache and beard.

He ceased his sawing at once and greeted the Inspector with a disarmingly cordial smile. "Oh, so it's you again, Inspector! I told Sheila I thought you'd be back. I suppose there's something else you wanted to ask us?"

Anderson politely returned his smile. "I daresay we're being a darned nuisance, but you may remember that when I was up here before, there was another call on my services and I had to dash away in a bit of a hurry . . . ?"

The Inspector lit up a cigarette and handed his case to Marchant, but the bearded man shook his head vigorously.

"Don't touch 'em, Inspector. Don't smoke at all, I'm pleased to say."

"Wise man," Anderson told him, and realized that the fellow was giving him a twinge of conscience. He smoked uncomfortably, acutely conscious of the steady unwavering gaze of the bearded man, the somewhat artificial smile enamelled to the mouth under the bush of dark hair.

Now, what was it he had asked the chap on that previous flying visit . . . ? Oh, yes, he remembered now. . . .

Shortly before the body of Mr X had been discovered, Mr and Mrs Marchant had actually been seen in a car very near the spot. It was Police Constable Chubb who had seen them, in fact. The Constable had informed the Inspector, and so Anderson had asked them if they had seen anyone—a suspicious character, a stranger—lurking near Braddock's bottom field that night.

The Marchants' answer had been in the negative. They had not seen a single soul.

"What else was it you were wanting to know, then, Inspector?" James Marchant was asking helpfully.

Anderson collected his thoughts. "Well," he said, "you and your wife will no doubt have seen the picture of the dead man in the *Gazette*. I'm wondering if either of you can recall his visiting the Hospice?"

Marchant shook his head emphatically. "I'm sorry, Inspector, can't help you there. We've both been racking our brains, but we're pretty certain he was never here."

"How can a man be a little island all on his own?" Anderson asked rhetorically. "Good God, the chap must have come from *somewhere* . . . *somebody* has got to know him!"

Marchant shrugged. "Well, we don't get the vagrants here like we used to. Something to do with the affluent society maybe. Only once in a blue moon will one turn up to claim his charitable bed and board. We would certainly have remembered him, Inspector, if he'd been here."

"Yes," Anderson said with a rueful sigh, "I daresay you would. I'm beginning to wonder, though, if the chap could make himself invisible . . .?"

"You remember my wife, I daresay?" Marchant broke in gently, and waved his hand.

The C.I.D. man turned. A young woman, probably in her late twenties or early thirties, was approaching them. He remembered her all right, although on the previous visit there had not been much opportunity to study her closely.

She had a shapely body, full breasted and full hipped, and a mass of dark tangled hair with enough natural curl to make its unbrushed condition unimportant. Her face was the soft, heavy type that would later become gross, but now, in its prime, had a sulky, provocative sensuality.

"Oh, hello, Inspector," she greeted him. "Do you find our Hospice so attractive that you can't keep away?" Her voice seemed to go well with her heavy body, throatily sensual and achieving something like a tangible caress.

The Inspector, who much preferred practical no-nonsense girls, didn't take to her very much.

Sheila Marchant was not able to tell him any more than her husband had been able to, and, presently, after pausing to look at their collection of miniature cacti in a glazed lean-to, Anderson left and returned to his headquarters in Burrowfield.

It was a stroke of fortune that he did this, instead of going straight home as he had earlier planned, because he happened to meet Woman Detective Constable Dorothy Whatmough. The latter wished to consult him about another case on which they were working, and he invited her into his office.

The policewoman's most ardent admirer, Sergeant Phelps, was still at his desk and he got up with a flamboyant display of chivalry as she came in with the Inspector.

The girl stood by Phelps's side while the Inspector riffled through some papers that had been left on his desk. Her eyes, which contrived to be both beautiful and busy, strayed to the wire basket on the desk of the young detective sergeant. In the wire basket was a copy of the *Burrowfield Gazette*.

"Hello," said Detective Constable Whatmough in a musical voice that brought up goose-pimples on the sergeant, "and what has James Marchant been up to, then?"

"Marchant?" repeated Phelps.

The Inspector glanced up, drawing his brows together. "Marchant?" he said.

"That chap who lives at the old Hospice," went on Dorothy Whatmough. "Warden or something. Isn't this him?"

She stared, frowning, at the newspaper. Then suddenly she broke into a laugh. "Oh, I see!"

Anderson came forward briskly. "Show me that!" He took the newspaper from the policewoman and stared at it. He glared sternly at Detective Sergeant Phelps for a few seconds and turned his attention once again to the *Burrowfield Gazette*.

Anderson stood staring at it thoughtfully for a while, tugging at the lobe of his ear. A curious thought process was churning and whirring in his active mind.

Presently he tossed the newspaper back into Phelps's wire basket with a cryptic grunt, and said to Policewoman Whatmough, "Now, my dear, you wanted to ask me something about that shopbreaking case . . ."

But very much later, sitting quite alone and sipping a glass of best bitter ale in the almost deserted snug-bar of the "Bull and Bear" public-house, Inspector Anderson was able to do some really profound thinking.

"You always need to think a thing through," he had once said paternally to Sergeant Phelps. "Think above, and below, and all the way round."

Being a man who always practised what he preached, the Inspector did just that, and on the following day he paid yet another visit to the ancient Hospice of Saint Theresa. This time, it was purely on the pretext of looking for his petrol-lighter.

When Anderson arrived, James Marchant was not there, but his wife Sheila was.

"Forgive me for butting in again," he said ingratiatingly, "but I've mislaid my petrol-lighter. You remember when I was in that glazed lean-to affair of yours, admiring your cacti? Well, I have a feeling I might have left it in there. . . ."

"Well, let's go back there and look," she invited him obligingly.

Of course, the petrol-lighter was not there, as he had known all along it wouldn't be, since it was reposing safely in his pocket. But when he finally left Sheila Marchant, thanking her politely (though she could never have guessed how thankful he was), the Inspector had something else in his pocket which had not been there on his arrival at the Hospice.

"I suppose you might call it a slight case of larceny," he said with a smile to Sergeant Phelps. "Naturally I shall return the stolen article in due course, and say that I somehow picked it up by accident. I'm pretty certain it will never be missed in the interim, Phelps."

"Would you like me to get the dabs taken off it, sir?"

"Yes, do that as quickly as you can, will you? And after you've got them, ask Ransford to come and see me."

"Yes, sir."

"H'm," Anderson mumbled to himself, "I wonder . . . I wonder . . ."

Ever since that day, they have spoken of the Marchant Case at the Burrowfield police headquarters as a local (if not a national) classic, a case that might never have been cracked but for a fortuitous accident, followed by a particularly shrewd hunch on the part of Inspector Anderson.

The Chief Constable himself, Sir Milroy Durnford K.B.E., made a special trip to headquarters when the news broke, to hear from Anderson first hand about the charge of murder which had been laid against Sheila Marchant and her lover.

"Yes, Sir Milroy, her lover," Anderson explained. "The man who was masquerading as her husband James Marchant is in reality a fellow called Patrick Blair. An amazing affair, sir. I very nearly dismissed the whole thing as too fanciful when I first played around with the idea.

"You see, sir, this man Blair *was* in fact a down-and-out who called at the old Hospice some while back. At the time he called there for his hand-out, the real James Marchant was temporarily up in London on business.

"Sheila Marchant carried on the usual tradition. She gave this tramp the customary food and shelter—and then, subsequently, she gave him rather more than the usual hospitality, sir. Blair stayed there four nights."

"I can well imagine what took place," the Chief Constable said with a snort. "Not, of course, that I am intimately acquainted with the lady in question."

"Naturally, Sir Milroy, naturally! Few people have ever got to know the Marchants really well. They kept themselves very much to themselves at all times. But Sheila Marchant, I need hardly point out, is a woman with physical appetites somewhat above the average. Her husband, James Marchant, was not at all satisfactory as a lover, being slightly effeminate, I understand, but the newcomer, Patrick Blair, was everything a virile lover ought to be."

"Ah . . . and therefore James had to be got rid of?" the Chief Constable prompted.

"Precisely, Sir Milroy. And the scheme was an exceedingly clever one. Marchant and Blair were of similar build and colouring, but there was one distinct difference. Marchant had thick dark hair and a fairly heavy moustache and beard—the locals, I understand, sometimes referred to him as Moses.

"To take the place of Marchant after he had been suitably disposed of, Blair had to grow his hair longer and cultivate a moustache and beard. He went away in order to do this, of course, and when everything was ready, he came back to the Hospice one night and James Marchant was got rid of by suffocation. A pillow or cushion was held over his face while he slept—hence that cyanosis, or the blue discoloration of the skin."

"Good God," murmured Sir Milroy.

"And then, sir, followed a rather grisly ceremony. The dead Marchant's moustache and beard were shaved off, leaving him quite clean shaven. His hair was dyed a lighter colour and cut short.

"And now, you see, Marchant became a total stranger, quite unknown to anybody. What a devilish plot this was, sir! There was nobody to be reported missing! James Marchant, to all intents and purposes, still existed—and so did Blair, who was now masquerading as Marchant, although he was a drop-out and lone wolf in any case.

"As soon as they had finished turning James Marchant into the non-existent Mr X, they rushed his body down to Braddock's farm, about a mile away, and dumped him behind a hedge in the bottom field.

"Actually, Sheila Marchant and her new 'husband' were seen near the spot in question by Constable Chubb, who reported it to me, because he thought that they might have noticed somebody or something unusual. They said they hadn't—naturally. I did rather wonder what they had been doing down by Braddock's place, which was a bit off the beaten track, but the couple were considered beyond reproach . . . the real Mr and Mrs Marchant, that is.

"It wasn't until young Sergeant Phelps started doodling, sir, that I began to do some really serious thinking."

"Doodling?" demanded the Chief Constable.

Inspector Anderson smiled.

"That's how he wastes his time on occasions, but not *this* time, Sir

Milroy. You remember the photograph of Mr X they put on the front page of the *Burrowfield Gazette*? Phelps drew a moustache and beard on it!

"Policewoman Whatmough saw it, sir, and jumped to the conclusion that the picture was of James Marchant. That put ideas into my head. I wondered if there was something up at the Hospice which had belonged to James Marchant, if we assumed that Marchant was dead . . . ?

"Well, there *was*, sir—a pipe. It was lying on the bench in a lean-to, among a collection of cacti. I knew that it couldn't belong to Sheila's lover, because the chap told me that he never smoked at all.

"I pinched that pipe, sir—well, let's say I borrowed it for a while—just to take the dabs off it, the fingerprints, I mean. We had already taken the prints off the body found in the field, to see if they matched any in our Records. They didn't, of course. But they *did* match prints we found on that pipe!"

"Excellent, Inspector. After that, you were laughing, as they say."

"Yes, Sir Milroy. But Sheila and her phoney husband were not."

"They tell me," the Chief Constable said, "that this Sheila Marchant is quite a 'dishy piece', to use a modern phrase."

Inspector Anderson shrugged.

"If you like them that way, sir," he answered, and added hastily, "not that you do personally, sir, of course!"

GONE....

Peter Godfrey

He stood at the far end of the long salon, his back to the enormous canvas I call "Eruption" and therefore facing me. He couldn't have seen me, though—I was standing partly behind drapes and the lighting my end was dim. He was surrounded by young people—students, I suppose—and he said: "The key to Tom Burt's technique is that he hears with his eyes."

He was so right. There I stood, 25 metres distant, stone deaf since birth, but my keen sight picked up every flutter of his lips and facial muscles. If I had had the auditory gift, I would probably never have heard a word; through my eyes what he said was a well-articulated shout. I was amused. I focused to hear more.

"As I told you before," he said, "Burt's work has attained a degree of visual impact unprecedented in art. His abstracts have an intense emotional force. His shapes are sharp and yet inexplicably plastic. His colours, in tantalising glints and flashes, show something beyond normal human perception. Just as some blind men achieve superhuman subtlety of hearing or touch, so I believe Burt's deafness has stimulated his sight. And that is where his genius lies. He converts sound into colour."

Again right, I thought, and felt the bitter frustration rising in me. Why only so far and no further?

His words echoed my thoughts. "But Burt has now reached his peak. For the last three years there has been no new development, no shattering outburst of perception. Each new work he produces is still magnificent because his technique is incomparable, but he repeats old images."

Someone must have asked a question. He paused, head fractionally cocked, listening. Then: "I'll give you a specific case. This." He pointed to an area of the canvas behind him. "It's quite a distinctive shape. It could be a flat-topped mountain, a rock, a piece of a jigsaw puzzle—anything. It has no significance to us, but to Burt it obviously symbolises something emotionally fundamental. It appears in every single painting he has ever done. I'll show you."

He moved with his group into silence.

Shape? I knew of no shape. Except for the last few years, all my paintings had been totally original. Even my technique had evolved, stabilizing something new with each canvas.

Suddenly, I felt afraid.

As soon as I could, I examined the portion of "Eruption" he had indicated. There it was, the shape—and there it was, too, on all the other canvases. Different angles, different positions, but always there.

I knew it. I recognized it.

His second guess had been right. A flat rock at the top of a dune on an undulating beach.

A rock on which a bright, happy girl had once stood, beckoned teasingly, stepped down and disappeared.

Completely. Forever.

My night had been sleepless, old memories and doubts emotionally shattering, my dawn resolve to do something about it sharp and compelling. Yet now, after a full hour on a psychiatrist's couch, I felt somehow empty and doubtful.

Dr Allen's words were neutral, neither believing nor disbelieving, and very matter-of-fact. He said: "Let's summarize your fears. They are all questions you want answered. What happened to the girl? What was her name and where did she come from? Was there really a girl, or is she some distorted figment of your own imagination? If so, are you mad or going mad? And—apparently the most important of all—in what way is her disappearance tied in with your present artistic infertility?"

He added: "At this stage I admit I don't really see the significance of your last question."

"I'll try to explain," I said. "First, you must remember I was only twelve at the time. I was stone deaf, and everyone—myself included—thought I was a mute. I could write and understand a few simple words only—those that could be taught by showing me characters and pictures. I could handspeak, but the language of the hands of necessity deals only with broad generalities.

"When she disappeared and I was unable to find her, it was shattering. I *had* to tell someone, but nobody could understand what I meant. The hopelessness was unbearable, crystallizing after many weeks into an uncontrollable impulse to communicate.

"I began to draw . . . My first sketch was of a rock with a girl on it; next to it I drew the rock, but no girl. Nobody translated my message. I tried again. This time I drew three rocks. The girl stood clearly on the first, was dim on the second and missing from the third. My head was patted approvingly for the quality of my drawing, and other pictures placed before me for copying.

"The continuing frustration made me cunning. Deliberately I pushed all memories of that smiling girl to the back of my mind. I told myself that first I must learn to communicate, then I could tell her story. I drew and drew, striving always for some method to convey subtleties. It was still not enough. I began to be conscious how normal people moved their lips and throat muscles. I imitated them. One day, quite suddenly, I learned the trick of making sounds.

"This was a real sensation. The cabbage had evolved into someone who not only could draw, but also could be taught to talk. It was exciting for me, too. I was sent to a special school. I drew, I painted and mouthed real words that others could hear. I learned to read lips. It was slow and hard work, and in all this activity I somehow forgot the motivating reason. The girl."

"Until last night," said Dr Allen.

"Yes. And with this realisation came another thought. I have been dissatisfied with my work for some time. I seem to have lost an element of basic creativity. And, somehow, I feel that that loss is tied in with the mystery of the girl. If I could only find her, speak to her . . . But then, as you suggest, she may be only an illusion . . ."

Dr Allen said, briskly: "Perhaps we can make sure." He hesitated. "Would you be willing to undergo hypnosis?"

"Anything, if it will help."

"Right. Now I am going to induce in you a state of complete relaxation. It will be as though you are pleasantly dozing, but your eyes will remain open. You will at all times be able to read my lips. You will tell me every detail you can remember of that morning you met the girl. When I bring you out of your trance, you will remember every word you said. Are you ready?"

"Yes," I said.

It is my twelfth birthday or, rather, the twelfth anniversary of the day I was brought to the Home. I think I am probably a year or even more older than that, but this is the day Lady has chosen as my birthday, and it is a special time. I am being given a treat. Today I sit in the truck, loaded with the wicker chairs and tables the older ones make, and Tall Man is taking me on his rounds.

We do not communicate. Tall Man cannot handspeak and drive, but I am happy. The sun is shining, the fresh wind blowing against my face, and the ground running backwards away from us faster than a rabbit. We go on for half the morning, then Tall Man stops, and we both get off the truck. We sit at the roadside and drink a soda. To one side there is a steep footpath leading down to a stretch of sand which in turn leads to the sea. The road we had taken runs alongside the sea most of the way, but all there had been before was rocks. The sand is something new. I keep looking at it.

Tall Man notices my fascination, and smiles. He gives me a packet of sandwiches and another can of soda. His handspeak is not good, but I understand. He points to the sand, makes motions that I should go there, perhaps paddle in the water, explore. He points to the position of the sun, indicates where it will reach when I must return to the road and wait for him.

The road has been lonely, and the sand is even lonelier. Not a human being in sight, and this is good. Some humans are nice but others look at me in a strange way. Being by myself with air and sand and playful water is great happiness. I wave goodbye and scamper down.

Almost immediately, sand gets in my shoes. This is uncomfortable. I take them off. There is nobody here to show me what to do. On impulse I shed my clothes, all except my underpants. I run down to the sea, letting the sand curl between my toes, then paddle them clean at the edge of the water. At first I am afraid of the waves, but they are small and do me no harm. Soon I stalk them as they retreat and then flee madly as they turn and chase me.

My legs grow tired, my feet are wet and cold, but the breeze is fresh and lazy, and the sun lays a warm arm lightly across my shoulders. I amble slowly along the dry sand to where I have left my clothes, lie face down with my head on my arms, and doze.

A lessening of warmth—something—rouses me. I open my eyes and see a shadow on the sand. In fright, I swing round, sit up.

It is a girl with golden-brown hair and freckles on her nose. She is dressed in jeans and T-shirt. She is not shy. Her lips move, like those of Lady and Tall Man when they communicate. Involuntarily I make the gesture I have been taught, touching both my ears and then my lips.

I expect her to turn away. Instead she smiles and shows me she can handspeak. In a moment our wrists and fingers are fluttering like birds.

I ask her: Do you live near here? Do you come here often? Would you like some sandwiches? Share my soda? Who taught you to handspeak?

She answers: No, I live a long way that way (indicating a direction). This is my first time on this beach. Thank you. I am hungry and thirsty. I live with my mother who is also a mute, like you. We handspeak all the time. My father taught me when I was very young. He is dead now.

I ask: Where is your mother now? And she indicates her mother is at home.

How did you get here? When do you have to leave? Do you know how to get home?

And now the handspeak gets very complicated. I gather she was given the day off to visit a friend, but she wasn't really going to the friend, she was going to something ... something big and round and glorious, filled with strange sights. A neighbour had taken her to the town in a car, but when she got there, the big round thing was already packed up and moving on. She had thumbed a lift to near this spot, and then decided to rest a while on the beach. Later she would thumb a lift home.

We munch sandwiches and sip soda, and now she asks the questions. Who am I? Where do I live? How did I get to the beach? Do I know many girls?

I answer, and am sad because we live in opposite directions. I tell her about Tall Man and the treat, because it is my birthday. She smiles pleasure, tosses her curls with an almost defiant little gesture, leans forward, puts both arms around me and kisses me on the lips.

It is a new kind of kiss. It starts as a soft flutter, but then I feel a shiver stirring up to my mouth, to hers too, our lips squirm into each other, my arms come up round her.

Only a few seconds, maybe, but it seems a long time. I feel a strange urge to hold her forever and, mingling with this, is the sensation of small breasts pressed firmly against my bare chest.

She gently pushes herself away from me, looking at me with a strange half-smile. And in that instant I am suddenly conscious of shame that my clothes are lying next to me, that I am almost nude.

With a quick movement, she flicks my arm gently and turns and runs across the sand, looking at me over her shoulder. Every movement of her body calls catch me if you can.

I want to chase her, but my strange new emotions make me hesitate. Shall I first cover my nakedness? I compromise. I put on my shirt.

Now she is standing on a flat rock on top of a dune, watching me. As soon as she sees I am looking at her, she smiles happily, beckoning me with her entire arm to come. As I start to move, she gives a final gesture of encouragement and leaps off the far side of the rock out of sight.

I want to run, but I will feel foolish if I do. I walk slowly to the dune, climb it and stand on the rock. There is a short drop where the girl has jumped, and the marks of her feet where she has landed, and taken one running stride along the sand gently sloping to the sea.

After that, nothing. No girl. No other trace of her. And even as I watch, a random roller from the incoming tide washes away the last remaining footprint.

I weep.

"One thing is certain," said Dr Allen when I had composed myself. "You are not going mad. The incident was not a delusion or a symbolic memory—it actually did happen."

"But how? Where could she have got to? I looked everywhere."

"True. But you were in a state of shock. Your adolescent emotions had been prematurely stirred. Despite the limited extent of your apperception of your environment at the time, your admitted timidity, you experienced powerful adult urges centred on the girl. First love."

I said: "Yes."

"And, in a sense, you still feel that love, but coupled now with guilt and frustration. All the more because that single contact motivated you so fiercely in the pursuit of your talents. And, yes, I think you are right. Your present artistic sterility is due to the mystery that has dominated your life."

"Doctor, what should I do?"

"Solve the mystery. Go back to the scenes of your youth. Find the girl. She left you enough clues to follow. Talk to her—the explanation may be simple. And if you can't find her go back to the beach. Look around it again, as a mature adult. Something may leap into your mind you have never thought of before. But, in all events *do something*. Frustration can only happen when you allow action to be inhibited."

I felt a new excitement. "You're right. I'll leave first thing in the morning."

He said: "And the best of luck to you, Sherlock Holmes."

It had been 22 years since I had last seen Flensburg, where the Home had been. It was a village no longer, but a busy little town. I recognised nothing. At the municipal offices, the young woman who helped me search the records was very helpful.

She said: "The institution known as Silent Rest sold its house and land to a property development corporation 15 years ago, and removed itself to a new locality somewhere in the west of the country. The manager of the housing estate built on the site may be able to tell you exactly where. Mr Simmins has been there since the very beginning of the development. I'll show you how to get there."

Simmins remembered only that all details of the transaction had been dealt with by a lawyer in the capital city. Then: "But maybe old Paddy can help you. He used to work for them once. He has a cottage on the far end of the estate."

He was working on a patch of garden, but came over to meet me as my car pulled up. The years had broadened and lengthened me; they had turned his sandy hair silver, shrivelled him and pleated the flesh on his face. Tall Man actually looked up at me.

"Don't you remember me, Paddy?" I asked.

His eyes were uncertain.

"I'm Tom Burt."

"Tom! Yes, you're Tom. But you've grown, lad. And speaking! Did they fix your ears?"

"No, Paddy, but I can lip-read. My eyes hear you better than ears ever could."

Inside, over a mug of coffee, I asked him whether he remembered my twelfth birthday.

"My memory ain't what it used to be, Tom. No—wait a moment. Wasn't that the day I took you with me on my rounds?"

"Tell me about it, Paddy."

"Nothing much to tell. Dropped you off at a little beach about 30 miles up the coast road, with some food and drink. Thought you'd enjoy that more than a dusty journey to inland towns, seeing people who'd take you for a freak. Thought I'd be back in about three hours, but I was delayed some. Ripe old state you were in when I picked you up. Crying and waving your hands, trying to tell me something I couldn't make head nor tail of. Remember? What was the matter? Did you think I'd forgotten you? That you were lost?"

"Not me, Paddy," I said. "Someone else."

"When I finally managed to get you in the truck, I took you on my last call—a furniture shop in Bliss—and you started up all over again, waving your arms and jumping up and down. There was a young lad there—son of the proprietor—and you scared the hell out of him. Didn't sell a stick of furniture to the father—then or ever again."

I had vague impressions of the incident as part of the wave of black hopelessness in my mind at the time, but the wealth of detail fascinated me. "Do you remember the name of the man or the shop, Paddy?" I asked.

A blank look came over his face. "No, Tom. But my memory's like that, these days. Everything crystal clear, except the name. And he had been a regular customer before that," he added.

I set off along the coast early in the morning. Because Paddy may have been in error about the distance, I watched carefully all the way. I passed the 30 mile mark, then 35 and 40. I had seen no familiar landmark, and my frustration was growing. It was too far; perhaps the road had altered? No. I had recognised some of the earlier scenery—the rocks and the sea. Could some obstacle at the roadside have prevented me sighting the only little beach on the route?

And at this moment in my thoughts I came on a small town, and I remembered in a vivid flash the gesture of direction the girl had given to indicate the position of her home. This way. And there were other clues to follow.

I found a Social Services office. "Somewhere in this vicinity 23 years or more ago," I told the man in charge, "there lived a woman, a deaf mute, a widow with a young daughter. I don't know her name, but I am anxious to trace her or her daughter. Can you give me any ideas how I should go about it?"

He shook his grizzled head. "Was she someone who might have applied for help to this department?"

"I don't know. Perhaps . . . Look, I only met the daughter, a child of twelve or so. But her clothes were neat, comparatively new and tidy. I didn't have the impression there were economic difficulties."

"I'm afraid I can't see any way I can help you," he said regretfully. Then: "Wait a moment. There's a private old-aged home a few miles from here, run by nuns. Most of the people they look after suffer some sort of physical disability. If this woman you seek had any sort of private income, it's just possible . . . I'll get the Mother Superior for you on the phone."

"You'll have to speak for me. I'm afraid I'm completely deaf."

"I hadn't realised. Look, I'll phone and arrange an appointment for you. The place is easy to find—I'll show you the way."

An hour later I sat in an easy chair, putting my request to the smooth-faced old lady in the white wimple. She said: "Possibly I can help. But first I want to know why you want to see her."

A flicker of hope pushed aside all inhibitions. I told her my story, simply and from the heart.

She said: "I have seen your work, God has given you great talent. I believe He must have guided you here. Perhaps there is another soul you can put at peace."

She had been talking abstractedly, now suddenly she addressed me directly. "Mr Burt, it is possible the woman you seek is here. Her name is Mrs Grohl. She is a mute, a widow, and once had a daughter. She came here 22 years ago. She is old and frail, so please be gentle. I will send for her now. If you like, the Sister who brings her will stay and help you communicate."

"Mother," I said, "all my life I have been speaking to mutes." With my hands I added: "Thank you, thank you, thank you."

A Sister wheeled the old lady in, and left us together. I greeted her with a sign of friendship. There was something about the positioning of the eyes, the shape of the nose that made my heart beat faster. Still, I had to make absolutely sure. My hands said: "Do you recognise this girl?"

I pulled my chair next to her, put my pocket sketch pad on my knee, and rapidly sketched a young smiling girl beckoning from a flat-topped rock.

Mrs Grohl obviously preferred writing to handspeak. She took the pencil from me. At the foot of the sketch she wrote "Jane." Her eyes were full of tears. Then: "Have you news of her?"

The joy that had leapt to my heart suddenly turned cold. "I saw her only once, 23 years ago. That is how she looked, how I remember her."

She wrote: "That is how I remember her, too. She was dressed exactly like that, the day she ran away."

I pointed to the last two words, and raised my eyebrows in query. She flipped over a page of the pad. "I'm not blaming her. It wasn't much of a life for a normal happy child, looking after a mother who couldn't speak or hear. That's why I let her go to visit her friend Maude Emburg in Fless for a day. Just that one day—September 8th, 1957."

My birthday.

The pencil was moving on. "She never came back, never tried to contact me. Can you blame me if I'm a little bitter?"

My hands said urgently: "How do you know she ran away?"

"Maude told me."

As I rose to leave, she wrote: "May I keep this drawing?"

Maude Emburg still lived in Fless, but now she was Maude Hocking, plumply matronly with a schoolmaster husband and two extremely active children. From the expression on her face they were very noisy, too.

She told me about Jane. "We were close friends, seldom seeing each other, but often writing. Despite having to stay so close to her mother, when we did get together she was always full of fun and imagination. I think she had a great urge to get away from her problems, see the world, have adventure.

"My father dropped me for an afternoon at her house in the last week of August, 1957. I told her about the circus that had come to Fless, and all the wonderful things I had seen there. She was fascinated."

I thought of Jane on the beach and the great big round thing she had been trying to describe in inadequate handspeak. A circus. Of course.

Maude went on: "She told me she was going to see the circus, too. She would tell her mother she was visiting me, but would go to the big top instead. She had some money saved. She asked if I would back up her story. I agreed. She got her mother's permission there and then. I'll never forget her words afterwards. She said: 'If I like it as much as you, perhaps I'll never come back.' "

Maude paused. I asked: "And then? Didn't the police investigate?"

"Of course, but they found nothing. It would be easy for people like that to conceal a twelve-year-old girl."

I smiled. "But it didn't happen. When she got there, the circus had packed up and she never saw it."

"How can you know that?"

"She told me herself."

The incredulity in her gaze made me hesitate, but only for a second. After all, she was Jane's friend. I poured out the story to her, the whole sweet, bitter, shattering experience. When I had finished she looked straight at me with hard brown eyes, and said: "I don't believe a word of it."

"It happened," I said. "I swear it happened."

"Don't keep on lying. I knew Jane better than any other living person. Two things are quite incredible. One is the disappearance—even you admit that. The other is your description of what occurred between you. Jane might possibly have spoken to you, but kiss you? Never. She hated boys."

"But why?"

"Every boy she ever knew was basically cruel. They mocked her. About her mother."

I left Fless and drove at random along quiet country roads, trying to sort out chaotic thoughts.

Positive points emerged. The girl who haunted me was no longer just a memory, a sharp dream-figure. She was now a real person. Jane. Jane Grohl. And I was beginning to understand the spirit of fun, the frustrations, the longings and the loyalties that made up her personality.

Even more important, the first kiss that had galvanised my life had been her first kiss, too.

And I knew that what had stirred the impulse in her was that I could never be a mocker, because I was one of the mocked . . .

I felt a black bitterness. What else was left? Where could I go? All clues had petered into nothingness.

Except one. The beach. Now I *had* to find the beach . . .

And as I thought this I came on a small town, read the bright notice at the roadside: "You are now entering Bliss." That was the place Paddy spoke of, his last call of that dreadful day, where I had scared the hell out of his customer's little boy.

I pulled up at a service station, not merely to refuel my car, but to think. Paddy's last call . . . I remembered something now. He had picked me up at the roadside just above the beach, and we had travelled a short way in the same direction we had gone that morning, before turning off the coast road to the town. And I was sure that we had continued on the same road right through the town before rejoining the main road nearer Flensburg.

I went inside and bought a road map of the area. I was right. A turn-off from the coast proceeded in a loop through Bliss before rejoining the littoral highway. *The beach must lie somewhere between the two intersections.*

I had come into town by a different route, but it was easy to orient myself. I turned at an intersection, and drove through the town just as Paddy must have driven so many years ago. At the coast road I turned right, so I would be travelling in the same direction as on my original journey.

At first, nothing. Then I found myself approaching a roadside advertisement proclaiming the social advantages of becoming addicted to a particular brand of cigarette. It momentarily cut off my view of the sea. On impulse, I stopped the car.

I approached one end of the billboard and peered down. Bushes and rocks, but through gaps I caught a glimpse of sand.

At the far side of the hoarding there was a curved cement path. I walked down it slowly and, as I followed its curves, the perspective altered. On the right there were crude timbered change rooms and toilets. Next to them—but closed at the moment—was a garishly painted snack bar. The buildings altered the shape of the beach, but on the left, clearly and unmistakably, there was the dune with the flat rock on top.

I faced it, and immediately the buildings disappeared. All I could see was the same deserted undulating beach I had first known many years ago.

Carefully I manoeuvred on the sand until my view of the rock coincided exactly with my sharp-etched memory. This had to be the very spot where Jane and I had feasted on sandwiches, soda and a kiss.

Time slipped away. Here I was, a man of thirty-five, feeling again the emotions of a lad of twelve. As I slowly walked towards the dune I almost saw her standing there again, beckoning me to follow, leaping into invisibility.

I came to the rock, as I had come before, looked down the short drop, half-expecting to see her footmarks back again on the sand.

No footprints, but halfway to where her second stride would have taken her, quite out of sight except from the summit of the dune, was a closely-meshed barbed wire fence. On it large gouts of words screamed at me with garish discordancy.

I saw two shrieks. One was mine exploding into purple bubbles of shock from a maw of horror. The other was Jane's, as she must have screamed so many years ago, green lightnings of panic, bright amber shafts of desperation, barbs of angry magenta hopelessness.

And the shrieks mingled, hers and mine, twining in fiery spirals of anguish, bubbles and lightning coruscating through every colour of the spectrum and beyond, effervescing into a deep flashing-glinting, still but ever-changing deep lake of peace.

For the second time in my life I stood on the flat rock, with an orgasm of tears in my eyes.

Never again will I paint that rock, I thought. Now I will paint the new things I am able to see, like the sussuration of light that is the sound of waves. I will paint for Jane and her miracle of the opening of my eyes. The world would never be the same again.

Even the words on the notice were no longer garish and discordant, but sad and low-keyed, befitting the threshold of inevitability.

On no account must this fence be crossed, they said. *Danger. Extreme danger. Lethal quicksands.*

TWO FLOORS UP IN CHINATOWN

Ernest Dudley

JOE RAYBURN STOOD at the window over Gerrard Street, though he wasn't seeing the dark heads and yellow faces milling past the acupuncture clinics, the Arts of War and Iron Palm bookshops, and Wu Fat's take-away. He wasn't hearing Chinatown's chat—other faces, other voices chased round his skull.

Like Ricky Jerome's, who'd set up this meeting with Mrs Vincent. She believes hubby, who's loaded, is on the cheat, Ricky had said. If true, she'd take him for a bomb—which, flicking cigarette-ash off his mohair pants, would suit Ricky okay.

Joe Rayburn didn't push it. He wasn't into divorce any more, anyhow. It didn't pay off anything like Home Office Dirty Tricks did, or C.I.D. under-cover cowboys. Not unless it was something special. This was something special, Ricky had said.

The board in the entrance on the corner of Gerrard and Wardour Street lists missing persons' agencies; skip tracings, and personal and property recovery bureaux. Etc. What Mrs Vincent was looking for was Joe Rayburn's office. Second floor, Ricky had told her. The lift was out of order.

She found what she wanted, J. Rayburn Investigations, and went on up.

Rayburn turned as the door opened and this expensive-looking woman came in. He pulled out a rickety chair for her. He noticed she wore nice, slim legs.

She said: "My husband's being unfaithful to me. I want to know who with." Her husband was Hugh Vincent, he was a partner in an estate-agency.

When did she first suspect him? Several months back, she answered. He was being kept late at the office more often. Then he began going away weekends. That sort of crap.

Rayburn dealt himself a cigarette. He offered her the pack, tapping the label. Low tar. She shook her head.

He pulled a note-pad to him.

A half-hour later, she had finished uttering, gave him a cheque, and went. He phoned Ed McNeill. He would have the gear, he told Rayburn, no problem.

Rayburn phoned Doris Adams. She was the wife of an ex-Central
C.I.D. Dick, who'd had both knees taken out by a sawn-off. So she put in
part-time sleuthing for Joe Rayburn.

Over a sandwich and a drink at the Half Moon, he put her in the
picture. She had worked with Ed McNeill before. He was okay.

Back at his office, and Greggson from the Chelsea cop-shop looked in
for a friendly chat. He was operational on the Ice-Pick Murders. Three
girls slain with an ice-pick over the past couple of months. M.o. always
the same. Ice-pick, and the killer thought to be a male, a sex-maniac.

But the question was: Was that what it was intended to look like? Or
was it a syndicate put-off?

Greggson and Rayburn had been useful to each other before. Joe
Rayburn had a room off the King's Road. He knew the Chelsea mob; the
pushers and pimps, hookers and perverts. You name them, he knew those
you could buy, and knew no one you couldn't.

"The buzz on the Ice-Pick is like thin on the ground," Greggson was
saying. Rayburn asked him what did he have on his blotter on Ricky
Jerome? He knew the cop was heavy into phone-taps and bugs, no
matter how hard the top brass slapped his wrist.

The cop started to say something when the phone rang.

"His secretary's just phoned. He has a business-appointment this
evening," Mrs Vincent said. "So he won't be back for din-dins." She
expected the works on her husband, she said. Where he'd gone, who he
was screwing.

Greggson had caught her name.

"Same Mrs Hugh Vincent who lives in Jarman Street?" he asked. He
made it sound casual, but Rayburn saw he had started a sweat at his
hair-line. So what interest had this cop got in her?

He said, "I'm hired to check her husband out."

Greggson eyed him. Then: "Know who the body-warmth is?"

"That's what I'm being paid to know."

After he had gone, Rayburn remembered the cop hadn't given any
answer to the question he had put about Ricky Jerome. He'd started to
utter, hadn't he, then Mrs V's phone-call?

At 5.15, Doris Adams reporting in, from a call-box, corner of Sloane
Street and Cadogan Place. She had picked up the subject at the
Connaught Hotel, where he'd lunched with another man. He often
lunched there, business lunches. She had tailed him back to his office.
Time 4.30, she had picked him up leaving, and tailed him to a first floor
flat, Sloane Court.

The flat was Melissa Lambert's.

Subject had been a regular visitor the past six months. Two, three times a week. Weekends lately, when he had stayed overnight. There were other visitors. Like one who, her informant had said, smelt like a cop. There was another regular. Slim, 30ish; sharp dresser, mohair suits.

Rayburn put a name to him.

"Could be."

Doris had called in Ed McNeill, who had got into the flat next door. The occupants were out, and he'd punched a bug through into Melissa Lambert's bedroom. He had the van parked halfway between Sloane Court and this call-box. As for her, she said, she was calling it a day.

Rayburn said he would be along.

He was thinking about Ricky Jerome. The boy sort of got around.

At the first floor flat, Sloane Court, Melissa Lambert was also thinking about Ricky Jerome. She was keeping her eyes closed tight, while she held Hugh Vincent's head against her marvellous breasts.

Hugh was chuntering on about his wife. She broke off her thoughts about Ricky to put in a word. "Perhaps she'll go and get run over by a bus, darling . . . Or, how's about that Ice-Pick nutter catching up with her—"

She shouldn't have said that. He jerked away, with a stricken expression.

"Okay, darling," she said. "I was only joking—"

She put his head where it had been before, then the phone rang. Christ, she thought, Ricky phoning at this time? Her eyes fixed Vincent. He mustn't hear. She got the phone.

"Sorry, wrong number," she said. She hung up. To Vincent: "Sorry, darl—some idiot. Now, where were we—?"

She was dead worried about Ricky phoning.

He had never done it before at this time. He was supposed to think she was always out, the hairdressers, shopping, or whatever. If he was on to her and Hugh Vincent—Oh, my God . . .

In Ed McNeill's van were Ed, Joe Rayburn, and Greggson.

The cop had come along with Rayburn. He had called back at the office to answer the question, he said, what had he got on his blotter on Ricky Jerome?

Not so much. He'd got no form. He'd earned his bread as a pusher. Solo—but the syndicate was taking over, and solos were getting rubbed out like pencil-writing on paper. Ricky had looked for something safer.

Like rich wives who needed another male shoulder to cry on. Like Mrs Vincent.

Rayburn was giving her a passing thought, now. Like how she would blow her mind when she heard the tape—when he noted the sweat-beads again at Greggson's hair-line. Surely, he reckoned, the cop must have heard this sort of crap before?

He gave a couple of ideas a whirl round his brain, only half-listening to the tape.

The Melissa Lambert story broke next morning.

She was found by the daily help, who'd called the cops, then passed out. Television ran pictures of her. Newscasters broke in on the d.j. shows.

Rayburn's meeting with Mrs Vincent was at midday. He was looking at a news-seller in Jarman Street, when she came in.

"Coffee? No—?"

She was hellish nervous.

"A drink, then—?"

"Only when I can get it."

She got him a scotch, while he took the tape out of his pocket, and played her the bit that featured her husband and Melissa Lambert.

Like he'd expected, she flipped her lid. She paced up and down with jerky steps, her mouth opening and shutting without making a sound.

Then she stopped him halfway through.

She struggled to put some words together. "How much—?" A hand stabbed at the tape. "How much—for it—?"

"But," he said, "I can get you further instalments—"

She cut in: "You've got me all I require. How much—? Then get the hell out of here—"

She didn't argue over the price. She wrote out the cheque, then at the door, she said: "It's the only copy, isn't it?"

"Of course," he lied.

He bought a midday edition in Jarman Street. His meeting with Hugh Vincent was an hour later, at his office.

Joe Rayburn played him a copy of the tape he had played his wife. A few minutes of it were enough.

"You don't think I had anything to do with her death?" It was a cracked whisper. He spoke and moved more like some zombie than a human being. "I didn't, of course—I had every reason for wanting her alive—" He broke off, and turned away. Then, over his shoulder, he muttered: "But, if the police—"

Rayburn told him not to worry.

"Or, my wife—"

He hadn't got the tiniest thing to worry about, Joe Rayburn assured him. He asked for twice the amount he had asked Mrs Vincent for the tape.

Hugh Vincent gave him the cheque, and asked: "I suppose you don't know anything about who did do it?"

He only knew what he'd read in the paper, Rayburn lied.

*   *   *

An hour later he stuck his finger on Ricky Jerome's bell-push. Doris Adams had kept her eyes skinned on the flat in Cheyne Walk since early that morning. Ricky hadn't left the flat.

But he wasn't answering the bell.

Rayburn heard a noise which sounded like someone vomiting. He pushed the letter-box flap open. It was someone vomiting. He stuck his finger back on the bell, and kept it there until Ricky Jerome opened up.

His eyes were bunged up with weeping. He was holding a towel to his mouth.

Joe Rayburn went in.

"What he must have done to her—" Ricky groaned through the towel. He'd heard it on the lunch-time news, he said. They had been lovers, you see. The past two years. Mrs Vincent? Oh, she was just a meal-ticket— you knew that . . . He started retching again.

Rayburn followed him to the bathroom.

He took out the third copy of the tape. Only he didn't play back the bit he had played to Mrs Vincent, or her husband. This was a different bit of the tape.

And it stopped Ricky Jerome from throwing up.

When Rayburn left him, he had settled for weeping some more.

Doris Adams was minding the store, while she typed back the reports. There'd been nothing, she told him.

She got Greggson.

"How about *The Pier*," Joe Rayburn said. "Like around seven."

The cop's voice: "In aid of what's this?"

"In aid of steaks and chips, and a bottle of vino."

You could practically hear Greggson's brain oozing mingled curiosity and suspicion. Then: "Okay; see you."

Doris Adams had said, "Chow . . ." and he stood at the window and he put a flame to a cigarette. He wasn't seeing the dark heads and slanted-eyed, yellow faces milling below. He wasn't hearing the Chinatown chat. Other faces, other voices were chasing around his skull.

Like Mrs Vincent's—and her husband's. And Melissa Lambert's voice on the tape, a lascivious voice. Then, not so lascivious. And Ricky Jerome's face, and his voice muffled by the towel.

He called the Cheyne Walk flat.

A man's voice which wasn't Ricky Jerome's answered. It could have been a cop. The doc was with him—something Mr Jerome had taken. It was a stomach-pump job. No, he couldn't say if he'd be okay. Who was it speaking?

Joe Rayburn hung up.

The Pier overlooks Chelsea Embankment. Run by an ex-cop, it's a favourite water-hole for the Law and ex-cons, the syndicate goons and the C.I.D.'s Heavy Mob. Food and drink first-class, like the cigars.

Rayburn and Greggson worked on the steaks and wine. Over black coffee, Rayburn said: "Cheated on you, too, didn't she? Same as she did on Ricky?"

Beads of sweat glinted at the cop's hair-line.

"You bastard—what you been sticking your nose into?"

"I paid him a call, this afternoon. Throwing up all over, he was. On account of Melissa Lambert getting whacked by this Ice-Pick nut—"

"Ice-Pick nut—? How in hell—?"

"D'you know, I spoke with him about that. 'Funny,' I says, 'you should know about how she was done over. Because, you see,' I says, 'no one else knew. Except one or two. The media weren't told. That was deliberate, you understand . . .' Then, I played him the tape—"

Greggson shoved the table back. He looked in a hurry.

Rayburn told him to cool it—it was being taken care of. He said: "But you never mentioned he could lose his marbles, he'd get so crazy jealous. So, last night, he goes and does just that—"

Greggson was scowling. "You said you played him the tape—"

The stuff Ed McNeill got, Joe Rayburn told him, after they'd left. Ed had hung about, just in case something more had come up. Something had.

The other's scowl relaxed slightly.

"Like Lover Boy—"

Rayburn nodded. He'd rumbled her and Hugh Vincent, he said. He filled him in on the latest from the Cheyne Walk flat.

"If he hasn't croaked," Greggson said, "I'll fix him myself . . . Jesus, the poor, poor bitch." He sagged in his chair. Then, he looked up suddenly, passing a hand over his moist brow. "You haven't said who grassed on me."

Rayburn recalled the description given of him by Doris Adams's informant—he'd been the one who smelt like a cop. Information received, he told him.

The *real* Ice-Pick Murders?

Still on Greggson's blotter. Unsolved.

THE WORLD ACCORDING TO UNCLE ALBERT

Penelope Wallace

My UNCLE WAS mad about Sherlock Holmes.

Sometimes I just thought he was mad.

He had this enormous magnifying glass and, when he wasn't rereading The Master, he was cantering around the ample grounds of his country estate, waving it around. "A big dog's been through this thicket," he said.

"Yes, a Great Dane called Hound. *Your* Great Dane. You walked him through here this morning."

His embarrassment was fleeting. "I'd have known anyway, from the paw marks," he said scathingly.

"If you use that great thing in the afternoon sun, you'll start a fire," I told him. I'd just snagged my pantihose and I reflected for the hundredth time that the proper apparel for a stroll through Uncle Albert's underbrush was slacks.

Uncle Albert was against slacks. Women should look feminine and behave in a feminine way—preferably in high necks and long skirts as in dear old Sherlock's day. He didn't want an Irene Adler in the family.

I'd once pointed out to him that there were other crime writers. It was like telling a religious bigot that there were other churches.

I always explain to any visitors whom my uncle means when he speaks of The Master. We'd had a nasty interlude when one of my old school friends thought he was referring to Noël Coward.

I should, perhaps, explain that I live by myself in London, but Uncle Albert is my only living relative and, despite what he calls my aggressive modernity, he seems to like me, so I come down most weekends.

This Friday afternoon was particularly hot and, after my remarks about starting a fire, he reluctantly agreed that we retrace our steps.

He always wears an Inverness for these walks—just like you-know-whose—and he stowed the magnifying glass away in a large pocket. "About the party—" I began. But he bent suddenly over a thorny bush, dragging out his "eye of God" and peering intently.

"That's not Hound's hair," he announced. "It's some fine shreds and—yes, by Jove, it's blood!"

"Group 'O'," I told him. "Rhesus Positive."

He turned, amazed.

"How—?"

I pointed to my leg. "My blood," I told him. "And shreds of my pantihose."

He put away the magnifying glass and walked with me, rather huffily, back to the house.

I wondered whether I should apologize for scratching my leg or if I should have left a little notice: "Here lies the fine blood of Frances Stephen—wounded while on lawful pursuits."

Uncle relented when we were back in the drawing room. "Tea now, I think," he said, and rang the bell by the fireplace. "After tea I think I'll dip into *The Hound of the Baskervilles*."

The Great Dane uncurled himself at the sound of his name and ambled over to see if he was missing anything—like tea, I thought, the way that dog eats.

Poor Uncle. Mrs Hubbard, the housekeeper, had refused to let him buy a mastiff and, although Hound was large enough, he didn't have at all the temperament of his namesake.

Once I'd pointed out to Uncle Albert that the Great Man hadn't owned a dog and had, on occasions, employed a tracking dog called Toby, who was an ugly lop-eared mixture of spaniel and Labrador. Uncle had become frosty and Hound had looked sad. He wasn't actually the kind of dog who carries the burglar's torch—he was too lazy even for that.

"Uncle," I said firmly. "Not too much reading after tea. Remember, you're giving a party; the guests will start arriving about seven."

Uncle mumbled crossly, but I knew that he actually liked parties. It gave him a chance to quote The Master and recall a few occasions when he himself—in his humble way, as he put it—had made some startling discoveries and deductions.

"You're giving the party for me," I reminded him. "My nineteenth birthday party—although I'm not actually nineteen until the week after next. Roger and his wife will be coming from London. They'll be staying the weekend, and John Canning will be here for the night."

"Where's he coming from?"

"Six miles away, but you asked him when you met him last May. You said he was an unusually sensitive and perceptive young man."

"Oh, yes. I remember the boy. Reads The Master and congratulated me on some of my own achievements. Who else is coming?"

"Don's driving down from London with his sister and various others."

"Long-haired layabout."

"He's not a layabout; he works at the B.B.C."

Uncle Albert muttered something about Lord Reith and inquired whether they were all staying the night.

"They'll drive back to London after it's over," I told him.

"So few people," he said mournfully.

"I thought *you'd* asked some guests as well."

"The vicar and his wife and Dr Spence and the Paynes and Mrs Caxton, but they won't stay long after dinner. Oh, yes, and an author fellow I met last weekend—he lent me one of his books—I can't say I think much of it, but he seems a decent chap. Quite young too.

"I've got your mother's jewellery in the safe—you will wear some of it, won't you? I remember when your mother wore it at her parties."

He'd said the same at my last birthday party and the one before and the one before that. Then, as now, I agreed.

"I'll get it out now," he said, and I followed him through the connecting door to his study—an indescribably untidy room, since Mrs Hubbard was allowed to do no more than vacuum the carpet. The safe was large, solid-looking, and very old. Uncle Albert started spinning dials. Usually he supported himself on the top while he did so, but on this occasion he kept well clear, with his left hand behind his back.

"Is it that dirty?" I asked him.

He hesitated. "Not dirty exactly," he said gruffly and I went forward to investigate. "Don't touch the door!"

I looked carefully at the safe door. "It's shinier," I said. "What have you done to it?"

"I suppose I might as well tell you. In fact, I'm rather proud of the idea. It's covered with a special fine grease. For fingerprints," he explained. "Of course, there are burglar alarms at the windows and doors and there's Hound, but someone might gain admittance by day when the alarms are off."

I recalled that they had been, at one time, left on by day—until one memorable occasion when the vicar, waiting for my uncle in the drawing room and presumably stifled by the heat, had flung open the French windows—and all hell had broken loose. Mrs Hubbard, relating the event, said that even Hound had entered into the spirit of the thing, and fascinated villagers had seen the vicar running down the main street with his hands clapped to his ears and his bony legs clearly visible through the rips in his cassock.

The safe was filled with envelopes and packages—rare first editions and what Uncle referred to as "memorabilia and ephemera". My jewellery was in a strong cardboard box on the top shelf. Normally, covered with oceans of sealing wax, it was held at the bank. Only for my birthday was it brought to this temporary home. As usual I chose to wear a small diamond pendant and, also as usual, I refused to bedeck myself with various rings and bracelets or to take the box back to London to "bring an aura of gracious living", as he put it, into my bed-sitter.

I had referred to my "birthday party" because that's how Uncle Albert thought of it, but it was really his evening. Some of his cronies, some of my more respectable friends—the others couldn't afford the fare or petrol from London—came in for a few drinks, dinner, and the birthday cake. Then, after a decent interval for coffee and recovery, the older guests would depart and Uncle would take himself off to the study and, as he said, "Leave the young people to enjoy themselves." Not surprisingly, the proceedings which followed lost spontaneity.

I was dutifully dressed, wearing the pendant, and downstairs by six-thirty. Roger and Jane arrived a few minutes later. Roger's father had been a friend of my father's; they were in their late thirties but determined to be young or, as Roger said, "with it". Jane was small and slim, but Roger's spread was definitely middle-aged. I had a standing invitation to visit them in London and felt rather guilty that I so rarely did. Roger's publishing house was reputedly going through a difficult time. Soon after they joined me in the drawing room for a drink, a tap on the door revealed John Canning. Apparently he had arrived when I was changing and had been shown to his room by Batty Annie, who came from the village to help Mrs Hubbard on special occasions.

I had only met John Canning twice before, and he didn't improve with the third meeting. He had impressed Uncle Albert with his knowledge of Sherlock Holmes and, when he heard that Roger was a publisher, he launched into the Meaning and Significance of the Modern Novel and the particular significance of Roger's publications.

Roger was puffing up nicely when Batty Annie flung open the door and let in the vicar and Mrs Vicar and Mr and Mrs Payne. The Paynes were in their seventies; they had known my mother when she was a child and I was very fond of them. I couldn't say the same of Mrs Caxton, who followed them in. She was a predatory forty-fiver, a widow whose target, I felt sure, was Uncle Albert. I didn't think she'd have any luck, noticing that when he joined the throng he had the wary look he usually has when she's around.

Dr Spence arrived next, as untidy as usual, with his neat sparrow wife. I wondered where Don had got to, and then Batty Annie brought in Uncle Albert's author—who turned out to be Simon Lantern—and I rather forgot about Don. I could see John Canning bestowing himself on one group after another and, during lulls in the conversation, I heard him discussing heart surgery with Dr Spence and God with the vicar. Predictably, he soon turned his attention on Simon.

"Mr Lantern," he said. "You have given a new dimension to crime fiction."

Simon gave an enigmatic smile and I hoped the subject would change, because although, of course, I'd heard of the great Simon Lantern I'd never read any of his books. In fact, I don't like crime books, although it seems terribly disloyal to Uncle Albert to mention it.

I was saved by Batty Annie announcing dinner. She wasn't really mad—I should explain—but had acquired the adjective as a result of a passing interest in spiritualism.

Uncle Albert had the problem of rudeness to my friends from London if we started dinner without them and offending Mrs Hubbard if we didn't. I assured him that Don's car had probably broken down and we certainly shouldn't wait.

Dinner was somewhat formal, with Uncle Albert at one end of the long table and myself at the other. I firmly put Simon on my right, the chair on my left was tacitly left empty for Don, and a block of four were left empty below Simon. It turned out they weren't all needed, because Don arrived soon after the soup with apologies—they *had* broken down—and with him were only his sister Susan and one other. Susan was wearing a scarlet blouse and purple slacks; I could see Uncle shuddering in the distance, but he should have seen the jeans she normally wore. With Susan was a new friend of hers named Sammy—I hadn't met him before, but Susan believed in variety. Sammy had a scrubbed look and I suspected that Susan had bathed him for the occasion; my suspicion was later confirmed when I passed to windward and was rewarded by the unmistakable smell of Pink Lilac talc.

"Only the three of you?" asked Uncle.

"Yes," said Don. "The other two fell out at the first roundabout."

There was a stunned silence, and I feebly explained that Don was joking. Nobody laughed.

Simon asked Don what kind of car he had and they immediately entered into the kind of dialogue which is common to males of all ages and races—I suspect it's what they beat out on African drums, and maybe those streams of little flags my naval friends refer to as "making signals" don't actually carry stirring messages about "England expecting" or instructions to "Form line of battle", but really read, "I'd just been passed by this Lotus Elan—"

Anyway, it gave me a chance to look around the table. Uncle Albert debating, as usual, with Dr Spence. Mrs Spence was chatting demurely with the vicar. Susan and Sammy were holding hands, which meant that Susan had to hold the soup spoon in her left hand. And John Canning was using what he thought was charm on Mrs Caxton, who was smiling and nodding. He certainly worked hard. Jane was working hard too, conversing with Sammy, but whereas I thought John Canning had ulterior motives I knew that Jane was just pursuing her affection for, and hopeful affinity with, the young.

The car conversation seemed to have petered out, or maybe Don and Simon had remembered whose party it was. "So how are you, Frankie?" asked Don.

I hoped Uncle hadn't heard—and I loathed it too. "I'm fine, thank you, Donnie."

I was happy to see that he winced slightly.

Dinner proceeded smoothly with Mrs Hubbard, as always, giving of her best. Her crowning effort was the birthday cake. The lights were turned out as she brought it in, firing on all nineteen candles, and put it in front of me with a large cake knife. Uncle Albert always insisted on champagne for my birthday dinner and, as the candles flickered, I began to wonder if I had let my glass be filled rather too often.

I stood up and thanked Uncle and Mrs Hubbard before starting to blow at the flames and it was while I was leaning forward, puffing, that someone remarked on the beauty of the pendant—I couldn't tell who it was in the dark. I heard a murmur of assent, and by the time the candles were out and the lights back on, Uncle Albert was holding forth about the beauty of my mother's jewellery and my inexplicable behaviour in refusing to take it to London and wear it. There were assents and reminiscences from the older members of the party and a tactful silence from the younger until Sammy, whom I had thought incapable of conversation, suddenly said that he thought I was right; that the trappings of wealth were no longer acceptable.

He didn't actually say, "Come the Revolution," but I could see Uncle Albert heating up—he has a low boiling point—and then Simon Lantern was coming to my rescue by pointing out the responsibility involved with valuable jewellery and the risk of theft. Someone mentioned the recent loss of a film star's emeralds and soon the conversation had generalized into talk of burglaries in general and of jewellery in particular, with Uncle quoting The Master's cases at appropriate moments.

Uncle Albert had a hankering for the port-and-nuts-for-the-boys segregation but I had talked him out of it the preceding year, so after we had finished the cake we all trooped into the drawing room for coffee.

By about ten the locals started to leave—but not, I was happy to see, Simon Lantern.

At ten-thirty, Uncle Albert retired to his study and the rest of us sat around talking—except for Susan and Sammy, who sat on the sofa still holding hands and apparently oblivious of all but each other. It was when

Don got into a political argument with Jane and Roger—with John Canning agreeing with both sides—that Simon said, "You haven't read any of my books, have you?" I admitted that I hadn't and apologized for the fact that I never read crime fiction. "There's one I think you would like," he told me. "May I send you a copy?"

I said I'd be delighted and he wrote down my London address, adding, as an afterthought, that perhaps I could dine with him the next time he visited his publisher and he could give me the book in person.

He was an undeniably attractive man—mid-forties, I thought, with black hair greying at the temples. It occurred to me that perhaps I should keep the diamond pendant, because I was sure he'd take me to dine at that sort of place. While I was telling him that I'd like that, I thought how part of his charm lay in the way he actually listened when people were speaking, his head held slightly on one side.

When the telephone rang about eleven-thirty, I didn't bother to answer it because I knew that Uncle Albert had an extension in the study and would deal with it there. It was a call for Simon, and Uncle invited him to take it in the study. Don took advantage of his absence to remark unkindly on him and suggest that he practised his air of attentive listening in the mirror each morning.

Simon wasn't long on the phone. We heard him speaking to Uncle Albert and Uncle saying, "Nonsense, my boy, no trouble at all," then he returned to explain that the call was from his sister. All the lights had failed and the electricity people had told her it was a cable fault that couldn't be mended until the following day. She was going to spend the night in the nearest hotel and advised him to do likewise but Uncle Albert had pressed him to stay the night here.

I thought his sister was taking rather drastic action but I only said that I had no idea he had a sister and asked why he hadn't brought her to the party. He replied that his sister wasn't good at parties, whereupon Don gave a baleful look at Susan and Sammy and said, "Nor's mine."

Around midnight Don said they'd better start back. It was a warm night and we all went out to wave them goodbye.

It was a dead loss, waving goodbye, because the car wouldn't start, and although Don and Simon both poked around under the bonnet it appeared that the problem couldn't be repaired without spares from the local garage. That meant three more besides John Canning, Roger, and Jane staying the night.

Proprieties had to be observed and Don and Sammy were given a twin-bedded room, Susan a smallish single room down the corridor. Uncle Albert doled out toothbrushes and pyjamas, and I gave Susan a nightdress. Uncle Albert then took the reluctant Hound for a short walk while I busied myself with sheets and towels and offers of help in making beds.

While I was thus skivvying, I heard Uncle return and the clanking of bolts as he locked up for the night. He always locked the doors from the passage to the drawing room and study and took the respective keys to bed with him. When I heard his footsteps on the stairs, I left Don to finish making his own bed. Uncle Albert has some old-fashioned ideas, and I hate to shock him unnecessarily.

My bedroom was in the middle of the corridor and there was a certain amount of traffic during the night which I took to be guests en route to the bathroom or Sammy en route to Susan. I didn't sleep particularly well and sometime in the early hours I remembered that I should have given the pendant to Uncle Albert so he could lock it away in the safe. Instead, I had left it on the dressing table by the window. Remembering the tales of robbery earlier in the evening, I got up and actually leaned out of the window to check for drainpipes and other furtive access to my room but I couldn't see anything that would help a would-be thief. My room overlooked the drive and I peered anxiously at the trees which flanked it, but I didn't see any suspicious shadows. I could hear owls hooting sadly and, somewhere to the front of the house, a faint hissing. For a moment I thought it was rain; then I remembered the Speckled Band Uncle Albert had insisted I read about in my early youth—but neither seemed applicable, so I went back to bed and, finally, to sleep.

When I woke, it was half-past nine and there was a lot of noise outside my window. I looked out and saw Don and the man from the local garage peering into the guts of Don's car while Simon sat in the driver's seat using the starter when requested. The car burst into noisy life for brief periods while the garage man poked about with an enormous screwdriver and Don watched anxiously.

I had a quick bath and dressed. My final look at the scene outside showed Don at the wheel—and no sign of Simon. I hoped he hadn't left.

I was halfway down the stairs when I saw Uncle Albert at the open study door.

"Frances," he called to me, and I followed him in. Simon was there. "I said I'd show Mr Lantern some of my treasures," Uncle told me darkly, "and when I opened the safe, I found that all your jewellery is missing. We've had a burglary."

I wasn't particularly upset for myself. I seldom wore it and had no doubt that it was well insured. But Uncle Albert was very unhappy.

"Come and see this, Frances," he said, and Simon and I followed him to the drawing room.

The French windows were open—apparently Mrs Hubbard had

assumed that Uncle had opened them before she cleaned the room, since the alarm seemed to be switched off. "However," said Uncle, brightening visibly now that he could start deducting, "the alarm was *not* switched off, someone disconnected it. And look there"—he pointed to the earth outside the window, which bore strange marks, fairly deep and spade-shaped—"you will remember," he said, "how in 'The Adventure of the Priory School' The Master realised the cow hoofprints were actually made by horses?"

Simon said he remembered it well.

"*I* deduce that those prints were made by a man walking on his toes."

"Why?" I asked.

"Because," he explained, "it would give less guidance to the man's size of shoes than would a full footprint. You can see the tracks he made coming in—and going out."

"So," I said with some relief, "it could have been any thief for miles around."

"I'm afraid not, Frances. I told you the alarm on this window had been disconnected. That could only be done from inside the room. And it was done yesterday, because I tested the alarm on Thursday evening when I brought your jewellery home from the bank."

"Anyone could have come in yesterday. The windows were open and we were out in the grounds. We wouldn't have seen anything."

"One thing we do know from the size of those footprints is that the robber returned to force open the French doors after it started to rain: the ground was very wet, which made the prints wide and deep."

"But," said Simon, "it didn't rain last night—or, if it did, it was a very light shower. I've been out in front trying to help Don with his car, and the ground's bone dry."

"Have you called the police?" I asked Uncle Albert.

He looked hurt. "Simon persuaded me to do so. I've called the C.I.D. at Midhampton. I think I'll just go and have a quick look outside before they arrive. They have to travel sixteen miles." He scooted through the open French windows, more or less avoiding the footprints, and disappeared behind some nearby bushes. He didn't ask Simon to go with him; maybe he just didn't see him as an obedient Watson.

We saw Uncle Albert emerge from the bushes holding something white, and as he came back through the windows we could see it was a pair of gloves.

"Look," he said proudly. "The fingers of the right glove are covered with grease. The burglar was left-handed. The left glove is quite clean and is obviously the one that came in contact with the dial." He turned to

Simon. "Who else aside from you is left-handed?" he asked.

Simon looked surprised. "I'm right-handed," he said.

Uncle was disappointed. "You picked up the telephone receiver with your left hand last night."

"I'm deaf in my right ear," Simon told him.

Uncle turned to me. "Your friend Susan," he said. "She held her soup spoon in her left hand at dinner."

I explained that Sammy had been holding her right one, and Uncle tutted a bit. "Anyway," I pointed out, "who's to say it's one of us? There are probably hundreds of left-handed burglars in the county."

A local bobby arrived at that moment. P.C. Brown was a keen gardener and, after one look at the footprints, opined that something funny had been going on, because it hadn't rained for three weeks and if someone had been using a hose it was strictly illegal.

"Of *course*," I said. "The hissing noise last night—it was either the hose or the garden sprinkler!" I explained why I'd been looking out of the window and Uncle Albert beamed at me.

"Excellent," he told me.

Don came in at that moment to say goodbye and P.C. Brown explained that Don and his party must wait for the Inspector from Midhampton. Uncle told Don about the burglary. P.C. Brown frowned at Uncle and Don swore. Reluctantly, the P.C. allowed him to telephone his excuses to London.

"Who else is staying in the house," P.C. Brown asked us afterward, "and where are they?"

Don had seen Roger and Jane heading toward the village, Sammy and Susan were packing—packing what? I wondered—and nobody had seen John Canning. "His car's still outside," offered Don.

P.C. Brown could never have played poker. Over his face there flitted the go-seek-and-round-up-suspects look, closely followed by a baleful stare at Uncle laced with the obvious thought—based perhaps on previous experience—that if he left the room Uncle would be off clue-hunting and Midhampton would be very displeased with the results. To his evident relief, Midhampton itself showed up at this point. The party consisted of a rather elderly and cynical Inspector, a sergeant who reminded me of a vicious terrier I'd once had, and a horde of experts who proceeded to search the grounds, take photographs, make casts of the footprints, and dust surfaces with grey powder.

The Inspector turned to Uncle Albert. "Have you found any evidence?" he asked in a sad voice. Evidently Uncle's fame *had* spread. Uncle pointed out the footprints outside the French windows. The Inspector peered out, looked for rather a long time at those on the periphery, and opined that Mr Holmes would have used a mat.

A convert!

Uncle beamed. He realised he couldn't always be as perfect as The Master. With a flourish he produced the white cotton gloves. The sergeant yapped, whipped a polythene bag out of his case, and dropped them in.

P.C. Brown, who was being upstaged, told the Inspector of the hissing noise I'd heard in the night.

"Not the Speckled Band," I interrupted and got a half smile from the Inspector and a rather hurt look from P.C. Brown, who battled on and was then sent to round up those of the party who could be located. The sergeant left with him and Mrs Hubbard appeared with coffee and biscuits, followed by the still-clasped Sammy and Susan, who sat together on the sofa.

We all heard a sharp yelp through the French windows. It wasn't the call of Hound. I suspected it was the terrier-sergeant hot on the trail. The Inspector departed in its direction and Uncle Albert said he must wash his hands. He reappeared some ten minutes later with a smug expression, a pair of binoculars, and Hound.

He hadn't been able to observe much from the downstairs loo—cloakroom, as he insists on calling it—even with the binoculars, because the window glass is opaque and the window is small and high, but he'd had a good view of the sergeant's back and heard him refer to faint scuffmarks at the foot of the drainpipe and yelp a second time when he spied some threads of material caught partway up the pipe.

A man had been dispatched for a ladder and Uncle had had to step away so that the climber wouldn't see him.

"It's definitely an inside job," he said. "Someone in the house climbed down the drainpipe after everyone was asleep, forced open the French windows—having earlier disconnected the burglar alarm—opened the safe, took the jewellery, and climbed back up the drainpipe to his room."

"Clasping the jewellery," I asked, "until such time as the police would arrive to take it from him?"

"He may have had an accomplice in the grounds," said Uncle, "or he may have concealed it in the house. In 'The Naval Treaty'—"

Jane and Roger came in at that point and Jane, wearing a well cut trouser suit which had Uncle tutting under his breath, helped herself and Roger to coffee. Uncle brought them up to date on the facts and on his deductions. Midway through his dissertation John Canning came in and explained that he'd been reading in his room until the police had turned him out to conduct their search. I gave him a cup of coffee.

Uncle moved to the window, his binoculars in hand.

"They've found something!" he said.

And Hound, who'd been lying peacefully on Sammy and Susan, obeyed some atavistic call, leaped to his feet, bounded through the windows, and was off at a speed I'd never credited him with. I could see that Uncle was as surprised as I was, but he was very loyal.

"They've found something!" he repeated. "They're holding it up—some sort of bundle—and Hound—yes, Hound's got the scent!"

I suppose I was the only other person in the room who knew that Hound could no more follow a scent than I could fly to the moon. Uncle retained his optimism.

"Yes," he cried, "and now he's coming back here!"

Hound came bounding back and sank, panting and exhausted, at Uncle's feet.

A few minutes later, the Inspector came in with a rolled-up bundle tied with garden twine. From it he drew a pair of loud check trousers. I'd always thought they were hideous since the day Uncle bought them.

"These are yours also?" asked the Inspector, holding up a pair of over-shoes. "And the gardening gloves?"

"Yes," admitted my uncle. "I keep them in the garden room for when I do the garden."

"The garden room," I explained, "is the one with the cracked sink and the broken lawnmower next to the—the cloakroom."

"And the room is not locked?"

My uncle looked sad and shook his head.

"I assume," he said, "that the thief wore my clothing to protect his own whilst climbing up and down the drainpipe—and then threw it out of the landing window."

"It would be one hell of a throw," I pointed out.

"Yes," agreed the Inspector. "It seems more likely that your uncle's clothes were hidden in the bushes sometime later, possibly early this morning."

"And why the hose?" I persisted.

"You will remember," said Uncle Albert, "that The Master could calculate the weight and possibly the height of a man from his footprints, but a man standing on very wet ground in someone else's overshoes—" A faraway look came into his eyes and I knew he was on the track—or, as he would have said, "deducting".

I tried to pull him back to the present. "Surely it would have been even more difficult if the ground had been bone dry."

Uncle responded with a proud smile. "I always keep that patch of ground slightly wet," he said. "Damp enough to hold footprints in the event of a burglary."

I saw Don looking at Uncle Albert and then at me. Well, I'm not the only person in the world with an eccentric relation.

"It's very interesting," said Don. "But may I ask when we shall be allowed to leave, Inspector?"

"You're all free to go now," was the answer.

Don galvanized Susan and Sammy and then his car into action. In minutes, they were speeding dangerously down the drive. Then John Canning made his polite departure, followed by Simon Lantern.

Our weekend guests, Jane and Roger, remained.

The Inspector agreed to join us for a pre-lunch drink. Uncle Albert looked portentous and frustrated until both Jane and Roger decided to tidy up before lunch. As the door closed behind them, Uncle launched into his theory.

"Of course it was them," he said. "Very sad, but Roger's firm is in need of money and the jewellery would fetch a very good price." He shook his head sadly and continued. "They are both familiar with the house. They knew where I kept my gardening clothes and where the hose was. They went out for a walk quite early, hiding my clothes in the bushes on the way. They're great walkers so no one would remark on the fact that they strode out to the village. No doubt they met an accomplice there. Of course it was Jane who came down the drainpipe—Roger's a little stout for a manoeuvre of that sort—and she had to make the ground really wet to disguise her lack of weight and inches. It all fits," he added. "And I hope that you will be able to apprehend them and trace the jewellery before the accomplice sells it."

He said it with a look which would have made Lestrade quail, but it didn't have that effect on the Inspector.

"We certainly hope to recover the jewellery," he said. "My men are watching the thief at this moment and they will see when he makes contact with his accomplice. In fact, we pretty well know who that will be, because he usually works with the same man."

"Usually?" My uncle was shocked. "You mean this isn't their first offence?"

"It won't be the thief's first offence—but the thief is neither of your two friends."

"I'm glad of that," I said with feeling, "but who is it?"

"I'll tell you that as soon as we're able to make the arrest," the Inspector promised.

It was a sticky weekend, with Uncle having to admit failure to himself and pretending like mad he'd never suspected Jane and Roger—who didn't make the situation any easier by constantly asking Uncle for his opinion on the theft. It was quite a relief when they left on Sunday afternoon, and even more pleasant when the Inspector rang in the evening and asked if he could call around. I'd refused a lift from Jane and Roger and decided to stay over and take an early train in the morning in case there was any news.

The Inspector brought my jewellery along for formal identification.

"Who was it?" I asked.

"Mr Canning."

"How did you know?" Uncle asked.

"It was quite simple. Canning had several convictions under other names and it was his style. He fit the general description. His fingerprints clinched it. Of course, the fact that he is a jewel thief didn't prove he'd stolen Miss Stephen's jewellery—we had to wait until he collected it from his accomplice."

"But how could you know?" I asked. "How could you know his style, what he looked like, who his accomplice was?"

"I didn't need to, Miss Stephen. Scotland Yard has a fine Criminal Records Office. A man with a police radio has a great advantage over a man with a magnifying glass."

Uncle Albert was very unhappy in the hours that followed the Inspector's departure and I was considering phoning the office in the morning to say my uncle was ill when he suddenly perked up.

"It was entirely solved by the fingerprints," he said. "Entirely. And, of course, The Master was one of the very first to realize their importance."

DEATH OF AN OLD DOG

Antonia Fraser

PAULINA GAVIN CAME back from the vet with a sweet expression
on her heart-shaped face. The little crease which sometimes—just slightly—marred the smooth white skin between her brows was absent. Her
eyes, grey yet soft, swept round the sitting room. Then they came to rest,
lovingly, on Richard.

"Darling, I'm late! But supper won't be late. I've got it all planned."

Widowhood had made of Richard Gavin a good, as well as a quick
cook. But Paulina had not seen fit to call on his talents before her visit to
the vet: he found no note of instructions awaiting him. Now Paulina
kissed him with delicious pressure on his cheek, just where his thick
grizzled sideburn ended. It was her special place.

From this, Richard knew that Ibo was condemned to die.

Viewing the situation with detachment, as befitting a leading barrister,
Richard was not the slightest bit surprised that the verdict should have
gone against Ibo. The forces ranged against each other were simply not
equal. On the one side, the vet, in his twenties, and Paulina, not much
older. On the other side, Ibo. And Ibo was not merely old. He was a very
old dog indeed.

He dated from the early days of Richard's first marriage, and that balmy
period not only seemed a great while since, a long, long time ago (in the
words of Richard's favourite quotation from Ford) but actually was. Even
the origin of the nickname Ibo was lost in some private joke of his
marriage to Grace: as far as he could remember the dog had begun as
Hippolytus. Was it an allusion to his sympathies in the Nigerian Civil
War? Based on the fact that Ibo, like the Biafrans, was always starving
. . . ? That too seemed a long, long time ago.

You could therefore say sentimentally that Ibo and Richard had grown
old together. Except that it would not actually be true. For Richard had
gingerly put out one toe towards middle age, only to be dragged backwards
by Paulina's rounded arms, her curiously strong little hands. And having
been rescued, Richard was obviously reposited in the prime of life, as
though on a throne.

His past athletic prowess (including a really first-class tennis game
which only pressure at the Bar had prevented him taking further) was

easy to recall, looking at his tall, trim figure. If anything, he had lost weight recently. And it was not only the endearing Paulina but Richard's friends who generally described him as "handsomer than ever". It was as though the twenty-five-year age gap between Richard and his second wife had acted upon him as a rejuvenating injection.

The same miracle had not been performed for the master's dog. Casting his mind back, Richard could dimly recall embarrassing walks in the park with Ibo, portrait of a young dog at the evident height of his amorous powers. Now the most desirable spaniel bitch would flaunt herself in vain before him. Like Boxer in *Animal Farm*, where energy was concerned, Ibo was merely a shadow of his former self. And he did not even have Boxer's tragic dignity. Ibo by now was just a very shaggy, and to face the facts fully, a very smelly old dog.

Richard stirred in his chair. The topic must be raised. Besides, he had another important subject to discuss with Paulina, sooner or later.

"How did you get on at the vet, darling?" he called. She had after all not yet mentioned her visit.

But Paulina, having skipped into her kitchen, apparently did not hear. Pre-arranged odours were wafting from it. Richard guessed that she would soon emerge having removed her apron. He guessed that she would be bearing with her a bottle of red wine, already opened, and two glasses on a tray. There was, he suspected, a strong possibility that supper would be eaten by candlelight.

Both guesses were correct. The suspicion was confirmed when Paulina artlessly discovered some candles left over from Christmas and decided on impulse to use them up.

"Why not? Just for us." She enquired to no one in particular, as she sat down at the now positively festive little table with its browny-red casserole, its red Beaujolais and scarlet candles. Then Paulina's manner quite changed.

"Poor Ibo," sighed Paulina. "I'm afraid the vet didn't hold out much hope."

"Hope?" repeated Richard in a surprised voice. It was not surely a question of *hope*—what hope could there possibly be for a very old, very smelly dog—but of life. It was the continuation of Ibo's life they were discussing, for that was all he had to expect, not the possibility of his magical rejuvenation.

"Well, *hope*," repeated Paulina in her turn, sounding for the first time ruffled, as though the conversation had taken an unexpected and therefore unwelcome turn. "Hope is so important, isn't it? Without hope, I don't see much point in any of us going on—"

But Richard's attention was distracted. There was an absence. He would have noticed it immediately had it not been for Paulina's charade with the dinner.

Where was Ibo? Obese, waddling, grey-muzzled, frequently flea-ridden, half-blind, where was Ibo? Normally his first action on entering the sitting room would have been to kiss, no, slobber over Richard's hand. Then Ibo, an optimist, might have wagged his stumpy tail as though, despite the lateness of the hour and his incapacity, a walk was in the offing. Finally, convinced of his own absurdity, he would have made for the fire, pausing for a last lick of Richard's hand. None of this happened. Where was Ibo?

Paulina began to speak quickly, muttering things about further tests, the young vet's kindness, the need to take a dispassionate decision, and so forth, which all seemed to add up to the fact that the vet had kept the dog in overnight. Once again Richard cut in.

"You do realise Toddie comes home from school tomorrow?"

This time an expression of sheer panic crossed Paulina's face. It was only too obvious she had quite forgotten.

"How can he be?" she began. "He's only just gone there—" She stopped. She had remembered. Toddie, the strange silent ten-year-old son of Richard's first marriage, was returning the next day from school to have his new plate tightened. The dentist had emphasized that the appointments had to be regular, and had thus overruled protests from Richard who wanted Toddie to wait for half-term. At first Toddie had taken the news of his quick turn round with his usual imperturbability. But after a moment he had suddenly knelt down and flung his arms round Ibo, a mat of fur before the fire.

"Then I'll be seeing you very soon again, won't I, you good old boy? The best dog in the world." It was a long speech for Toddie.

Toddie's embraces were reserved exclusively for Ibo. His father had tried a few grave kisses after Grace's death. Toddie held himself rigid as though under attack. Later they had settled for ritual handshakes. When Richard married Paulina he had advised her against any form of affectionate assault on Toddie, warned by his own experiences. For Paulina, the frequent light kiss was as natural a mode of communication as Richard's solemn handshake. Baulked of this, she had ended up deprived of any physical contact at all with Toddie. At first it worried her: a motherless boy . . . Later, as her step-son remained taciturn, not so much a motherless boy as an inscrutable person, she was secretly glad she was not committed to hugging and kissing this enigma with his unsmiling lips, and disconcertingly expressionless eyes.

Only two things provoked any kind of visible reaction from Toddie. One was crime, murder to be precise. No doubt it was a natural concomitant to his father's career. But Paulina sometimes found the spectacle of Toddie poring over the newspapers in search of some gruesome trial rather distasteful. It was true that he concentrated on the law reports, showing for example considerable knowledge of appeal procedure, rather than on the horror stories in the popular press. Perhaps he would grow up to be a barrister like Richard . . . ? In which case, where murder was concerned, he was making a flying start.

Toddie's other visible interest was of course Ibo.

Jolted by the prospect of the boy's return, Paulina now launched into a flood of explanation concerning the true nature of Ibo's condition. Ibo had a large growth, said the vet. Hadn't they noticed it? Richard clenched his hands. How long since he had brought himself to examine Ibo? Ibo simply existed. Or had simply existed up to the present time. Paulina went on to outline the case, extremely lucidly, for "putting Ibo out of his misery" as she phrased it. Or rather to be honest, sparing him the misery that was to come. Nobody pretended that Ibo was in violent misery now, a little discomfort perhaps. But he would shortly *be* in misery, that was the point. Richard listened calmly and without surprise. Had he not known since the moment that his wife pressed her lips to his cheek that Ibo was condemned to die?

What Richard Gavin had not realized, and did not realize until he conceded, judicially, regretfully, the case for Ibo's demise, was that the old dog was not actually condemned to die. He was already dead. Had been dead throughout all the fairly long discussion. Had been put to sleep by the vet that very afternoon on the authority, the sole authority, of Paulina Gavin. Who had then returned audaciously, almost flirtatiously, to argue her senior and distinguished husband round to her own point of view. . . .

The look on the face of Richard Gavin Q.C. was for one instant quite terrible. But Paulina held up her own quite bravely. With patience—she was not nearly so frightened of Richard now as she had been when they first married—she pointed out to her husband the wisdom and even kindness of her strategy. Someone had to make the decision, and so she, Paulina, had made it. In so doing, she had removed from Richard the hideous, the painful necessity of condemning to death an old friend, a dear old friend. It was easier for her—Richard had after all known Ibo for so much longer. Yet since Richard was such a rational man and loved to think every decision through, she had felt she owed it to him to argue it all out.

"Confident of course that you would make your case?"

Richard's voice sounded guarded, as his voice did sometimes in court, during a cross-examination. His expression was quite blank: for a moment he reminded Paulina uncomfortably of Toddie. But she stuck firmly to her last.

"I know I was right, darling," she said. "I acted for the best. You'll see. Someone had to decide."

There remained the problem of Toddie's precipitate return, the one factor which to be honest, Paulina had left out of her calculations. She had expected to be able to break the sad news at half-term, a decent interval away. But the next morning, Paulina, pretty as a picture in a gingham house-dress at breakfast, made it clear that she could cope with that too. With brightness she handed Richard his mail:

"*Personal and Confidential!* Is it the bank?"

With brightness she let it be understood that it was she, Paulina, who would sacrifice her day at the office—the designers' studio she ran with such *élan*—to ferry Toddie to and from school, although she had already sacrificed an afternoon going to the vet. The only thing Richard was expected to do, Paulina rattled on, was to return from *his* office, in other words his chambers, in the afternoon and tell his son the news about the dog.

Richard continued to wear his habitual morning expression, a frown apparently produced by his mail:

"No, it's not the bank," he said.

"Income Tax, then?" Paulina was determined to make conversation.

"No."

"Some case, I suppose?"

"You could put it like that."

"Why here? Why not to your chambers?" Paulina carried on chattily.

"Paulina," said Richard, pushing back his chair and rising. "You must understand that I don't exactly look forward to telling Toddie that Ibo is dead."

"Oh God, darling," cried Paulina, jumping up in her turn, her eyes starting with bright tears. "I know, I know, I *know*." She hugged all that was reachable of his imposing figure. "But it was for *him*."

"For Ibo?"

"Yes, for him. That poor dear old fellow. Poor, poor old Ibo. I know, I understand. It's the saddest thing in the world, the death of an old dog. But it is, somehow—isn't it, darling?—inevitable."

The hugging came to an end, and then Paulina dried her tears. Richard went off to his study, the large book-lined room which Paulina had created for him above the garage. He indicated that he would telephone his clerk with a view to taking the whole day off from his chambers.

One of the features of the study was a large picture window which faced out at the back over the fields to the wood. To protect Richard's privacy, the study had no windows overlooking the house. There was merely a brick façade. This morning, Paulina suddenly felt that both the study and Richard were turning their back on her. But that was fanciful. She was overwrought on account of poor Toddie. And of course poor Ibo.

Paulina reminded herself that she too was not without her feelings, her own fondness for the wretched animal. It had been a brave and resolute thing she had done to spare Richard, something of which she would not have been capable a few years back. How much the studio had done for her self-confidence! Nerves calmed by the contemplation of her new, wise maturity, Paulina got the car out of the garage and went off to fetch Toddie.

Of course Toddie knew something was wrong the moment he entered the empty house. He slipped out of the car and ran across the courtyard the moment they returned; although by re-parking the car in the garage immediately, Paulina had hoped to propel him straight into his father's care. As it was, she refused to answer Toddie's agitated question as to why Ibo did not come to greet him. She simply took him by the shoulder and led him back as fast as possible to the garage. Then it was up the stairs and into the study. Paulina did not intend to linger. She had no wish to witness the moment of Toddie's breakdown.

She had once asked Richard how Toddie took the news of his mother's death, so sudden, so appalling, in a road accident on the way to pick him up at kindergarten.

"He howled," Richard replied.

"You mean, cried and cried?"

"No, howled. Howled once. One terrible howl, then nothing. Just as if someone had put their hand across his mouth to stop him. It was a howl like a dog."

Paulina shuddered. It was a most distasteful comparison to recall at the present moment. She was by now at the head of the narrow staircase and thrusting Toddie into the big book-lined room with its vast window. But before she could leave, Richard was saying in that firm voice she recognised from the courts:

"Toddie, you know about the law, don't you?"

The boy nodded and stared.

"Well, I want you to know that there has been a trial here. The trial of Ibo." Toddie continued to stare, his large round eyes almost fish-like. Paulina turned and fled away down the stairs. No doubt Richard knew his own business—and his own son—best. But to her it sounded a most ghoulish way of breaking the news.

A great deal of time passed; time enough for Paulina to speak several times to her office (pleasingly incapable of managing without her); time enough for Paulina to reflect how very unused she had become to a housewife's enforced idleness, waiting on the movements of the males of the family. She tried to fill the gap by making an interesting tea for Toddie, in case that might solace him. But it was in fact long past tea-time when Paulina finally received some signal from the study across the way. She was just thinking that if Richard did not emerge soon, she would be late returning Toddie to Graybanks (and that would hardly help him to recover) when the bleep-bleep of the intercom roused her.

"He's coming down," said Richard's voice, slightly distorted by the wire which crackled. "Naturally he doesn't want to talk about it. So would you take him straight back to school? As soon as possible. No, no tea thank you. He'll be waiting for you in the car." And that was all. The intercom clicked off.

Upset, in spite of herself, by Richard's brusqueness, Paulina hastily put away the interesting tea as best she could. Still fighting down her feelings, she hurried to put on her jacket and re-cross the courtyard. But she could not quite extinguish all resentment. It was lucky, she thought crossly, that as Richard grew older he would have a tactful young wife at his elbow; that should preserve him from those slight rigidities, or perhaps acidities was a better word, to which all successful men were prone after a certain age. For the second time that day she recalled with satisfaction the moral courage she had shown in having Ibo put down on her own initiative without distressing her husband; there was no doubt that Richard was relying on her already.

This consciousness of virtue enabled her—but only just—to stifle her irritation at the fact that Richard had not even bothered to open the big garage doors for her. Really, men were the most ungrateful creatures, it was she, not Richard, who was facing a cross-country journey in the dark; he might at least have shown his normal chivalry to ease her on her way—taking back his son, not hers, to school. Reliance was one thing, dependence and over-dependence quite another. Still in an oddly perturbed mood for one normally so calm and competent, Paulina slipped through the little door which led to the garage.

She went towards the car. She was surprised that the engine was already running. And Toddie was not in the passenger seat. In fact the car appeared to be empty. She tried the door. It was locked. Behind her was the noise of the little side door shutting.

About the same time Richard Gavin was thinking that he would miss Paulina, he really would: her cooking, her pretty ways, her office gossip. Habit had even reconciled him to the latter. In many ways she had been a delightful, even a delicious wife for a successful man. The trouble was that she clearly would not make any sort of wife for an older man dying slowly and probably painfully of an incurable disease. This morning the doctors had finally given him no hope. He had been waiting for the last hope to vanish, putting off the moment, before sharing the fearful burden with her.

Really, her ruthless and overbearing behaviour over poor Ibo had been a blessing in disguise. For it had opened his eyes just in time. No, Paulina would certainly not be the kind of wife to solace her husband's protracted deathbed. She might even prove to be the dreadful sort of person who believed in euthanasia "to put him out of his misery". He corrected himself. Paulina might even *have* proved to be such a person.

Back in the garage, the smell of exhaust fumes soon began to fill the air. Still no one came to open the garage doors. Even the side-door was now apparently locked from the outside. Paulina's last conscious thought, fighting in vain to get the garage doors open, was that she would really have to arrange automatic openers one of these days—now that Richard was no longer as young as he was, no longer eager to help her.

A couple of fields away, in a copse, Toddie was showing his father the exact spot where he would like to have Ibo buried. Richard had been quite desperate, as he would tell the police later, to cheer the poor little chap up. It was a natural, if sentimental expedition for a father to make with his son. A son so bereft by the death of an old dog. A son so early traumatised by the death of his mother (a step-mother was not at all the same thing, alas).

And when the police came, as they surely would, to the regrettable conclusion that the second Mrs Gavin's death had not in fact been an accident, well, it really all added up, didn't it? Exactly the same factors came into play and would be ably, amply, interminably examined by the long lists of child psychiatrists to whom Toddie would be inevitably subjected.

But Toddie, Richard reflected with a certain professional detachment, would be more than a match for them. What interested him most about his son was his burning desire to get on with the business of confessing his crime. He seemed to be positively looking forward to his involvement with the police and so forth. He was certainly very satisfied with the way he had compassed his step-mother's death.

Richard was also quite surprised at the extent of Toddie's knowledge of the law concerning murderers. You could almost say that Toddie had specialised in the subject. Whereas he himself had never had much to do with that line of country. Richard realized suddenly that it was the first time he had ever really felt interested by his son.

Under the circumstances, Toddie very much doubted that he would have to spend many years in prison. He intended to end up as a model prisoner. But there might have to be a bad patch from which he could be redeemed: otherwise he might not present an interesting enough case, and the interesting cases always got out first. No, Toddie really had it all worked out.

"Besides, Dad," ended Toddie, no longer in the slightest bit taciturn, "I'm proud of what I did. You told me how to do it. But I'd have done it somehow anyway. She deserved to die. She condemned Ibo to death without telling us. Behind our backs. No proper trial. And killed him. Ibo, the best dog in the world."

"PENALTY, REF!"

Jeffry Scott

IN A HUGE bowl of turf, stone, brick, concrete, a little glass and much galvanized iron, a monster with 12,743 heads was in fitful song.

From a distance it sounded like a storm dwindling. At close range, where ridged sheets of iron create special acoustics, the monster could have been an alien musical instrument in a science-fiction film.

The bowl holds people willing to watch football in the British style, paying the most for the least in the way of comfort, services and cleanliness. For this is United's ground, a minor shrine of England's secular religion, opened in 1907 and according to rumours, repainted once or twice since then.

There is a grandstand, looking a mixture between bloated garden shed and a Victorian railway station that wandered away in the night, losing its lines and trains. But most spectators prefer the C-shaped range of broad concrete steps surrounding nearly two-thirds of the pitch.

Stan Dalgetty had never set foot in the place before—and knew it well. A bachelor Scotsman earning his living in London, he attended soccer matches all over the city.

The floodlights, peering down from steel pylons giving the ground a prison-camp air, were turning a raw autumn afternoon into a faintly eerie one. Artificial sunlight, powerful yet wan, when the sun ought to be down.

At the hooligan end of the terraces, a band of United supporters were anxious to assure the visiting team's star that they were aware of his presence. They'd draped a grimy sheet over the low fence dividing spectators from playing area. "BILLY NAGLE STEALS UNDERWEAR" was the spray-painted slogan on their banner; true, as a recent, much-reported court case proved, but unkind.

Dalgetty sniffed disapprovingly, hoping that the sheet's owner would get paint all over his backside when going back to sleep on it that night, as he very likely would. That banner and occasional pointedly obscene chanting apart, it was a tame afternoon by London soccer standards. A small but determined cloud had just wandered over and mizzled on everybody, and the game was pretty boring.

Charging out of the goalmouth, the youth in the green jersey leaped like a dolphin to capture the ball, succeeded . . . and dropped it.

Cheering changed quality in an instant, becoming a growl of frustration—then, just as quickly, a communal blend of gasp and moan. Obsessed by the ball, Wilby Town's striker was hacking at it and the goalkeeper, by now down to earth, on all fours.

The impact could not be heard. Thousands fancied they felt it. Even Dalgetty, no stranger to knocks, hissed and shook his head. The boy in the jersey curled into a foetal position; the striker fell over him, sprang up and made to kick the ball instead of the goalie's collarbone (most people can get things right, second time of trying) before running out of decision and movement.

Players and crowd waited for the ambulance men. "Animal," a fat man, standing next to Dalgetty, observed with relish. "Typical North London rubbish, that Town side. All kick and rush. No art, no science, no poetry—and woe betide any poor sod as gets in their way."

Dalgetty made a neutral, throat-clearing noise. The London borough of Rexton—which United represents in the Third Division of the Football League—is South London, though only just. North London, of which his neighbour spoke in the tone of a Roman dismissing Picts and other barbarians, lies a few miles away. In any case, the majority of both Wilby Town and Rexton United players were non-Londoners.

He shared the thought, diffidently. "Ah, now you're splitting hairs, incher?" The fat man's face was florid in a neon fashion, blue as much as red. Bearing the costly varnish of countless Quick Ones, Little Sharpeners, and Ta-Mine's-a-Doubles. "Soon as they get in the Town side, they pick up all those naughty North London ways. Evil communications corrupt good manners," he added surprisingly, "and that's in the Bible, chum."

Play resumed with a substitute goalkeeper, but Dalgetty hardly noticed it. He wondered why the fat Bible-invoker reminded him of fish and chips, though dressed like a respectable businessman in dark overcoat and glossy shoes. Mainly, however, Dalgetty was scanning faces and listening hard.

He'd been thrown into Rexton at short notice, after Hydell's appendix burst, aided by a kick from an Iranian pimp extremely reluctant to exchange courtesies with the police, far less assist their evil imperialist enquiries. Detective Inspector Dalgetty believed the fastest way to take a strange patch's temperature and heartbeat was to watch the natives watching their gladiators.

Rexton's heartbeat seemed steady. Superintendent Blake of the uniformed branch had already told Stan Dalgetty as much.

Talk of the devil, there was Blake now, pacing the cinder strip between crowd barriers and pitch. The Super looked straight through Dalgetty, of course.

"Old Bill." Superintendent Blake's first name was Harold but the fat man was using Cockney slang for the police in general. "Too mean to pay at the turnstiles like honest folk do."

"He seems more interested in us than the game," Dalgetty commented, all innocence.

"Well, he would be. All nose, Old Bill is. Dead inquisitive, the law, it's a character defect."

Suddenly the critic was shaking his fist, vibrating with operatic rage. "Bloody hell, Jack the Ripper's at it again!" Town's No. 11, Nagle—he of the lingerie—having been outrun by a United winger, had just tapped the rival's heels together in tribute to his speed.

Soothed by the referee's award of a free kick against Town, the fat man sighed meditatively. "He won't be content with the goalie, ruddy little psychopath. It's like an Agatha Christie book, this is . . . Where Will The Killer Strike Next?"

Apparently elated by the hurricane of booing, No. 11 collected the free kick when it rebounded from a United player, raced thirty yards along the touchline and popped the ball into the net.

"That was a fluke," the fat man mourned. "Three-nil down, and I only just got here, what a life!" Adversity made him sociable, it seemed. "My name's Cyril, by the way."

"Stan, pleased to meet you."

Cyril deployed a hip flask with the martyred expression of a man taking vile medicine. "What's your line of work, then, Stan? Or are you here on your holidays from Bonnie Sco'land, och aye? You're a Jock, see, I can always tell an accent."

Dalgetty felt as if a giant squeaky pencil had been raked down a slate big as Buckingham Palace, but he managed a smile. "Clerical—you know, office work and that. Bit of driving and so forth. This and that."

Cyril shook the flask, decided against sharing it, and frowned down at the pitch. "Is it my imagination, or is Old Bill coming on strong this afternoon?"

A few yards below, on the cinders, Blake had been joined by a brace of boyish constables and a dog-handler reassuring a dejected Alsatian. As a show of strength, it struck Inspector Dalgetty as less than impressive.

"Prolly my imagination," Cyril answered himself. "Sensitive about Old Bill, at this moment in time, me."

Good anglers don't jerk the rod the moment their line tautens and the float quivers. Dalgetty yawned and forced interest in United's best player nearly making a brilliant pass.

"But there *is* a lot of law here," Cyril persisted, thinking aloud. "Not just the regular Filth, neither. I was chatting up a mate of mine, on the way in, and he reckoned there's a C.I.D. bloke circulating—a plain-clothes snoop."

For a heartbeat, Dalgetty thought he'd been made the target of a laboriously prepared joke. But Cyril wasn't accusatory. What he was, undoubtedly, was a man so worried that he had to share the concern.

Dalgetty winked at him. "Try this one out of the Bible: *The wicked flee where no man pursueth*. In other words, relax, mate, and you'll live longer."

His new friend shrugged dubiously. "Maybe. Funny, all the same . . . soon as you get a dodgy bit of business on the go, a trans-bloody-action that's a bit aromatic as you might say, everybody seems to be staring at you."

Again Dalgetty refused to be curious. "You're staring at me, for that matter." He turned his shoulder to the other man, hearing an audible rasp as Cyril—whose grooming, like his elusive tang of fried stuff and cotton-seed oil used repeatedly, didn't match his posh clothes—rubbed his chin.

Dalgetty knew that he was being studied. Good luck to Cyril, who was seeing a toughish looking fellow, evidently not prosperous, with a cast in one bleak grey eye giving him a promisingly shifty expression.

Cyril reached for his flask and came to a decision. "Would you happen to have a van, Jock?" he asked abruptly.

Slapping the pockets of his abominable trench coat, Dalgetty grinned. "Not on me."

"Very droll. I'll put it another way. If you've got a van, or the use of one, you're on for some nice tax-free earners. Hundred quid, in the hand, say nothing."

It was Stan Dalgetty's turn to say, "Maybe." Which was enough to make Cyril lose interest in his favourite team, slandering them as a bunch of pansy no-hopers not worth watching. And he knew of a nice little pub round the corner . . .

This turned out to be a very nasty little pub, almost as dank and nearly as smelly as a public lavatory, which its tiled decor suggested.

"The thing is," said Cyril, "I've got to shift some stuff tonight. Not electric stoves, but hot enough to cook on, get my drift? And I can't drive."

He held up his left hand; for the first time, the policeman noticed that it was wrapped in a handkerchief.

Cyril named a spot where one vehicle would be lost among several. "Be there at eight tonight, eight sharp, mind. You'll be picking up half a dozen cartons, easy lifting, and it won't take you an hour to get 'em to . . . well, somewhere else, I'll say where, later. Hundred quid when the job's done, and be there, don't let me down."

His earnestness, in any other context, might have been comic. His husky voice squeaked.

"Wouldn't miss it for worlds," Inspector Dalgetty assured him. Still speaking the truth.

"Cyril, Cyril . . ." Superintendent Blake mused. They were in his office at Rexton police station, and the Super had his boots up on the fender before a popping gas fire, his chin on his knees. Cap off, Blake looked grandfatherly, bald dome soaring above the pressure marks left by his headgear.

Dalgetty's portrait was laconic. "Fat chap, fiftyish. Spends a bit but slovenly with it. Could hang around a fish-and-chip shop. Hard drinker, smokes too much."

"Cyril Donks," Blake crowed. "I saw him chatting you up on the terraces. And you think he's up to strokes?" The disbelief was manifest.

"Sure of it. He's getting a consignment of stolen goods tonight and he thinks I'm shifting it for him." Dalgetty sketched in the earlier conversation. "So I'll have him, and whoever delivers the hot consignment. Nice little pull, for my first few days on the patch."

His smugness wavered. "What's the matter, sir?"

The Superintendent met his eye. "I'm not one of those jealous berks and I've no time for C.I.D. versus uniformed branch feuds. But I don't like the smell of this."

Dalgetty prodded, "This Cyril Thingy . . . Donks . . . he's a villain, isn't he?"

Blake's smile was sardonic. "On this patch, everyone is to some degree, except us. And no cracks about *that*, ta very much. Oh, Cyril's got form but he's an antique. My son used to have a saying for the likes of Cyril—yes, that's it, 'A blast from the past.'

"Now, we've got a few bad lads and hard cases around this manor, no two ways about it. Extortion, the old protection racket, that's on the upswing. But Cyril was never up to that, taking and driving away a motor vehicle was his biggest coup, as I recall. Hasn't been active since around 1963, he's got this transport cafe at Fellsdown, last stop before the motorway. Going straight."

"Fellsdown," cried Dalgetty, "that's where I've got to meet him with the van. He *is* fly, our Cyril. Gave me to understand the stuff would be brought to the car park behind the cafe . . . never told me he owned the place."

Superintendent Blake replaced his cap, becoming at once sterner and fifteen years younger. "Silly old fool, starting up again at his time of life. Nice little business he's got, too. Those lorry drivers are good spenders. What's your plan?"

"I'm taking Sergeant Pryke, he seems to know what time of day it is, and he's a big lad. Pryke's getting hold of a pick-up truck, he can hide under the tarpaulin in the back. Two of us should be able to handle Cyril and his supplier—no need to make a big production out of this and go along mob-handed."

Blake nodded abstractedly. "I can't get over it, Cyril Donks being such a twit! Fancy recruiting the first bloke you run into at a football match, when your whole future depends on it . . ."

Dalgetty sniggered into his muffler. "If they were clever, I reckon both of us might be looking for easier ways to earn a crust, Super."

"There is that," Blake agreed heavily. "Best of luck then, Stanley."

They parked the Mini pick-up beside a juggernaut lorry, and waited. The transport cafe was a modern building, as much windows as walls; Dalgetty in the driving seat, and Sergeant Pryke under the tarpaulin, had an excellent view.

The cafe, like its park, was almost deserted. Most lorry drivers tried to be at home over the weekend—somebody's home, anyway. If foiled in that, they were looking for hard drink and soft women, not mugs of tea and chips with everything.

Dalgetty clicked his tongue, suddenly recognizing the portly man in whites and a chef's hat, thirty yards away across the park and behind the counter, as Cyril Donks. Donks must have registered the pick-up truck's arrival but was ignoring it.

The park was large, and Dalgetty had long since rejected the other vehicles waiting there. The car or van bearing the stolen merchandise, he was ready to bet, was not among them. Nothing could happen until it turned up, and Donks committed himself.

Dalgetty thumped the partition between cab and cargo area, Sergeant Pryke thumped back: they were all set.

They were all set at two minutes to eight, ten past and twenty past. Dalgetty fretted, unable to approach Donks and ask about the delay. The difference between a policeman in plain clothes and an *agent provocateur* is arguable at the best of times.

Then he had stiffened, only to slide down on the seat. A Volkswagen micro-bus, faded white paint livid in the amber-streaked semi-darkness between street lamps, was rolling into the park. Ignoring the herringbone lines marking suitable spaces, its driver kept going until the front bumper was nudging the cafe and his vehicle half blocked the entrance.

One, two, three—hell! Five burly men were alighting and marching into the place.

One of them stood at the counter and the rest fell in behind him, a loose, almost military and certainly menacing formation.

Other customers—a lorry driver still chewing, a prostitute in a gaudy plastic raincoat and boots run down at the heels, a bearded hitch-hiker— were leaving in a hurry. Scuttling past Dalgetty without seeing him. Sergeant Pryke was out of hiding and squatted beside the pick-up's cab.

"The big feller, sir, you know him?"

"They're all big fellers," Dalgetty joked feebly. "Go on, I'll buy it—tell me, share the good news, Sarge."

Pryke was removing false teeth and stowing them in his breast pocket. "That's Willy Corner, sir," he lisped. "A rough customer . . . Mr Blake reckons Corner's behind this protection racket that started last year."

Dalgetty, objectively noting that his heart and pulse rates were up, his palms sweaty, admitted: "I've been taken for a mug. Try to raise the nick on your personal radio."

He was watching a silent movie projected on the brilliantly lit windows of the cafe. Corner, even with his back to the observer, was obviously making demands and threats, gesturing imperiously. Chef's hat flopping in time with a busy lower jaw, fat Cyril was equally obviously telling Mr Corner to do something that would be painful if not physiologically impossible.

"Cavalry's on the way, sir," Sergeant Pryke reported cheerfully. "But I don't give much for poor old Custer's chances, in there."

They looked at each other, conversing silently. Both knew that some policemen would now discover urgent business elsewhere, or be stricken by blindness. Cyril Donks, Dalgetty thought savagely, deserved a bloody good thrashing, for being too clever by half . . .

Everything, as is customary in such situations, happened pretty much at once. Willy Corner abandoned formal negotiations and attempted to break Cyril's W.C. Fieldsian nose. The cafe owner, swaying out of range, continued the movement to snatch up a pan of scalding fat and hurl it over the gangster.

Corner's four soldiers surged forward.

"Come on," Dalgetty yelled. Far too soon for his liking, he and Pryke were inside, back to back and fighting against a brace of thugs each, while Willy Corner, a few wizened chips scattered on his ruined silk shirt, writhed and cursed among the feet and Cyril Donks bellowed and made not particularly spirited attempts to clamber over the counter and join battle.

If you can't take a joke, you shouldn't have joined. That gem of Metropolitan Police humour occurred to Inspector Dalgetty—zipped through the back of his mind like a bullet, making him snarl—as Thug One kicked him in the knee and Thug Two brandished a sawn-off pickaxe handle.

Dalgetty shut his brain to the agony in his leg, tasted wet saltiness, ducked the blow and barged Pryke out of danger in the same frantic spasm. The club, missing both policemen, cracked Thug Three's arm and he collided with Thug Four who reeled back and trod on Willy Corner's hand, causing the maddened Corner to bite him in the calf and send him into the path of a two-fisted swing from Sergeant Pryke . . .

Dismal and craven, the voice in Dalgetty's head whimpered that it wasn't fair; it had been going on such a long time, too long, and it *hurt* and they'd got Pryke on the deck and—

The cafe was full of blue uniforms.

As in a dream, Dalgetty saw his prime attacker swept up by Superintendent Blake, easily as a bundle of dirty laundry, and hurled across the room. For a bald-headed old buzzard, the Super could put himself about a bit. Dalgetty wanted to kiss him.

Staunching a bleeding nose with the back of one hand, Dalgetty squinted at his watch. The encounter had lasted less than sixty seconds from start to finish. And it *was* finished, no error. Blake and his uniformed boys were striding about like lion tamers—only with truncheons instead of chairs and whips—and the Willy Corner lobby was subdued, not to say rueful.

The same went for Detective Inspector Dalgetty. "Thanks, Super. You must have come here by jet or something."

Superintendent Blake's long yellow front teeth nipped a loose triangle of skin from his knobbly knuckle. "Tell you the truth, Stanley, I was only round the corner—followed you here, on the off-chance."

Turning his head away, politely, the Super spat neatly. "Not like Cyril Donks to tell his life story to the first personable stranger he meets . . . so I took the liberty of sticking my oar in."

"Thank God you did. Sarge, are you okay?"

"Hang about, an' I'll tell you," Pryke panted. He was examining his dentures, with childlike anxiety. "Ah, not broken. Roast pork for dinner tomorrow, see, and I do love that crispy crackling."

Feet on the fender, Superintendent Blake ticked points off on his fingers. "Assault on police officers. Malicious damage. Making an affray? Shouldn't wonder . . . Of course, Willy Corner and his mob ought to be done for extortion, but our Cyril will never admit they were after him for protection money. Still, with Corner's form, what we do have will put him away for a good while."

He paused, head on one side, benignly wolfish. "And *that* was what army officers call 'the object of the exercise', from Cyril's point of view," he said gently.

Inspector Dalgetty's tongue stopped testing a loose tooth, and he blushed. "Right dummy I made of myself. Donks knew who I was—*what* I was, anyway—as soon as he clapped eyes on me. Right?"

Blake beamed, pipe releasing acrid smoke signals. " 'Fraid so, son. Classic con trick, eh? Always tell the mark what he's longing to hear."

Dalgetty groaned, not wholly theatrically. "Pile it on, sir, I deserve it. Con trick is right—I'm going to have him."

"Unwise." The Superintendent shifted his pipe. "Put Cyril in court, tell your story, and he'll say it was all a misunderstanding. He offered you a legitimate haulage job in good faith, the rest was your imagination. Um . . . was he so far wrong?"

"Damn!"

"See it his way, Stanley. Blokes like Cyril Donks are out on their own, they'll never be respectable citizens. They can't—they *feel* they can't—run to the law for protection. Cyril would sooner die than turn grass, be an informer.

"But Corner was at his throat, ready to bleed him dry. In Cyril's book, tricking you into being there when he stood up to Willy Corner . . . well, it wasn't exactly grassing. It gave him a fighting chance."

"Except we did the fighting." Dalgetty brightened, and smiled grudgingly. "At least this way, we get five real villains instead of one tiddler. Well, it's me for a hot bath, aspirins and bed. I feel awful."

Blake made his pipe gurgle disgustingly. "You want to stay away from football matches, son. Read the papers—it's a terribly violent game."

DEAD GIVEAWAY

Dan J. Marlowe

STEPHANIE BLAKE WAS on her way to bed when she heard the door chimes. The faint hum of the air conditioning accompanied her into the front hall. Outside the condominium-apartment on Ponchatoula Street in New Orleans, the oppressive summer night's heat was almost like a substance with weight.

She was surprised to see George Henderson when she looked through the peephole. "Good to see you up and around again, tiger," he greeted her when she opened the door. "I need my tennis partner before I start fattenin' up." He moved past her toward her study, as he always did, his target the wallcase containing the collection of antique swords she had inherited from her father.

"Insomnia, George?" Stephanie inquired, watching as he opened the case and took down the weapon she called the Ardennes Sword. It was an early Roman relic.

He didn't answer her. "Man!" he breathed reverently, slicing the air in whistling slashes with the two-edged fighting steel. Its massive hilt fitted his big hand in a manner that suggested there must have been giants in those days, too, Stephanie reflected. George Henderson was a forthright mountain of a man. He stood six feet four inches tall, and he weighed 280 pounds.

"Now there's a *sword*!" George exclaimed, continuing his cutting and thrusting. "Nothin' like the cakecutters we use at the club."

George was a homicide bureau detective, and a good one, but his admiration for the sword was no affectation. He might look like an ex-athlete running to fat, but twice in the past three years George had been state sabre champion. His wrists resembled the upper arms of an ordinary man.

"Insomnia?" Stephanie tried him again.

George returned the sword to the case reluctantly. "How you feelin', Forehand?" he answered her question with a question. He called her "Forehand" because it was the basis of her steady tennis game.

"Fine," she lied.

"That's not what I hear from your associates in the legal profession," he returned.

Four months earlier while on a Central American assignment for the law firm in which she was a junior partner, Stephanie had picked up a bug from whose devastating after-effects her system seemed unable to rid itself. She was still on sick leave.

George cleared his throat. "Seen much of your neighbour down the hall lately? Wilhelm Hegel?"

"Not since I came home from the hospital." Stephanie tried to assess George's tone. "Why?"

He removed a newspaper clipping from his shirt pocket and handed it to her. CORPORATION OFFICERS MYSTERIOUSLY SLAIN, the headline said. DIRECTORS OF KROELICH IMPORT-EXPORT FIRM FOUND DEAD. Stephanie handed the clipping back. She had no need to read the text. There had been almost nothing else on radio and television for the past 36 hours, but she had forgotten that her neighbour, Wilhelm, was an officer of the Kroelich Company. "I know Wilhelm wasn't killed, because I saw him in the foyer this morning," she said. "You think he's involved?"

"Got to be," George said, scowling. "I know you corporate types don't keep up with our local crime waves, but five people were just about obliterated inside the Kroelich soundproofed boardroom. There were five bodies inside, only we couldn't tell was it three, five, or seven till Doc sorted 'em out."

He paused for emphasis. "Look, there's a twelve-foot ceilin' in the boardroom, an' there was blood on *it*, an' on the walls, an' on the crystal chandelier over the table they sat around. They were whacked to pieces with a chunk of lumber, but there wasn't a sign of it except for the wood fragments adherin' to the bodies. An' you want to know the screwy breaks you get on a case like this? The lab says they can't identify the wood fragments. They claim they're not native."

"Not native to the area?"

"Not native to the country!" George snorted. "Ever hear anything so crazy?"

"So you're making no progress with your investigation."

The big man grimaced. "In reverse I'm makin' it. I'm in trouble with the lieutenant right up to my oversized tailgate. The press kept buggin' me, an' he overheard me tellin' a couple of 'em I thought an elephant had done it. Would you believe they halfway went for it? An elephant on the eighteenth floor of one of the biggest office buildings in the city?" He brooded for a moment. "At that, it makes as much sense as anything else I've come up with." His tone changed. "I want you to get me in to see Hegel."

"Wilhelm?" Stephanie's surprise was reflected in her voice. "Don't be ridiculous, George. He's more of an acquaintance than he is a friend. We play chess occasionally, have a drink together. I have no right to disturb him, and I won't."

"He might appreciate the chance for a quiet talk here rather than an official session downtown."

"No," Stephanie said. "I've no right to do it."

"Call him," George urged her. "Let him decide."

She resisted further, but the force waves emanating from the big man almost literally drove her to the telephone. "This is an imposition, Wilhelm," she said when she had him on the phone. She explained hurriedly.

"Bring him over," her neighbour said quietly.

"Great!" George enthused when Stephanie hung up. His ear had been within three inches of hers. "Let's go!" She found herself being hustled down the hallway. Wilhelm Hegel stood at his opened door. He was tall and slender, with thick blond hair that looked shaggy. His appearance was boyish. Stephanie noted with misgiving that behind his horn-rimmed glasses his eyes appeared anxious-looking.

Neither man offered to shake hands when she introduced them. "This meeting is perhaps as well," Hegel said. "You will come inside, please?"

Stephanie could see George mentally filing away the phrasing in Hegel's speech that indicated a language other than English as his mother tongue. She was turning to leave when she realised that Wilhelm was looking at her expectantly. "You want me to come in, too?" she asked uneasily. "As counsel? I'm not well enough qualified in criminal law to—"

"As a friend," Hegel said. "I have not that many."

She went inside, finally, despite a strong disinclination to become involved. Hegel led them to a sitting room and waved them to chairs. "I have a strange story to tell," he said, "and I would as soon a friendly ear heard it as an official one."

George's voice filled the room. "What is your capacity with Kroelich, Mr Hegel?"

"None." Wilhelm's tone was firm. "At the present time," he amended his answer in response to Stephanie's look of surprise. "Originally, I was one of the founding partners."

"Your partners bought you out?"

"My partners and I were eliminated." Hegel said it bleakly. "We became entangled with financiers. I could not describe how it was managed, but we were frozen out. Completely."

"And the people who froze you out—?"

"Are the people whose deaths you are investigating."

Stephanie didn't like what she was hearing. "George, since all this is very irregular, I suggest—"

His heavy voice overrode hers. "There was hard feeling over the ouster, Mr Hegel?"

"Naturally." It was sharp and biting.

"Your partners' names?"

"My partners—" Hegel hesitated. "There is a Helmut Fritsch. There was a Manfred Fritsch, his father."

"Was?"

"Manfred recently became—" Hegel hesitated again, "—irrational. He had to be institutionalised. Three days ago he died." He put out a hand in a defensive gesture. "I realise how this must sound to you. And there is more, which you should hear from me rather than from another."

He drew a quick breath, visibly bracing himself. "Helmut has been under a doctor's care himself. He has telephoned me to speak of a recurring dream, a persistent nightmare that has tormented him. He tried to explain it to me, but I'm afraid I'm a man of limited imagination. Helmut became impatient with me."

He removed a small, flat package from a pocket of his jacket. Stephanie could see an address label and cancelled stamps. "I received from Helmut yesterday a tape recording of his dream." There was a sheen of perspiration upon Hegel's forehead. "It is not pleasant. It is not—not natural."

"Your friend Helmut flipped out like his old man?" George demanded aggressively.

"That is not for me to say." Hegel said it stolidly. "I say that it disturbs me. I do not understand it, and I pride myself that I am a practical man. I would like you to hear it. I have your permission?"

Without waiting for it, he picked up from the floor beside his chair a leather case Stephanie had taken for a briefcase. He opened it, disclosing an expensive-looking tape recorder into which he inserted a cassette. "I give you Helmut's dream," he said, his husky voice betraying an inner tension that alarmed Stephanie.

He snapped on a switch, and a slight mechanical scratchiness was succeeded by a voice so harsh, so overwhelming in its metallic vibrancy, that it impacted upon Stephanie's hearing as sound without meaning. "Too loud?" Wilhelm asked. He fiddled with a dial. "Helmut has an unusual voice. He is a powerful man."

"I'll just bet he is," George muttered. He fell silent as the switch clicked again. Even at the lower level the blaring strength of the reverberant voice was such that it took Stephanie a moment to catch up.

"—sunrise was on the hillside when they dragged us out, naked in our chains, a soldier on each arm. There were three of us: Molhir of Alesia; the boy, Luctor; and I, Esserac, son of Molhir. Above the morning mists rising from the moat about the encampment the spiralling smoke still rose skyward from the breached walled town beyond."

George Henderson sat erect in his chair, a frown upon his blunt features. He glanced toward Stephanie, then back toward the intently listening Hegel, shrugged, and folded his huge arms.

"The freshening breeze came to us with the persistent taint of death on this third day," the tape-recorded voice continued. "The legion was drawn up in marching order behind the dais upon which the chosen centurions were closely grouped about the purple-cloaked imperator. The camp was struck. The stakes were down from the earthern breastworks, returned to the soldiers' packs. The imperator's tent was in the baggage train, the cooking fires extinguished. There remained only the disposition of us, the last of the vanquished chiefs. Death had been the decision of the council. That we had been told. Death to the vanquished, in the sunrise, within sight and sound of the shattered walls they had fought to defend."

George Henderson cleared his throat as if about to say something, then subsided. Stephanie didn't think Hegel heard him.

"They thrust forward my father, Molhir of Alesia, who had fought them so long and so cunningly. Like a slave they rushed him toward the dais, and they forced his palms flat against his cheeks while the iron collar clamped his wrists to his neck. Beside me, Luctor gasped, paling. They dragged my father not to the block with its heavily encrusted axe, but to the post, fresh timbers embedded in the earth with a crosspiece between. So for us it was not to be the merciful axe, but death under the rods."

Wilhelm Hegel had slumped deeply into his chair. His pale features glistened damply as the torrential tape-recorded voice thickened with passion.

"They suspended my father between the posts, and two soldiers removed heavy rods from wet sacking. They stepped up behind him and struck heavily, right and left. My father bit chunks from his upraised arms to keep from screaming, but that could not last. When the first set of soldiers cast aside the bloody stumps of their rods and stepped back to be replaced by fresh men with fresh rods, the twitching mass between the posts had become a slobbering animal. It is not easy to kill a man beneath the rods."

The voice rose until it hurt Stephanie's ears. "God, how I hated them! The posts shook from the force of the blows, the left more than the right, and from between them there came only a sick moaning. Upon the dais, the imperator dictated to his scribendi, who wrote hurriedly upon his tablet, then rushed off. At its leisure the purpled arm rose languidly, and the crimson thing between the posts was cut down and dragged to the block. The same instant the soldiers' arms tightened upon my arms, and I was wrestled to the posts, close enough for my chest to scrape the blood-wet bark. There was a pause then while all eyes turned toward the block."

The voice had become such a guttural, snarling torrent of sound that Stephanie could barely keep up.

"I stood there with the hate of the world in my heart, and as the axe flashed downward, I seized the weaker left post. It came free in my hands at the second ripping lunge. I hoisted it high, scarcely feeling the blow on the head from behind as I wrenched post from crosspiece."

Wilhelm Hegel rocked slightly in his chair, eyes closed.

"I charged the dais with the post in my arms, scattering the soldiers. I was amidst them before they realized it, the four chosen centurions who had led the final assault upon the walled town that had been my birthright, and the imperator whose face turned the lemon-yellow of any other frightened man. I smote them, and smote them again, the joyous strength of twenty within me. I heard a ringing shout of command from in front of the drawn-up legion, and I tried to turn to charge them—" A solid chunking sound cut off the raging voice abruptly. It was followed by a drawn-out, gasping sigh, then two distinct thumps, one heavier, one lighter.

Stephanie could picture the upraised post falling, and then the man. George Henderson's big hands were tensed upon his chair's arms preparatory to propelling himself to his feet when the tape-recorded voice spoke again, weakly. "—I pity the—boy, Luctor, left—to the swords of—the legion."

There was silence then. Complete. It filled the room. The snap of the switch when Hegel turned off the recorder sounded like a pistol shot. Hegel stared at them, ashen-faced. "Each time I hear it—" he said raggedly, then stopped.

George was on his feet, his voice hard. "Cute sound effects there at the end, Hegel. How'd he manage it?"

"It is not my dream," Hegel said soberly. "You will have to ask the man who had it."

"Let's you an' me go do just that," George said briskly. "Have you talked to Fritsch since the massacre?"

"He does not answer his telephone." Hegel turned to Stephanie, his voice and expression wistful. "For a little while you nearly believed?" Stephanie didn't answer. She couldn't. Her ears were still filled by the sound of that haunting voice.

They rode across town to Helmut Fritsch's address which had been furnished by Hegel. The night air was close and humid. Stephanie had been included only at her own insistence. "You're not able physically to go out yet," George had protested.

"If I don't go, Wilhelm doesn't go," Stephanie said with finality. "I can't let him go with you without representation."

George braked the unmarked police car in front of a long, massive-looking building that extended out over the river. "Damned if that looks like an apartment building," he observed.

"It's a warehouse that Helmut converted into an office and living quarters for himself," Hegel explained.

"A warehouse!" George echoed. His voice said that the statement told him all he needed to know about Fritsch's sanity.

Sounds of the river current sucking at pilings were audible as they stood at the front entrance. Hegel produced a key, and George looked at Stephanie significantly as the blond man used it. The place was cavernously gloomy inside, tremendously high-ceilinged. George marched from area to area, calling for Fritsch. There was no response. Stephanie became conscious of an increasingly swampy odour that clung to the nostrils.

The cement underfoot turned to dirt, then to a black-looking muck. George's flashlight played upon odd-shaped shrubs, small trees, snake-like vines, flowering lianas, and menacing-looking plants of types Stephanie had never seen before. Increasingly, the growth filled the area as they advanced. The place had the dank, marshy smell of the forest primeval. Stephanie could hear George muttering to himself as he pushed his way through the thicket.

The farthest corner of the building had been set aside for office space. An incongruously rich-looking rug covered a twenty-foot square. A desk and three filing cabinets were ranged against the rear wall. George stopped so suddenly that Hegel ran into him. Stephanie, following, bumped into Wilhelm. They all stared down at a bearded, naked body face down upon the carpeting.

Hegel's breath hissed sharply. The deadly-looking shaft of a bone-handled knife protruded from beneath the left shoulder-blade. George dropped to one knee to examine an outflung arm, palm up on the rug. Stephanie could see bark and bits of wood clinging to fingers and palm.

"Turn on the lights," George said to Hegel. Wilhelm groped his way beyond the desk and located the switch. Stephanie turned away as the light lent stark reality to the situation which in the glow of George's flashlight had resembled a scene upon a stage. Off to one side she saw on the rug a stout timber, shaggy-barked, one end of which was black with the swamp-muck surrounding them. The other end was also darker than the intervening stretch of bark between.

"Tell us about it," George said curtly to Hegel.

"I don't know what you mean," Wilhelm replied.

"You quarrelled with Fritsch about what happened at Froelich's," George said. "It was Fritsch's idea, and you were afraid you'd be involved. You came over here, one thing led to another, and you killed him. Right?"

Hegel firmed his lips in the manner of a man who has said all that he intends to say. Stephanie was glad to see it. George went to the telephone on the desk and called homicide headquarters. Then he drew Stephanie aside. "I shouldn't say it, but if the loony jumped Hegel, you can probably plead self-defence, or at least manslaughter," he said in an undertone.

The long ride across town had tired Stephanie more than she would have believed possible. She felt light headed. "Why does it have to be Wilhelm who killed him?" she asked.

"Who else?" George rebutted. "He had a key. He was leary of Fritsch ever since Fritsch's old man jumped his trolley, especially after the phone calls about the dream."

Stephanie's eyes went again to the bearded face on the carpeting. Even in death it was a strong face. That high-cheekboned death-mask could certainly have hated with savagery and passion.

George pushed the medical examiner hard when he came. "Don't rush me," the medical examiner kept complaining. "All right, all right," he said finally. "A single knife thrust, by an expert. Plus a nasty bruise on the back of the head."

"You noticed his hands, Doc?"

"I noticed. It will have to be checked out, but for a guess, this is your berserker from the boardroom."

"One man could have done all that?"

The doctor hesitated. "One maniac," he said at last.

Before they left, Stephanie watched George peel off a strip of bark from the fallen timber. Outside, George tried to place Hegel in a cruiser with three detectives while he urged Stephanie toward his own car. She resisted his hand on her arm. "Wilhelm rides with us or I'll report you to the district attorney's office in the morning!" she said hotly. She didn't like the sound of her own voice. It was too high-pitched, too hysterical. She didn't even know if she was within legal bounds in making the demand.

But George shrugged and waved the car of detectives away. Hegel climbed silently into George's car and sat like a stone image in a rear seat corner. Stephanie sat beside George. "That tape, George," she began. "Fritsch—"

"Hegel found the tape there after he killed Fritsch," George interrupted her. He was using the same undertone he had employed before. "He added the sound effects at the end, then mailed it to himself. Neat. A tape-recorded alibi."

"You *know* all this?"

"Wouldn't you have, if you'd been him?" George countered.

A shudder began in Stephanie's central nervous system and rippled through her. "*Listen* to me, George! How do you explain Fritsch getting the timber out of the boardroom unseen?"

"He didn't," George said calmly. "An' in about five hours I'll tell you who saw him. The stenographic pool's just outside that room. Fritsch just bought himelf three or four people."

"But the *tape*, George! Isn't it possible—"

"Whoa up, there, tiger!" George said it sharply, but then his voice softened. "If you don't believe me, just ask yourself what it is you're tryin' to make yourself believe. Okay?"

Stephanie subsided, her mouth dry.

The balance of the ride was completed in silence. A corner of Stephanie's mind was still listening to a tape-recorded voice. George's men escorted Hegel to his apartment in the small elevator. George and Stephanie had to make a separate trip. Outside her door, he snapped his fingers loudly. "Forgot somethin', Forehand. Open up an' let me make a phone call, okay?"

When she let him in, he walked straight to the study and took down the Ardennes Sword in the familiar ritual. Stephanie started to tell him to get on with his call, then realized suddenly that he had none to make. George had decoyed her away from Hegel's apartment while George's men worked on Wilhelm.

Stephanie hurried through her hallway and down the corridor. "Hey!" George shouted. She could hear him pounding along behind her. At Hegel's partly-opened door, she caught a quick glimpse of Wilhelm sitting stiffly in a straight-backed chair, wooden-faced, while the three standing detectives fired hard-voiced questions at him.

George's big body bumped Stephanie to one side. She shoved at him angrily, but it was like shoving at a pyramid. He was still carrying the sword, but, oddly, he didn't look strange with it in his hand.

"The man has rights!" Stephanie panted. She felt dizzy.

"Don't get shook," George attempted to soothe her. "The loony might not have jumped him." His tone was firm although his manner was discomfited. "We got to know."

"Not in any such manner as—" Stephanie began, then stopped. From inside Wilhelm's apartment a high-pitched, keening wail rose to a scalp-prickling crescendo. George whirled from Stephanie to face the room's interior. She pushed herself into an eighth of the doorway beside him.

The detective team around Hegel stood frozen. The blond man had risen in a half-crouch. Unnatural sound poured from him in unnatural volume. Then he plunged through the knot of men and ran head-down toward the doorway.

"Here, you!" George commanded, and pointed at him. Wilhelm Hegel, unheeding, ran hard against the point of the Ardennes Sword in George's extended hand. The shock jarred even his mountainous body backward a step as Hegel was jolted to a stop, spitted on the sword, the point of which emerged from beneath his armpit in back.

Stephanie heard someone screaming as George Henderson eased the sword's burden to the floor.

Then hands on her arms led her away, but not away from the sound of the screaming.

THE RECKONING

Margaret Yorke

ON THE MORNING of her husband's seventieth birthday, a Thursday in September, Ellen Parsons rose as usual at seven o'clock. She went quietly down to the kitchen and put on the kettle. While it boiled, she laid the table in the dining room: blue and white Cornish crockery, honey and butter, on a linen cloth.

This was the last meal at which she would sit across the table from Maurice, and she hummed under her breath as she made the tea. She carried the tray upstairs, setting it on the table between their twin beds, and poured out two cups, with two lumps of sugar in Maurice's. But nothing sweetened him.

"Tea, Maurice," she said, and took her own into the bathroom, where she dressed out of his sight.

Maurice did not reply, but she knew that he would now sit up, yawn, and drink his tea in gulps. She would return to the bedroom to do her hair, in time to pour his second cup. When he was ready to rise, she would be downstairs, cooking his daily bacon and egg.

She had decided to kill him in church one Sunday morning a year ago, hearing the words from Ecclesiastes: *To every thing there is a season, and a time to every purpose under the heaven: a time to be born, and a time to die . . .*

I have not lived yet, Ellen had thought.

Her mind ranged back over the years of her marriage to when she first met Maurice. Her father, a widower, had died after a long illness, through which she had devotedly nursed him. Maurice, then junior partner in the firm of solicitors acting for her father, had advised her to keep the house for the present, and Ellen, weary from the strain of her father's illness, set about restoring the neglected garden, and washed curtains and paintwork indoors.

Maurice watched both her and the house revive under this treatment. One day he brought her some violets: another time, a book of poetry. She looked forward to his visits; he had a sweet smile.

Soon she exchanged one form of bondage for another. She and Maurice, after their marriage, continued to live in the large, old house on the edge of the village, and here their only child, a daughter named Priscilla, was born. Priscilla, against her father's wishes, had married a young farmer and the couple had immediately emigrated to Australia.

Priscilla wrote every fortnight; she urged Ellen to come out for a visit and see her grandchildren, but Maurice would not go himself and would not permit Ellen to go without him.

The smile that had once charmed Ellen was seen rarely after their marriage. Maurice insisted that meals be punctual to the second; arguments were not allowed; and only his own opinions might be expressed. He controlled the money that Ellen had inherited from her father, allowing her small amounts for personal needs.

Priscilla, as a child, was allowed no parties, and her friends were not encouraged to visit the house. It was not surprising that she had escaped as soon as she could. The only guests approved by Maurice were his business acquaintances.

Ellen's fragile links with other people grew weaker after Maurice retired. If she invited anyone to tea he would sit scowling and looking at his watch, finally leaving the room with a remark like, "See that dinner is on time, Ellen," in front of the guest, humiliating her.

But now, all this would end. The resentment that had simmered for so long had at last boiled over. The house was hers; and all the money, both what she had inherited and what Maurice had made, would be hers, too.

The days of our years are threescore years and ten.

Ellen had read the words many times. Maurice had now ended his allotted span; she had made her plans and at last the time had come to carry them out.

She gave him her present when he had finished breakfast—a thick, wool dressing-gown. She had bought it with Ben, the jobbing gardener, in mind, for Maurice would not live to wear it. Maurice thanked her without enthusiasm, saying he would have preferred camel colour to maroon. Ellen knew that cheerful Ben would like maroon better.

Each morning, Maurice went to his study, while Ellen did her chores. Today, after she had made the beds, she went into the garden and cut three large, ripe marrows; Maurice had pointed them out to her the day before. She carried them into the house and down the flight of steps leading to the cellar. The door was locked and bolted. Ellen took the key from a hook beside the door and unlocked it; she laid the marrows on a stone ledge inside.

Strings of onions already hung on the walls but, otherwise, the cellar was bare; it was dark, lit only by a tiny window high on one wall.

The marrows deposited, Ellen left the cellar; she closed the door, which opened outwards, but did not lock it.

Now it was time for her weekly shopping expedition; every Thursday Ellen went into town, her only outing. She backed the car out of the garage until the corner of the rear bumper and the exhaust pipe were exactly opposite the cellar window which, seen from outside the house, was a narrow slit a few inches above the ground, the glass protected by chicken wire which was now rotten with age. There was a blackened area, caused by exhaust fumes, on the brickwork around the window, for the car was always reversed into this position.

But, today, Ellen reversed too far and broke the window. She smiled as she switched off the engine and uttered a shriek.

As she knew he would, Maurice had heard the crash. He came storming out of the house to inspect the damage to the car, which was nil; the corner of the bumper had gone straight through the rotten wire and the glass. Ellen had practised the manoeuvre until she could have done it blindfold. She stood wringing her hands and apologising meekly while being scolded. Maurice, furious, went to discover what had happened in the cellar, into which most of the glass had fallen, and Ellen followed him.

Automatically, he reached for the key and found it missing from its hook. It was in the lock already.

"You've been down here this morning, Ellen," he accused.

"Yes, Maurice. I brought those three marrows in. You told me yesterday to cut them."

"You didn't lock the door. How many times must I tell you everything?" he exclaimed, opening the door and striding angrily inside.

In an instant Ellen had slammed the heavy, close-fitting door behind him, turned the key and thrust the bolt across. For a moment she leaned against it, her heart pounding. It had been easy! She had spent hours devising the perfect scheme, thinking of first one plan, then another. Now, she could truthfully say, when she was questioned, that she had forgotten to lock the cellar door after taking in the marrows and had returned to do it. How could she have known Maurice was in there?

She hurried up the stairs before he had time to begin beating upon the door. In a few minutes she had started the engine of the car, reversed it still closer to the wall, so that the exhaust was tight against the broken cellar window, and left it to run, leaving the choke well out.

Maurice always insisted that she warm the car up thoroughly before driving away. The rich mixture filling the cellar with fumes would make Maurice unconscious very quickly; a mere five minutes in a closed garage with a large car could prove fatal, she had discovered during her researches in the public library, and Maurice was due for a much longer diet of fumes from their medium-sized saloon.

She left the car and walked away, for there were sounds coming from the cellar, shouts and cries, and she could not stay to listen. There was nothing Maurice could stand on to reach the window far above his head, and he would not be able to break the door.

Ellen went to the garage and fetched a bottle of distilled water. She returned to the car, not hurrying, opened the bonnet and topped up the battery, concentrating on the task, ignoring the cellar. There was no sound now, apart from the car's engine which was beginning to run evenly as it warmed up.

She pushed in the choke, put away the distilled water and closed the garage; Maurice would never allow it to be left open when the car was out, for fear of passing thieves, although it was behind the house and could not be seen from the road. Then she went into the house. She could scarcely hear the car now; its engine purred so sweetly.

She went to her sewing-box and took from it the wad of leaflets about travelling to Australia which had lain hidden there for weeks, under her embroidery. How should she go? By boat, she thought: a large and luxurious liner which would call at exotic ports on the way, and first-class, of course.

No one came to the door while she turned the pages of the brochures; the only regular callers were the milkman and the postman and, on Tuesdays, the cleaning woman; few door-to-door salesmen or flag-sellers bothered to come to the isolated house at the end of the village. Occasionally, she rose to listen to the car; it still ran, without stalling.

At last she decided she had waited long enough and went out to it; it had got rather hot. Ellen moved the car forward. She laid a sheet of slate that normally covered the kitchen drain against the broken window-pane to keep in the fumes. No sound came from the cellar.

Then she drove to town and did her shopping.

When she returned, more than an hour later, Ellen removed the slate and replaced it over the drain. She backed the car up to the window again and left the engine running while she unloaded her shopping. Finally, she opened the garage doors and put the car inside.

It was now time to prepare lunch, and, for once, it would not matter if the meal was late. How wasteful, she reflected, peeling Maurice's usual two potatoes and slicing runner beans, fresh from the garden. She had made his favourite pudding, cream caramel, the day before: a birthday treat. She put the grill on for the chops. Soon, she would have to start looking for him.

She could spend some time searching the house and garden, and then go up to the village to enquire if anyone had seen him. She needn't think about the cellar until later, much later; perhaps she need not think of it at all, until she told the police that he was missing.

That was the part she dreaded: finding him. But, by then, he would have been dead for a long time; most certainly by now he had been dead for hours. He would not have suffered for long, though his hands might be torn and bruised if he had clawed at the cellar door.

She dished up the meal and put it in a low oven. Then she went upstairs to wash and do her hair before calling him, as she always did. She never saw the sleepy wasp among the bristles of her hairbrush as she raised it to her head; she felt only the sharp, searing stab of the sting above her temple.

Ellen grew giddy almost at once. Three years ago she had been stung on her arm, fainted, and had recovered only because Maurice had been there, seen her apoplectic face, and called the doctor instantly.

This time, he could not save her.